Oscar curved up his tail and whacked his own back, all the time beckoning with his foreflipper.

"Hey, wait!" Hawthorne got the idea. He hoped. "Wait, do you want me to come for a ride?" he asked.

The cetoid blinked both eyes. Was the blink the counterpart of a nod? Hawthorne straddled him, grasping a small cervical fin and leaning back against the muscular dorsal. The long body glided from the station. Water rippled sensuously around Hawthorne's bare feet.

The motion was so smooth that Hawthorne was finally startled to glance behind and see the station five miles off. Then Oscar submerged.

POUL ANDERSON

DIALOGUE WITH DARKNESS

TOR

A TOM DOHERTY ASSOCIATES BOOK

DIALOGUE WITH DARKNESS

"A Chapter of Revelation," in *The Day the Sun Stood Still*, ed. Lester del Rey, Thomas Nelson, Inc., New York, 1972, copyright © 1972 by Poul Anderson.

"Sister Planet," *Satellite*, May, 1959, copyright © 1959 by Renown Publications.

"The Life of Your Time," *Analog Science Fiction*, September, 1965 (as by Michael Karageorge) copyright © 1965 by Condé Nast Publications, Inc.

"Time Heals," *Astounding Science Fiction*, October, 1949, copyright © 1949 by Street and Smith Publications, Inc.

"SOS," *Worlds of If*, March, 1970, copyright © 1970 by Galaxy Publishing Corporation.

"Conversation in Arcady," *Analog Science Fiction*, December, 1963, copyright © 1963 by Condé Nast Publications, Inc.

"Dialogue," in *Faster Than Light*, ed. George Zebrowski and Jack Dann, Harper and Row, New York, 1976, copyright © 1976 by Poul Anderson.

"The Communicators," in *Infinity One*, ed. Robert Hoskins, Lancer, New York, 1969, copyright © 1969 by Poul Anderson.

First printing: February 1985

A TOR Book

Published by Tom Doherty Associates
8-10 West 36 Street
New York, N.Y. 10018

Cover art by Tom Kidd

ISBN: 0-812-53083-7
CAN. ED.: 0-812-53084-5

Printed in the United States of America

Contents

A Chapter of Revelation

Tuesday 14 June

(Chairman Wu Yuan of China warned today in an internationally telecast address that the presence of American warships in the Yellow Sea is an intolerable threat and provocation. "Unless this trespass upon the territorial waters of the People's Republic cease forthwith," declared the head of the Chinese state, "it will become necessary to take measures fraught with the gravest consequences." At a special press conference called within hours of the speech, U.S. Secretary of Defense Jacob Morris insisted that the American fleet is staying well outside the twelve-mile limit and is in that area only in response to the Korean crisis. Heavier fighting was reported along the 38th parallel, but officials refused to give newsmen any details.)

* * *

Simon Donaldson stumbled a bit as he entered the living room. His wife glanced up from her seat before the television. "Why home so early?" she asked—and then, having looked more closely into his face, rose and hurried to him.

"I knocked off," he mumbled. "Wasn't getting anything done. Couldn't think." She reached him. He caught the warm slenderness of her and held it close. "Oh, God, darling!"

She, understanding, did not try to kiss. Because they were both tall, she could not well lay her head on his breast; but her cheek rested on his shoulder and his nostrils filled with the clean scent of her hair. He ruffled it.

"Yeah," she said after a while. "I'm getting scared too."

"We'd better not delay any longer. Tonight we load the camping gear in the car. Tomorrow you buy groceries and start north."

"Not without you, buster."

"You'll have to. I can't get away. Listen, Johnny's only ten, Mike's only eight. We owe our kids their lives."

"*And* their dad. Why can't you phone in sick and come along?"

"Because—" Donaldson sighed. "Our project's at a critical stage. I can't tell you more. Look at it this way. I'm a soldier in the technological war. The war that's being fought in the laboratories, on the proving grounds, to keep the balance of power stable enough that the war of missiles won't get fought. My friends on the Hill aren't running. Neither can I, if I want to keep any self-respect."

Gail stepped back a pace. Her eyes, blue beneath yellow bangs, sought his. "I know about lead times," she said. "Whatever you're developing can't be in production for five or ten years. The Korean business is this minute."

"Things may not explode," he said. "However, I want you three at Fort Ross, outside the fallout ellipse, for a week or so . . . in case."

She forced a smile. "What say we relax over a drink, so we can have dinner instead of a refueling stop, and argue later?"

Exhaustion overwhelmed him. "Okay."

Nevertheless his gaze followed her rangy gait until she had disappeared in the kitchen. After twelve years of marriage he went on considering himself lucky: he, awkward, rawboned, bespectacled, perpetually rumpled, a competent physicist and a bravura chess player but bookish, given to long rambles alone, no good at small talk—he got Gail Franklin!

And Mike and Johnny. A subdued clatter from the rear of the house showed they were at play, probably building further on their imaginary world Rassolageeva, not much chilled by that which lay across the world Earth.

Donaldson lit a cigarette, inhaled raggedly, prowled to the picture window and stared out. His house stood well aloft on the range that forms the eastern side of Berkeley. From there he saw over roofs and trees, gardens and uninhabited slopes gone tawny with summer, immense beneath a still more enormous blue, down to the cities. He could not see Lawrence Radiation Laboratory, where he worked, but he glimpsed the Campanile, poised on the University campus like a spaceship ready for long voyages.

The Bay gleamed sapphire and emerald, through a trace of mist snowlike under sunlight, San Francisco dream-vague on the farther shore but the Golden Gate Bridge arching clear to vision in a few fine brushstrokes that could have been done by a Chinese artist. . . . *Chinese, God help us, nonexistent God. The great mother of the East and the son and heir of the West, with guns at each other's temples.*

"—our next guest—"

The too-hearty voice scratched Donaldson's nerves. He moved to switch the television off, then stayed his hand. *Maybe I need a counterirritant, till Gail has the anesthetic mixed,* he thought. *Besides, she likes this show. What's it called? Oh, yes, "Pulse." Local talk program. People write in and whozis picks whoever seems likeliest to help fill the bored housewife's hour. No, I'm being unjust. After all, the show is popular, including among bright folk like Gail. It beats dangling on the lips of some half-hysterical news commentator.*

"Mr. Louis Habib of Oakland," the MC (Dawes, yes, that was his name) announced. Teeth glittered above his modish tie. "How do you do, Mr. Habib. Welcome to 'Pulse.' "

"Th-thank you." The other man could scarcely be heard. Stage fright, doubtless. He must have something a bit unusual to offer, if he hadn't been weeded out in audition. Donaldson peered at the screen. Habib was stiffly and shabbily clad, squat, dark, big-nosed, balding. His eyes were his best feature, the long-lashed gazelle eyes of the Levant.

"Let me see, Mr. Habib, you have a garage, don't you? The Motor Man Garage, 1453 Murphy Street, Oakland, right? Commercial pause, ha-ha. Well, tell us something more about yourself, if you please. You're married?''

"Yes. I'm not important, though," the short man blurted. "M-m-my message . . . no, too big a word . . . what I'm here about—that's what matters.''

"Our audience does like to get acquainted," Dawes said. "Your idea, the letter you wrote, is certainly very interesting, but we want to get to know the man behind it."

"It's not my idea," Habib stated in a kind of desperate valor. Donaldson made out how sweat channeled the makeup they had put on him. "It's as old as . . . oh, Moses, or older, I dunno. And I'm not important. Nor are you.''

That rocked Dawes back sufficiently for Habib to confront the camera. His look seemed to spear the watcher. "Listen, please listen," he begged. "Sure, I'm married. Three children. Friends. A whole world. Everything to lose. Same as you, all of us. This thing in Asia—this way the human race's been living on the edge of the pit, far back's I can remember, and I'm forty-four. What's wrong? We're crazy, that's what. Else we'd see how no . . . uh . . . i-deology, no power, no pride, nothing's worth blackening this beautiful world we got and frying little children alive.''

Dawes tried to get back control. "As I understood your recommendation, Mr. Habib, you do not propose we surrender.''

The round head shook. "No. We can't. Or we won't. I realize that. Don't say we should, either. There aren't many countries left with any freedom in them. Though maybe a lot don't agree with us about what freedom is, any more than we agree with their notions.

11

"But arguments don't mean we, the Chinese, the Russians, anybody has to fight. Least of all fight with weapons that won't leave much to quarrel about, afterward. We could, uh, settle somehow. Live and let live. Except we don't. Why? Because we're crazy. And what's made us crazy? I think it's that we don't know God.''·

Dawes, in a valiant effort to restore smoothness: "You indicated, Mr. Habib, you feel man has a need of faith as great as his need for food. He craves to believe in something higher than himself, something he can give himself to because it gives meaning to the universe. At the same time, you are not a conventional evangelist. Am I right?"

"Sort of." Habib continued looking straight into the camera, out of the screen. "I'm not a Bible thumper. Haven't been in church for years. But, well, I always figured there has to be a spirit behind creation. People used to believe. That didn't, uh, necessarily make them good or kind or wise, I know. But then, they had nothing but faith to go on.''

He lifted a finger. "That's my point," he said. "In the long run, faith wasn't enough. Maybe it should've been, but it wasn't. When science didn't find any reason to suppose the world was more than atoms and chance, why, faith eroded away. And people felt, well, empty. So they started inventing faiths, like communism or fascism in politics, or these nut cults you see around. But those just made 'em crazier, same's they went crazy when the old Catholic religion was, uh, challenged. Then they burned heretics and witches and they fought like devils. Today we make concentration camps and atomic rockets and we fight like devils.

"And maybe we Americans—and, uh, western Europeans too, I guess—maybe we're the worst off. We haven't got faith in anything, not even progress. Why's this country been so terrified, these past days? Isn't it on account of nearly everybody thinks, in his heart, he thinks nothing exists worth dying for?"

A curious power filled the stumbling words. Donaldson found himself listening and weighing, barely aware that Gail had returned with two martinis and was likewise quiet at his side.

"You suggest—" Dawes began.

"We need a sign," Habib told them. "We need proof, scientific proof, the only kind we can accept any more, proof that God is."

He hunched forward where he stood, fists clenched at his sides. "We won't get it free," he said, hoarsely now. Sweat soaked through his jacket. "Maybe we won't get it at all. Then we'll just have to live or die, as best's we can. But why not ask for a sign? Ask for some proof that there is a God, Who cares; that there is something bigger and brighter than our squabbles, our greeds, our want to make our fellowmen into copies of us. Then maybe we can begin to see those things for what they are, and—"

He did not quite ignore Dawes, but rather hurried on before the host should get a chance to soften his one occasion: "Let's pray together. That way, if the sign happens, we'll know God listens. A week from today. Tuesday noon. Midsummer. Around the world, whenever noon comes to you. Stop a minute and pray for a sign. If you don't believe, well, then speak your wish to yourself— your wish we will be shown while time remains. Even if you're an atheist, can't you dare to hope?"

13

Wednesday 15 June

(Dr. Nikio Sato, head of the Radiological Institute at the University of Tokyo, has confirmed that monitoring teams under his leadership have detected the explosion of "a sizable nuclear device not far southwest of Cheju," an island below the Korean Peninsula. The news blackout imposed by Washington, Peking, Seoul, and Pyongyang continues.)

Louis Habib entered the shop almost timidly. Joe Goldman, his assistant, was laying out tools. "Hi, boss," the mechanic said.

"How're you?" Habib started to remove his jacket. Morning sunlight streamed in the entrance, hit a fresh oil slick on the concrete floor, and melted in rainbows. Morning traffic rumbled and whirred past in the street. Smog was already acrid. "Gonna be bad today, the air," Habib said. "Wish I was out fishing."

"Yeah, if you know a stream the pollution hasn't killed." Goldman cleared his throat. "I, uh, heard about your show yesterday. My girl friend saw it."

"Oh, that." Habib hung up his jacket and took his coverall off its hook. His ears smoldered. "Damn fool thing to do, I guess."

"Hey, now, you can't mean that, Lou."

Surprised at the young man's vehemence, Habib dropped his glance and said with difficulty, "No, sure, I meant it, all right. Only I never—well, I sort of wrote in on, uh, impulse, and my jaw really hit the floor when they called and asked. . . . I'd never've had the nerve myself. But Helen insisted. You know how women are. Especially when I was promised twenty-five bucks for appearing and the dentist's gotten a little impatient about his bill.''

"Seems like a good idea, though," Goldman said. "What can we lose? I think I'll phone in and ask 'em for a replay one evening when I can watch."

"Aw, Joe, come off it."

"No, seriously, Lou. I don't go to services and I'm a good customer for ham sandwiches. But things look so ugly. My girl says— Anyhow, okay, next Tuesday noon I'll take a minute off to ask for a sign. If we're still here.''

"Well, well . . . thanks." Habib buttoned his coverall fast. "Meanwhile, the transmission in that Chevy *is* here."

He took refuge in his hands.

Thursday 16 June

(President Reisner admitted today that the American fleet in the Yellow Sea has suffered heavily from a missile described as being "in the hundred-kiloton range." He denounced the Chinese move and vowed "appropriate response." Peking had made public several hours earlier that it launched the weapon at units it declared were "in flagrant violation of territorial waters, preparing for a sea-borne invasion of the People's Republic of Korea." Heads of state around the world issued pleas for restraint, and Secretary-General Andrei Dekanović called an emergency session of the United Nations.)

Simon and Gail Donaldson stood, fingers clasped together in hurtful tightness, and stared down at the night cities. Lamps, windows, electric placards were nearly lost among headlights, which did not move and did not move.

"No," he said. "We put it off yesterday and now we're too late. Be as dangerous to join that stampede as to stay here."

"What can we do, then?" she whispered.

"Keep your packsack loaded and the bedrolls handy. Be ready to hike with the boys into Tilden Park, hills between you and the Bay. Hope too many people haven't gotten the same idea."

"At once?"

"No. The enemy might settle for a counterforce strategy, and the fallout from places like Vandenberg and Hamilton might not blow this way. Or, conceivably, a general war will be avoided. We sit tight for a while."

"And pray?"

"If that'll make you feel any better."

"I'm not getting religion, Si. But that funny little man on TV the other day—What harm can a prayer do?"

"What harm can anything do, by comparison? Sure. I'll join you. Probably be home anyway. The Lab's tumbling into chaos much faster than I expected."

Friday 17 June

(United States bombers today launched an atomic attack on Chinese rocket bases on the Shantung Peninsula. President Reisner declared that the weapons used were of strictly limited yield, for the strictly limited purpose of taking out installations which, he said on television, had "murdered an estimated ten thousand American sailors and left a greater number in the agonies of burns, mutilations, and radiation sickness." He pledged no further strikes unless further provocation occurred and called for a conference to

16

settle the Korean problem and "other issues which have brought civilization to the rim of catastrophe.")

The network representative scanned the room, as if an assessment of it would explain what he had just heard. It remained a room: yellow-plastered, wood-paneled in the pseudo-Maybeck style of older Eastbay houses; furniture which years of use had contoured to individual bodies; threadbare carpet; obviously homemade drapes; television set; a few harmless paperback novels and how-to books, newspaper, *Life, Reader's Digest;* no Bible in view; some family pictures, a mountainscape clipped out of a magazine and framed; everything clean but unfussy.

"Maybe you don't understand, Mr. Habib," he said. "We're not simply offering to fly you to New York and pay you money. We're giving you a chance to present your, ah, appeal before the whole North American continent. Maybe the whole world."

The short man shook his head and drew on his cigar. "No, thanks," he repeated. "I don't want the publicity. If my, uh, suggestion seems to've, uh, caught on . . . if it's spreading around . . . why, that's plenty. I'm no preacher. When Mr. Dawes asked me to come back—"

"But this is *national,* Mr. Habib!"

"Yeah. And a fine idiot I'd look, stuttering in front of a couple hundred million people. Right, Helen?"

His wife squeezed his arm. "You never were much of a public speaker, Lou." To the representative: "Be warned, sir, and don't waste your time. Once his mind's made up, he can give cards and spades to a mule."

The representative considered her. She was of Mexican

descent, though California born: cheekbones wide and high, flared nostrils, almond eyes, olive complexion, hair sheening black. Those features had a delicacy; she must have been damn good-looking when she was young, before she put on weight, and she wasn't bad yet. "You're invited too, of course, Mrs. Habib," he said.

She laughed. So little laughter was heard of late that the noise startled him. "What have I to tell them? I'm a Unitarian, mainly because several of my friends are. Lou doesn't belong to any church."

The representative looked past them at their children. He'd been briefed. James, seventeen, skinny, long-haired, a frequently self-proclaimed conservative, that being the latest style in adolescent rebellion; Stephanie, twenty, student at California College of Arts and Crafts, who had inherited her mother's plumpness and her father's face; Richard, twenty-two, likewise plain and stocky, but the most promising of the lot since he was studying for the Episcopal ministry. . . . Behind his parents' backs, he smiled slightly and shook his head

"You've got to tell them something!" the representative exclaimed. "What would be an unmistakable sign, a miracle nobody could explain away?"

"How should I know?" Habib answered. He squirmed. "I, uh, no, who'm I to tell God what He ought to do? But . . . well—no, I won't."

"Go ahead," his wife urged gently. "It's not a bad idea."

"J-j-just a thought," Habib said. (How luminous his eyes were.) "You know, we, well, we're back in a very crude stage now, I think. We've got a lot of fine science

18

and, uh, technology, but we've put behind us all that thinking, that experience, over thousands of years—you know, theology, that nobody except a few like my son cares about any longer. We've really no better notion of God than, uh, some Hebrew nomad before Abraham. I know I don't. We've got to start over. Not the still, small voice, but something big, flashy—oh, like, how's the line go? 'Sun, stand thou still.' If God would stop the sun a while, maybe we'd get the idea. Because we sure can't understand a Sermon on the Mount any longer. Don't you agree?''

A reporter from the Oakland *Tribune,* quietly present, made a note.

Saturday 18 June

(Soviet Premier Nikolai Isaeff today asserted that his country would stand firmly beside China in any major conflict with the United States. He warned that further attacks upon the Chinese mainland could bring massive retaliation by Russian forces now fully mobilized.)

They weren't demonstrating before the White House. Not exactly. They were praying. Most of them were black. Their chant was so many-throated that it rolled past the fence, over the lawn and through the wall, into the bones.

"They could get out of hand, Mr. President," the Secret Service officer fretted. "We can hold them off, naturally, but the casualties . . . Are you sure we shouldn't disperse them?"

"That would make casualties too," William Reisner

replied. "No, let them stay. They don't menace anything except Pennsylvania Avenue traffic." His lips dragged upward. "I might follow their example, come the time."

Sunday 19 June
(Pope Benedict, in a sermon delivered at St. Peter's, today added his voice to the growing number of religious leaders who have urged their followers to pray for a token of God's presence at noon on Tuesday. At a press conference afterward, he was asked whether or not he meant noon, daylight saving time. "Follow your clocks," he said wearily. "God made time but man made the hours. Unless God help us, it may be man will end them.")

"Not the Tibetans, what remains of them," said the head of the political police. "Nor the Russians. Their reactions might have been foreseen. But the thing has spread like cholera across our own country."

"How did it happen?" Chairman Wu responded. He forestalled a reply. "Do not answer. There is no single, simple answer. Not in an age of transistor radios and relay satellites. The fact is, the average Chinese is as reluctant as anyone else to see his children turned to corpses and his land to ash. He grasps at archaic straws."

"What shall we do, honored leader?"

"Do? Why, nothing. Let them beat their gongs, burn their incense, yes, flock to their churches and pagodas if they wish. When no sign comes—but when their government, a few mortal men armed only with courage and correct principles—when *man* rides out the storm—they will have had a most valuable lesson."

Monday 20 June

(President Reisner has declared martial law throughout the United States. National Guard units, now federalized, are instructed to restore order among hordes fleeing the cities.)

"No power," Donaldson said. "Well, we've got candles."

"No fresh groceries," Gail told him. "Store's been bought out." She paused. "Remember, when we were first married and poor, what I could do with potatoes? We have quite a few spuds left."

He looked out into darkness. "You sure we shouldn't start walking?"

"Quite sure. To judge from what news I hear. No, darling, we stand fast and wait for tomorrow noon."

He regarded her in astonishment. "You know," he said after a moment, "I believe you're seriously expecting a miracle."

"Aren't you?" she asked.

"No. Certainly not. A miracle's a suspension of natural law. Can't happen."

"But you will join the boys and me. Won't you?"

"Oh, yes. Psychological effect. The idea does seem to've traveled fast and far. And Szilard once defined a miracle as an event with less than ten percent probability. Okay, us, the Europeans, Asians, Africans, Australians, everybody, let's hope together. The little man was right as far as that goes. We do need something bigger than ourselves to live by."

Tuesday 21 June

(Help.
Namu amida Butsu.
Om mani padme hum.
Hare Kirshna.
Eli, Eli.
Ullah akbar.
Our Father Who art in Heaven.
Minoké ago Legba.
Cosmos.
Man.
Luck.
Give us a sign.
Help.)

The strangest thing had been the way things kept going. For the most part, the riots, the panic flights, the destructions and breakdowns happened to you on TV and in the paper. Oh, you saw the smoke pall above West Oakland, and a troop carrier growl by full of Guardsmen who looked pitifully young under their helmets, and the looted remnants of a couple of shops in your own neighborhood; various businesses were closed and traffic had thinned and mail delivery was irregular; electricity was often out for hours in a row; your wife took what foods she could find after tramping from market to market, at police-guarded prices, or gave in to backdoor slinkers who had the goods at a thousand-percent markup; you quit using the phone, since lines were always jammed—but you and most of those like you continued on your rounds. You worked, you coped, you ate and bathed and went bowling on your usual night, you actually joked (thinly) and slept (badly) while the hours wore into days.

Joe Goldman had demanded, "What's holding us here?"

"Our jobs," Louis Habib had replied. He chose his words with care. "I won't get mad if you light out. I do advise you against it. The countryside can't support as many as have run. You'd be just another animal, to herd into a refugee camp and try to feed somehow. You'll help, instead of adding a burden, if you stand pat."

Goldman shifted a wad of chewing gum around in his mouth. "How can I be less of a man than my boss?" He grunted.

Over Habib's objections, he did insist on having a radio tuned to the news Tuesday. While they worked, the descriptions came in, hour by hour: crowds had gathered in Piccadilly Circus, a special service had been held on a battleship in mid-Atlantic, Times Square was jammed with humanity as on a silent New Year's Eve, rain fell in Chicago but nevertheless a gathering. . . . "Don't want to go downtown?" Goldman inquired. "Or maybe back to your folks?"

"No," Habib said. His heart stuttered. *God has to be everywhere, and we one in Him. Right? I don't know. That damn fundamentalist preacher who's been pestering us* . . . "At the Mormon Tabernacle in Salt Lake City—"

Bells around the Bay. No sirens; that would have been gruesomely dangerous. Noon bells, though, tinkling, mewing, clanging, striding. Cars, buses, walkers come to a halt. Heads bowed, heads uplifted to a blank sky. A shadow across the shop floor, cast by the pillar of a hydraulic lift. *God, Spirit, Whoever made the world, You can't have made it in vain. Show us. Please. Stop the sun, or do what else is best, but show us that You are, because we've failed ourselves and nobody is left except You.*

"Sun, stand thou still," Joe Goldman muttered.

Afterward he and Habib avoided each other's eyes and spoke no more than they must. Neither ate his lunch. Disappointment was too thick in their gullets.

Earth spun eastward, nightward. About four forty-five in the afternoon, the first wild rumor came out of the radio. Habib stood a moment. Then he laid a wrench on the floor, at the exact point where shadows joined of a rack and the automobile it upbore. He and Goldman watched for several minutes before they were quite sure that the shadow had stopped. Goldman broke into harsh, inexperienced sobs. Habib stowed tools, locked doors, got into his car, and drove home. At least, his body did.

Wednesday 22 June

(For one sidereal day, a trifle more than twenty-four hours, the sun remained moveless, at zenith in Mid-Pacific, precisely over the International Date Line.

Rather, Earth's rotation period was slowed to a value identical with Earth's year. As nearly as could be told, this happened instantaneously. It is certain that none of the sensitive instruments prepared and manned by what scientists had not gone more or less mad for the duration were able to measure any finite time in which the old spin was resumed at the end of that endless day.

Nothing else changed. The planet moved on in orbit, as did its moon. [This made every calendar in existence obsolete. But if Earth had actually stopped, Luna would have fled, become an independent globe on a wildly eccentric path. As was, its light fell icy on otherwise lightless Washington, New York, Brasília, Buenos Aires, London, Paris, Rome, Capetown, Cairo, Tel Aviv, Leningrad, Moscow, New Delhi.] Weather and tide patterns grew somewhat confused, but the term was insufficient for disaster to be generated. Wildlife was troubled; circadian rhythm disturbed, untold organisms went hungry until the familiar night-and-day returned; but few, if any, died.

Man took the matter worse. A thousand generations of historians would fail to record the whole of those hours and their immediate aftermath. Yet death, devastation, injury, collapse were held within astonishingly close bounds. It helped that worldwide dread had, beforehand, brought about worldwide activation of disciplined forces—police, firemen, militia, political cadres, private organizations. Then, too, the magnitude of what happened, the infinitely greater magnitude of what it meant, stunned violence out of all save the most foolish and brutish. Oftener than not, loss occurred because minds were turned elsewhere than to everyday [everynight] maintenance work.

The pilgrimages by torch to the Ganges, by candlelight to the Western Wall and the Mosque of Omar, by furnacelike sunlight to Our Lady of Guadalupe, were not frantic in any true sense of that word. They were awesome: men, women, children by the millions flowing together and becoming a natural force.

Nor did everyone enter such a tide or such a congregation. Some cleaved to the routines, others to the purposes which had always been their lives.)

Helen Habib thrust a sandwich into her husband's grasp.

He took it without noticing, where he sat by the window in his old armchair and stared out at the empty pavement.

She shook him. "Lou, you must eat," she said.

He blinked at her. "Now?" he answered, as if from very far away.

"Yes, now. When we've no faintest idea of what will come next. Eat. I'll make coffee."

"How long?" whimpered Stephanie in her corner while a marble-fronted clock, brought from Lebanon by her great-grandfather, bonged midnight. Around the house lay afternoon, listless leaves upon trees, shadows that did not stir. A dog loped by, outrageously unaffected.

"How should anyone know?" Richard retorted.

"You, dad," she said for the fiftieth or hundredth time. "You prayed for this. So pray for sunset."

"Yah, yah," Jimmy jeered. He was hunkered before the television, trying to get a program. But there had been no broadcasts for hours except replays of a tape whereon President Reisner told America to stay calm. "Just like that."

Dick's knuckles stood white around a Book of Common Prayer. Back and forth he paced. One shoe squeaked. "You seem to think your father's a magician, Steffie," he lectured, likewise repeating himself. "I tell you, divine inspiration is something else."

Habib shook his whole body. "Me? Inspired?" Their attention snapped to him; he had scarcely spoken before. "Can't be."

"The Lord chooses whom He will, father," Dick said; and then: "No! I've got to get off this pomposity. I was a glorified agnostic, a social-gospel churchman who saw

26

God, if ever I saw Him, as a—what'd somebody call it once?—a kind of oblong blur.'' Breath sucked between his teeth. " 'It is a fearful thing to fall into the hands of the living God.' ''

"But me!'' Louis Habib climbed to his feet. The sandwich dropped on the floor. He groped, as if blind, toward Helen. "Me,'' he pushed out of his lips. Sweat ran off him; they could smell the sharpness. "Me who figured there must be a God, but till the war scare never thought it made much difference—not since I was a kid, when I used to make fun of the sisters in my mind—hell, when I wrote that letter, I really thought we needed faith. Not that we needed God. The difference—''

He caught both his wife's hands and stood before her weeping. "I cheated on you once, Helen. I'd've done it more if the chance had come. Sometimes when a pretty girl went past, I'd imagine—I, I, I play poker, I go off bowling or fishing when maybe you'd rather have me home, I vote the straight party ticket b'cause that's easier'n thinking, I've chiseled on the income tax as much's I had the guts to, though th-th-that's not much—''

She kissed him. Nobody quite noticed the pain which had crossed her. "If you've nothing worse to confess, Lou, stop moping and . . . and eat, blast it!''

A drumbeat on the door called their minds away. Dick looked relieved. He went and opened it. A neighbor stood on the porch. "Why, hello, Mr. Olstad. Come in.''

The man entered behind a shotgun.

"What?'' Dick sprang back. Stephanie shrilled. Jimmy started to lunge, checked, and retreated, hands high. Their parents stood in the middle of the floor, moving no more than the shadows.

27

"Okay." Olstad's cheeks were unshaven, his hair uncombed. He croaked rather than spoke. The twin barrels of his gun jittered about. "Bring back the night."

Habib could merely gape through his tears.

"You did this, damn you." Olstad stabbed the gun in his direction. "I remember. Well, undo it. Or I'll kill you."

"Stop." Habib let go of Helen, thrust her behind him and took a step toward the intruder. "I did . . . maybe I did suggest praying for this sign . . . first, I mean. Or maybe not." As the words came forth, strength seemed to rise in him. He squared his shoulders. "Ideas like that get in the air. We never really know who begins them. Sam, do you believe one monkey like me can control this planet? That any one man can? I heard a commentator guess a billion people were praying. *They* were heard. Not me."

"Then start them praying again," Olstad said.

"Sure," Habib answered. "Glad to. Tell me how."

For a minute they faced each other. Suddenly Olstad pitched the shotgun through a window. Glass rang and tinkled; one chamber crashed off on the lawn. "Martha's half out of her head!" he screamed. "Billy's not come back from his Scout trip! What'm I s'posed to do?"

Habib went to him, gave him a brief hug, and said, "You start by having a drink, Sam. I've got a little Jack Daniels somewhere."

There was not much talk until after Olstad had left. Then Jimmy ventured, "Uh, dad, that went cool. You know, though, we could get a whole lynch mob. Couldn't we?"

"What do you propose?" Habib asked.

"Well, we hide out, like with friends or—"

This time the rapping was more controlled. Jimmy darted into his room for a sheath knife. When he came back, he saw his father confronted by two men. They were dressed like solid citizens, young and hard.

"Mr. Habib?" one said. "How do you do. We're from the Federal Bureau of Investigation." He flipped a wallet open to show his credentials. "You will all come along with us."

Thursday 23 June

(Heads of state around the world called for public thanksgiving at the return of day and night. Most agreed that mankind has indeed been granted an unmistakable sign that a personal God exists. Exceptions included the government of China, which had no immediate comment other than broadcasts and wall posters directing citizens to resume their duties and the Kremlin, which issued a terse statement that "this extraordinary phenomenon must be soberly and scientifically evaluated.")

Gail Donaldson had spent most of those twenty-four hours holding fear at bay in Mike and Johnny. When they, exhausted, fell asleep, she rejoined her husband in the living room but soon dozed off herself. Waking from fitful dreams, she found him still at the picture window, his eyes locked west across the afternoon light on the waters. Her attempts to talk foundered on his frozenness.

When finally the sun moved again, she had once more been preoccupied with the children. "Look, we're getting our night back! Soon you'll see the stars." On the whole, she thought, she had succeeded in making this experience a marvel to them rather than a root of future terrors. Simon's shock remained to be dealt with.

While the eastern range turned purple and the Bay argent, the ruddy globe sank beyond the Golden Gate and Venus gleamed above, she made drinks for them both and brought them to him. He accepted his, not altogether as mechanically as he had taken the food she prepared. Twilight smoked around them.

She raised her glass and grinned lopsidedly. "Here's to God."

"Uh." Donaldson stared at her for a moment, and at his martini, before he made jerky response. "Yeah."

"No disrespect intended, of course," she said. "I simply . . . am ignorant yet . . . about sacraments."

"You believe?"

"What, don't you?"

"I don't know." His hand trembled, so that the drink slopped over.

"The evidence, darling. You prayed too."

"I, well, I took part in a rite. Yes. My thought was, if people around the world could unite in an appeal . . . at this time in history . . . I mustn't hang back. Yes, I hoped for a miracle, but in Szilard's meaning. A mass conversion of some kind, conversion to sanity. Instead, we got—" His gesture chopped at the dusk. City lights were twinkling forth; large patches of darkness lay between, but no doubt full service would presently be restored and meanwhile the sky stood clear.

"Why're you so bothered?" she asked. "You never were a dogmatic atheist."

"No," he said slowly, scowling, though at least becoming restored somewhat to his old self, even to a touch of humor. "An agnostic, i.e., a polite atheist. I did believe in a natural order. That the universe, however mysterious, made sense."

"What's that line from Eddington? The universe is not only queerer than we know, it's queerer than we can imagine. Something like that. Isn't a God one more element of an always strange cosmos?"

"Not the same kind of element." His tone roughened. "I've heard and read too much drivel through the years, about how quantum uncertainties or evolution or whatnot prove there has to be a Creator or an afterlife or whatnot—when in fact they prove nothing of the sort. And what's happened now doesn't prove a God either. It only mocks all reason. A discontinuity. An impossibility. Either the laws of nature are subject to meaningless suspensions—are, maybe, mere statistical fluctuations in howling chaos—or else a Being is able to abrogate them at whim—and in either case, *we'll never understand.*"

"Do we have to?"

"I have to," he told her. "That was the horror of the war building up. You know how I rejected peace petitions and the like for the garbage they were, and held that old-fashioned realism, plus basic goodwill, gave us a fighting chance of winning through to a better order of things. Then Korea erupted, and suddenly events were beyond human comprehension or control. Disaster seemed inevitable regardless of anyone's wish, knowledge, power. Our helplessness was nearly as hard for me to take as the blowup itself would be."

31

He had been sipping while he talked. In his worn state, the alcohol took quick hold and hastened his tongue: "We may have been rescued, temporarily anyhow. But the helplessness is now like burial under a mountain. Think! If Earth can slow down its spin and then regain it—more than six times ten to the twenty-first tons of mass, accelerated instantaneously, which is even a logical contradiction; and no released energies to melt the ground and boil the oceans, not so much as a hurricane or a quake—which means that cornerstones of physics like conservation of energy and momentum were removed, and later replaced, with no noise, no fuss, no trace—how can we ever dare look to the future?

"A child might, on impulse, rescue a beetle about to drown. Later, on impulse, he might step on it. Or if there is a plan behind all this, what?" Donaldson shuddered. "Arthur Machen once defined absolute evil as when a rose begins to sing."

"You're no more certain of evil or chaos than you are of good and . . . and an order that includes purpose," Gail said. "Less, in fact." She set down her glass and offered him the reality of her hands.

He tossed off his own drink, straightened, and said, "Maybe. Maybe the impossibility . . . can be fitted in . . . somehow."

"That has to be your working hypothesis, doesn't it? And you're just the man to do the work." She kissed him.

He said at last, "Thanks more than I'll ever be able to speak, for giving me back some guts." After a hesitation, he added, "Do you mind if . . . if I go back to the lab already tomorrow?"

"Of course not, silly. You need to." After dinner she fed him a sleeping pill and held him in her arms till he drowsed.

—That had been the Wednesday sunset which ought to have come on Tuesday. Driving the winding hill streets on the belated early morning of Thursday, Donaldson dialed a local educational radio station, hoping for more than the inanities which blatted on every other waveband, save for those which played half a dozen religious compositions to death. A professional voice:

"—indubitably a conscious decision, therefore a conscious intelligence, stood behind the event. Would some blind, random process have halted the globe so that midnight fell exactly over our arbitrary prime meridian? And I suspect more was intended than that token. Consider. Almost the maximum land surface was held in darkness: the eastern United States, South America, Africa, Europe, most of Asia. True, the western United States enjoyed day, if 'enjoy' is the proper word; but most of China did also, as if to balance the two great antagonists. Does not a strong hint lie in the fact that mainly the part of Earth which stayed beneath the sun was innocent Oceania?

"Perhaps we have been given a symbol in the very dating. Besides the solstice, with all its associations, we have the occurrence lasting from Tuesday to Wednesday. Or, in Romance languages, from the day of Mars to the day of Mercury. In either case, from the god of war to the god who conducts away the souls of the newly dead. A warning? I don't know. I can merely suggest we close our ears to the rising chorus of partisan claims and, in this respite which has been given us, humbly set about our affairs in a more decent fashion than hitherto.''

At the head of Cyclotron Road, Donaldson was inspected closer than usual by the guard at the gate. ''Shucks, Bob, you know me,'' he protested.

''I don't know what I know,'' the guard answered. ''Lemme have your badge a second, please.''

The physicist found his office empty; the secretary he shared with a couple of other men hadn't reported in, nor had they. The laboratory he chose was likewise hushed. Instruments stared, apparatus loomed like idols of an abandoned faith. He wasn't sorry. It was good to use his own fingers on an elementary job. For a start, he wanted to measure terrestrial magnetism. The suspension of rotation must have affected it . . . maybe. . . . He sought his office again, phoned the main switchboard, found a girl on duty and asked her to put him in touch here and there across the country, as soon as possible. Beneath every shakenness he thought: *If ordinary laws did otherwise prevail, a fresh value of H, at a lot of different points around the planet, should give us insights about the core that we might never have had.*

A man in Army uniform, colonel's insignia, entered. ''Dr. Donaldson?'' He held out his hand. ''My name's Heinrichs, Ed Heinrichs. Excuse the intrusion, but this is important. They told me in Administration that of the workers here who're present today, you're our best bet.''

Donaldson gave him an uneasy clasp. ''What's the problem?''

''Well—'' The colonel was no model of assurance either.

He shifted his feet and stared at the floor. "The fact of the matter is . . . you know this Habib fellow? The guy who seems to have started it all?"

"I know who he is," Donaldson said warily.

"Well, we've got him here. And his family." The colonel raised a palm. "No, please hear me out. What else can the government do? We have to try to get some idea of what's happened, what's likely to happen, and he's our only handle on it. Isn't he? Besides, he needs protection. If you'll tune in the news on TV, you'll probably see a helicopter shot of the mob around his house. Not a hostile mob, so far, anyway. More like a . . . an old-time revival meeting, I guess, except the quietness is eerie." He gulped. "The police have the house cordoned off. They didn't get to Habib's garage in time. That's been stripped. Right down to the ground. Souvenir hunters, relic hunters, I don't know what."

Donaldson recalled the brisk medieval trade in pieces of the True Cross.

"Anyhow," Heinrichs said, "the word from Washington was to take the whole family into protective custody for a while. Could be Russian or Chinese agents after them. Or ordinary psychos. We can house them here, temporarily, secretly. A scientist—"

His eyes did not command, they pleaded.

Friday 24 June

(I. M. Leskov, noted astronomer and member of the Soviet Academy of Sciences, today proposed that the pause in Earth's spin was due to beings from outer space. "We cannot equate superstition and explanation," he declared in

35

a statement which had the cautious endorsement of the Kremlin. "The requirement of minimum hypothesis practically forces us to assume that what happened resulted from the application of a technology centuries beyond ours. I find it easy to believe that an advanced civilization, capable of interstellar travel, sent a team to save mankind from the carnage threatened by an imperialism which that society outgrew long ago.")

William Reisner sat still behind his desk for some time before he said, most quietly, "I don't want to suppose you're insane, Stan. I'd rather suppose I misheard you. Would you repeat?"

Gray-faced, the spokesman for the Joint Chiefs of Staff answered, "You didn't hear me out, Mr. President. True, the Korean fighting is still in abeyance. But the Chinese are using the chance to pour in reinforcements. Besides troops, mobile ICBM's. I have the reports here, air reconnaissance, space surveillance, ground-based intelligence. They understand as well as we do, no ICBM is worth a spent bullet, except for wanton butchery, till we reprogram every computer and adjust every navigational system. I don't give that tacit cease-fire another week. They have an overwhelming superiority in manpower and armor."

"But we have the same in bombers."

"Even so—"

"We retaliated for what they did in the Yellow Sea," Reisner said. "A so-called preventive strike is something else again. Its proper name is murder."

"There is also such a thing as responsibility toward our own men and allies. I don't argue for hitting their cities. I advocate it, but know better than to argue for it. A sharp, local warning *now*—"

"Will either make Peking respect our will enough to negotiate . . . or confirm Peking's belief that we are monsters who cannot be negotiated with. How about morale, discipline, organization among the Chinese? They must be pretty badly shaken themselves."

The military man shrugged and said bitterly, "Did you catch the news from the Middle East, Mr. President? Seems that Palestinian mullah who's preaching a jihad against Israel . . . seems he's got men swarming to him, yelling that Allah has shown He wills it. And that militant rabbi in Haifa—"

"I know," Reisner interrupted. "Still another consideration. We dare not spread ourselves too thin. But I asked you about the state of the Chinese."

"I can't tell you, sir. In spite of a hundred contradictory predictions from as many psywar experts, I've no idea what shape the American reaction will take, let alone the Oriental. I was just pointing out that the . . . miracle . . . didn't include putting brotherly love into all human hearts."

"Yours, Stan?"

"Sir, I'd go to chapel occasionally, but God always seemed comfortably distant from it. Today . . . He's here. Only what is He? I keep thinking of Jehovah the Thunderer— the Crusades—Don John at Lepanto, saving Christendom with sword and cannon— Suppose we sent a couple hundred squadrons over North Korea to buzz them? Simply buzz them; no shooting, no bombing, unless they shoot first."

Saturday 25 June

(A startling new theory about the stoppage of Earth's rotation was published today in China over the signature of Chairman Wu Yuan. According to it, the occurrence may have been a matter of ESP. "Such phenomena as telepathy [mind-reading], telekinesis [moving objects by mental power], and precognition, [foreknowledge of the future] are claimed by many reputable scientists to have been observed in the laboratory," said the widely distributed pamphlet. "The mind of man may have tremendous abilities, once liberated from the blinkers of the past. More than a third of the contemporary human race is guided by Marxism; more than half this number has for more than a generation been under the tutelage of wholly correct principles. Thus the massed concentration of the peace-loving peoples may well have triggered cosmic energies to produce those events which have halted the imperialists in their bloody track and thrown them wallowing back into the basest superstitions.")

Richard Habib sat down uneasily at first, in Donaldson's office, till the physicist opened a drawer and took out a bottle. "Care for some?" Donaldson invited. "Frankly, I need a drink."

"Wouldn't mind, thanks," the young man replied, almost too low to hear.

Whisky gurgled into Dixie cups. "Water down the hall if you want," Donaldson said. "No ice or soda handy, I'm afraid."

"This is fine, thanks."

Silence hemmed them in. Few were at the Radlab today and none, seemingly, in this building. The room lay bleak, hardly relieved by a picture of Gail and the children on a desk, a Peanuts cartoon Scotch-taped to a wall, a window open to mild air, sunlight, and concrete.

Donaldson sat down, lit a cigarette, filled his lungs with what he knew was carcinogenic pungency, and said, "I hope you're not too uncomfortable. They had to improvise quarters."

"Not bad, sir."

"Call me Si, will you? I'm, uh . . . you realize I was co-opted? I don't think they're right to hold you incommunicado like this, and I'm leaning on them to change that. Until they do, however—"

Richard Habib nodded. He was dressed in incongruously colorful sports shirt and slacks. Well, he hadn't been ordained as yet, had he?

Donaldson glowered at his ashtray. "The thing is," he said, word by word, "I'm a lousy choice. Too stiff. I've spent the last couple of days trying to get acquainted with your father, your mother. You saw the result."

"You're too shy, really, sir," Dick said.

Startled, Donaldson glanced up. After a moment, wryly, he replied. "Uh-huh. I've requested they bring my wife in on this. She understands people. Meanwhile, okay, I want to get on with my job . . . more because that's essential to my own sanity than for any other reason . . . but what is my job?"

"An impossible one, I'm afraid," the young man told him in a sober voice.

"Could well be. We can take EEG's and tissue samples and I don't know what from your father, we can give him psychological tests till hell wouldn't have it—" Donaldson stopped. Dick uttered a chuckle. Donaldson swallowed and plowed on: "For the time being, while they scramble around in Washington drawing organizational charts, Project Habib, *c'est moi*. My word's bound to carry weight in proportion to what results I can show before the bureaucrats descend on us. Well, I'm as anxious as you to keep the proceedings humane, to respect the rights of your father and his family. I'm also anxious to get some answers, or at least a notion of what the unanswerable questions are."

"I'm no authority."

"You are your father's son. And an almost-graduate of a seminary. And, they tell me, broad-minded. That makes you the natural lead piece in this game. Won't you tell me what you think happened?"

"A miracle." Dick's gaze was direct and calm. "I mean in the sense that Thomas Aquinas used, *praeter naturam* or *supra et contra naturam* or, in plain English, a supernatural thing. Therefore unexplainable by science. But verifiable by it."

"Hm?" Donaldson drew hard on his cigarette, grimaced, and took a sip of whisky. It glowed on the way down. *If you want quotations*, he thought, *I'll give you "Malt does more than Milton can."* Aloud: "I guess I see what you mean. Spell it out, though, will you?"

"What happened was a genuine, physical, observable event." Dick leaned into his chair, which creaked, looked out the window, and spoke with care. "I've had to come to terms myself, these past few days. Suddenly what had looked like a nice cozy symbol became reality. Well, it's happened before. Hume was more willing to assume that

40

testimony had erred or lied than that the laws of nature had been set aside. On the other hand, the Roman Church in modern times has taken pains to investigate alleged miracles, establish their empirical authenticity. As Saint Paul did in the beginning.''

Donaldson waited.

"First Corinthians," Dick said. "By now I have the passage memorized. He realized that the Resurrection is the central fact of Christianity. If you can believe that a corpse rose from its tomb, walked and talked, ate and drank and lived for forty days, why, then you can swallow anything, ancient prophecies, virgin birth, wedding at Cana, instant cures of leprosy—those are mere detail. The Resurrection is what matters. 'And if Christ be not raised, your faith is vain; ye are yet in your sins.' Paul went to considerable trouble to find eyewitnesses; he names them and lists the reasons for trusting them.''

After a second he continued, "And that was a subtle miracle. I think my father caught onto one truth when he remarked that today we're so far gone into spiritual savagery that nothing except the most primitive, public sort of demonstration could touch us.''

Donaldson took off his glasses, which made the world blurry, and polished them. He needed something to do. "As if we'd flunked quantum mechanics and been sent back to roll balls down inclined planes?''

Dick smiled. "I suppose. You must know better than I how much science is taken on faith. How many crucial experiments have you carried out yourself?''

"Uh-huh. Or how many theoretical developments have I traced the math of, step by step? Precious few. Still, in principle I can. Or could, till this week.'' Donaldson hunched forward. ''Science always had its differences of interpretation. Einstein never did feel the Bohr-Heisenberg discontinuities could be right, though he had no fast proof. Remember? *'Raffiniert ist der Herr Gott, aber boshaft ist Er nicht.'* ''

''I'm afraid I don't know German.''

''Oh, take the usual version. 'God does not play dice with the world.' Well, has He here? If He's been around at all? Or suppose He exists, suppose He did what He did for a purpose, like to save us from ourselves. Why this way? He could better have put some sanity into us.''

''And taken away our free will,'' Dick responded. ''Turned us into puppets. No, I think He would rather give us a fresh chance to make our own salvation.''

''Free will!'' Donaldson's fist thumped hurtfully hard on his desk. ''We could spend a whole day rehearsing the tired old arguments about that pseudo-problem.'' He stubbed out his cigarette as if it were a personal enemy. ''Salvation? What is salvation? Playing harps through eternity? Or simply being righteous? I've read a little biblical commentary too. In most of the Old Testament, they don't seem to have imagined we live past the grave.'' He gulped more liquor. ''*What* God wrought the miracle, if any did? The Christian God? If so, what version? A medieval one surrounded by saints and angels, a Calvinist one Who plans to cast most of us into perdition, a simpering Positive Thinker, or what? How do we know it wasn't the Jewish God . . . one of the Jewish gods? Or Moslem, or any of a thousand Hindu deities, or what?''

''We don't know,'' Dick said. ''Except by faith. Saint

42

Paul grasped that as well as the need for facts—the absolute necessity of faith if we're to have any intellectual coherence. Read his Epistle to the Hebrews, for instance.''

"And so we're back where we began!" Donaldson shouted. "Faith! Believe and be saved! What to believe? Take your choice of dogmas, each full of logical holes big enough to drive a camel through; or meaningless 'non-sectarian' mush; or science, a painfully built and always changing house, made by human hands alone—which has just had the foundations knocked from under it!''

Sunday 26 June

(As this day moved around the globe, churches were filled to overflowing. Where no more room was available, outdoor services were attended by thousands each. This was as true of most Communist countries, including the Soviet Union, as of the West. Non-Christian faiths draw similar hordes on their own special days. Rumors of a vast religious revival in China seep past a censorship which has put foreign journalists under virtual house arrest. On the whole, sermons have urged rededication to peace; but some have emphasized other matters.)

Los Angeles. The Reverend Matthew Thomas Elliott paused for a sip of water, which presented his aquiline profile to the television camera, before he tossed back a lock of hair with the well-known gesture of his head, leaned across the pulpit, and said into the faces and faces that crammed the auditorium:

"All right, my people, now I'm going to speak plain, the way God wants me to speak. I know it's going to

shock the liberals. Oh, you'll hear them squeal like stuck
pigs, exactly the way the Commies want them to squeal.
And the children of Shem won't like it any more than the
children of Ham; you know what I mean? But God has
made me His vessel. If He spoke His own will—and how
could He speak plainer than by stopping the sun as He did
for Joshua, Joshua who fought the good fight—if He spoke
loud and clear on behalf of His chosen people, honest
working Americans, the people of His promised land that
the Comsymps want to give over to the hosts of Moloch—if
God spoke, can Matthew Thomas Elliott remain silent?
Can you? Let's hear you, folks. Let's hear you speak out
for the Lord!''

The ''Amen!'' shivered the walls.

Oakland. Brother Hughie Aldrich looked up, as if to see
Heaven beyond the banners which hung from the ceiling.
He let silence grow until the breathing of his crowd was
like surf, their sweat like incense. Then, slowly, he looked
downward and caught their eyes.

''What did God stop?'' his famous organ tones demanded of them. ''The world? Oh, yes. But that was a
tiny thing. What He really stopped was this rich man's war
that was getting started when the bombs of white Amer-
ika''—he formed the K with his fingers, a gesture that had
become his trademark—''struck our Chinese brothers. The
rich man's war on the poor, the white man's war on the
black, the brown, the yellow, the red. Well, brothers and
sisters, we've been given the sign we prayed for in our
agony. If the Man can go so far that God Himself has to
cry 'Halt!' . . . why, then the Man can start undoing part
of the misery, slavery, poverty, torture, and death he's

visited on us these past four hundred years—he can do that or perish, perish beneath the wrath of God and the people!''

''Right on!'' chanted back at him. ''Right on! Right on! Right on!''

Sacramento. ''And who was the prophet chosen by God?'' asked the lay speaker. ''Was he some wild radical? Was he some dirty dropout? No, friends, he was a law-abiding, free-enterprise American businessman, struggling to pay the taxes to support his bloated government the same as you and I must struggle. Could God have given us a clearer sign of His will?''

San Francisco. ''What has become of Louis Habib?'' cried he who delivered the keynote address. ''Where is he? What have the capitalists done with him, his wife, his children? Why have they hidden him away from the people? Because they're afraid of the message an honest working-man has to bring us, the same as fascist Rome was afraid of the message a carpenter named Jesus had to bring. If we don't want another crucifixion, we'd better act fast.''

Portland. ''In the presence, brethren, in the very presence of this awesome manifestation of God's power, Satan's agents continue to gnaw like rats at the heart of faith, morality, and society. These atheists, evolutionists, free-love swine, boozers, tobacco smokers, dope fiends still try to hide from us the plain truth of God's word as revealed in the Holy Bible. Why else have they cast His chosen prophet into a nameless dungeon?''

Seattle. ''Like, God's told the establishments what He thinks of 'em. Every establishment, dig? Every last unhuman suppressive polluting corporate monster, in America, in Russia, in China, in Europe. When He stopped the Earth

45

spining, He told them, 'Rotate.' Now they're scrambling to save their corruption. That's why Louis Habib, our guru, ain't here today. You dig?''

Tijuana, San Diego, Bakersfield, Eugene, Walla Walla, Vancouver, Honolulu, and points north, south, east, and west. "When God's word came to me and I called upon the people of the world—"

Peking. "After Chairman Wu's thought had massed the minds of the peace-loving peoples of the world—"

Monday 27 June

(The Soviet government today announced its willingness to take part in a great power conference for the purposes of defusing the Korean powder keg and working out arrangements for arms control and broadly based international cooperation. Public unrest and spontaneous meetings throughout the country, in defiance of prohibitions and calls to official rallies, are believed to have influenced the Kremlin's decision. There has been no direct Soviet response to riots in the European satellites, from which most Russian forces have withdrawn in the course of the last few days. Since these have not been deployed in the western USSR, observers think they are hurrying to the Manchurian border in alarm at the massive Chinese buildup.)

Alice Haynes Prescott, wife of the Senator, frequent contributor to magazines, television panelist, former United States ambassador to Belgium, president of the Women's League for Social Justice, vice-president of Americans United for Law and Order, inevitable on every best-dressed list, beamed with long but dazzling teeth and said, "You can't imagine how hard it was to learn where you were and be admitted. My husband the Senator and I had to—if I may use the expression reverently—move heaven and earth.''

"Nice of you," Louis Habib mumbled.

She patted his hand. "The arrogance! The sheer stupidity! Though'' (a delicate moue) "I must say I would expect no better of the present Administration."

"Oh, they did what they figured was right. We've not, uh, been mistreated. In fact, the Donaldsons are damn nice—begging your pardon."

She measured out a laugh. "Well, quite as I thought. The holy man is human."

He swallowed and looked from her. It was bright, gusty weather. Clouds scudded small on a wind which roared in the eucalyptus trees. Sun-flecks and leaf shadows danced on crackly-carpeted ground; pungency whirled through the air, which was cool. Below spread the Radlab complex, and hills toppled down into Berkeley, the Bay danced aglitter, San Francisco rose white, Marin County lifted heights that were blue-hazed with distance.

He had grabbed the chance to go for a walk when this woman desired it. The two guards who came behind didn't spoil the day much. Now he wished he'd crawled into the darkest corner of the quarters hastily rigged for his family and shoveled old newspapers over himself.

"I'm not a holy man," he said, half strangled. "I've told 'em and told 'em till the words turn me sick. I got no visions, not then, not since, never. I don't feel any different. Sure, I'm glad to learn there is a God and we matter to Him . . . I guess we do. But I don't know anything about Him, I tried to say daily prayers but felt too silly, I'm no kind of priest and don't want to be.''

47

"I understand, Lou. You're the man of genius, exactly as I described him in my article for *Civilization* magazine. The real geniuses have all been unpretentious men and women, you know. When somebody is bombastic, like the composer Richard Wagner, it proves he isn't a genius."

"Who says I thought of the idea first?" He waved his arms. "I been watching TV, what times they aren't quizzing me or putting me through their stupid tests. Quite a lot of guys claim they had the original notion. Could be. Why not? An idea sort of floats around when the time is ripe, don't you think?" He pounced at what seemed an opportunity. "In fact, Mrs. Prescott, the more I think about it, the more sure I am that I was a Johnny-come-lately. This guy back east, says he was pushing for everybody to pray together these past three years—sure, I'll bet I heard about him somewhere and, uh, subconsciously . . . No?"

She shook her head firmly. The wind had displaced no hair upon it. "No, dear," she smiled. "Cranks and false prophets we have always among us. They don't count. The overwhelming majority of the Free World knows that the inspiration came to you. *Vox populi, vox Dei.* That's Latin and means, 'The voice of the people is the voice of God.' "

"Uh, I don't know much, uh, theology, but I doubt—"

"Besides," Alice Haynes Prescott told him, "you have a patriotic duty. Don't you realize what would happen if you, the American seer, disowned yourself? Haven't you heard of Wu Yuan's preposterous assertion that *he* is responsible for the event? You can't let such a madman go unchallenged, especially when the international situation is

48

so critical. My husband the Senator is preparing a major speech on the subject; that's why he isn't here today. For my part, I intend to make good use of my appearance on the 'Forefront' show Wednesday night. And you must back us up in the clinches, Lou.''

''Well . . . well, I never went in for politics, Mrs. Prescott.''

''Alice.'' Again she patted his hand. ''Never fear. Some of the most talented speechwriters in the country will be at your disposal. And—don't breathe a word of this, Lou— Rance Rockstone called me personally from Hollywood and offered his services in any coaching you might need. No, not a peep out of you. I know this sounds terribly, terribly insincere, but the fact is you can't put your sincerity across without professional help. Besides, Rance is one of the most sincere persons alive. You'll find out.''

''We better go back,'' he said. ''I better ask my wife.''

''Oh, come along a while. A lovely day. Naturally, you should consult Helen. I want to myself. I'm sure she'll have thousands of good ideas for the gala we'll give in Washington to celebrate your arrival, as soon as my husband the Senator has won your release from here. And your children . . . what fine young persons. Did you know that I'm on the board of the Minerva Foundation? Among other things, it gives college scholarships to deserving students, very generous ones, if I do say so.''

Tuesday 28 June

(The call for a People's Crusade, a mass descent on Washington to insist on ''peace and equal rights under God,'' is gathering adherents from all walks of life with terrifying speed. By now an estimated million individuals are on the move, and more are added every hour. Authorities express concern at the health hazard and at the violent tone of many spokesmen, like one who declared, "This is Armageddon." Already they have trouble maintaining order, especially when groups of would-be demonstrators encounter such militant newly formed rivals as White Americans for Christ, Angels of the Judgment, United Anarchists, and the Religious Freedom League [atheist].

In a press conference, President Reisner deplored what he termed mass hysteria. He also warned against a quieter but, he said, still stronger tendency for workers to quit their jobs and seek a religious life of some kind. "When vital and complex negotiations on the highest levels are to be undertaken," he stated, "the American government must not be weakened at home." He refused comment on the rumor that desertions from the armed services are taking place at such a rate that many units have become completely ineffective.)

"Similar phenomena are not unknown in history." The psychiatrist had to raise his voice above the cocktail-party hubbub. The smoke made him cough a bit. "Consider the medieval dancing manias or the Reformation witch hunts. Today, thanks to global electronic communications, a piece of news, an attitude—a conversion—can spread at the speed of light."

"Everybody saw the sun halted in its course," the chemistry professor pointed out.

"Yes, yes. The difference from the past, had it occurred

in the past, is this. Virtually no individual, certainly no community, could decide in privacy and at leisure what it meant or how to react. Everybody saw, or at least heard on a radio, the most spectacular things that everybody else was doing. Of course you get a lemming effect! The trend's been visible for decades. It changed the character of politics before you or I were born. Today, however, it's gained a new order of magnitude. Some fascinating depth-psych studies wait to be done.'' The psychiatrist grimaced. "If we survive."

"Oh, I'm sure we will," the professor said comfortably. "I can't imagine the miracle was passed for any reasons except two, and one of them was to prevent us from destroying ourselves."

"What was the other?"

"To give us further information about reality." The professor held his glass out to a passing waiter. While a filled one was handed him, he chose a canapé. "You know I was not a devout man before the event," he said. "And I don't suppose I am yet, in any conventional sense. I've positively no intention of becoming a Mormon. Nevertheless, the Mormons do have something in their doctrine of continual revelation: the idea that the Cosmic Force (which term I prefer, tentatively) has not given us any last word but speaks further to us when it deems us ready for the next stage of comprehension."

"Hm. Pretty noncommittal this time around, I'd say."

"No, no. Far from it. You see, we were given a scientifically measurable phenomenon, precisely in an era of so-phisticated instrumentation and analytical techniques. I expect a flood of papers on every aspect. For example, I happen to know that personnel aboard our manned space laboratory took close observations on changes in its orbit due to the pause in terrestrial rotation. Not to speak of meteorology, continental drift, solar wind, et cetera. Now let's organize these data in various ways, crank them through suitable computers in search of patterns—d'you see?''

The psychiatrist blinked. ''You hope to . . . find clues to the nature of God?''

''Precisely,'' said the professor. ''I don't claim a coded message is buried in fluctuations of the Van Allen belts. Such things are conceivable and we must check them out. But the fact that the Cosmic Force has operated in *this* manner rather than *that*—d'you see? Just as man went from astrology to astronomy, he's about to move from theology to theonomy.'' He nudged his companion. ''Ah, please keep this confidential, but I've put my grad students to work and I expect soon to have a proposal which'll make NSF spring for as hefty a grant as ever was dreamed of. Really, you ought to get something in yourself before the rush begins.''

Wednesday 29 June

(In a lightning predawn move, Israeli troops struck deeply into Jordan and Syria. Premier Levi ben-Zvi asserted that the massacre at Jericho was only the last straw and his government intends to reach a final solution of the feda-yeen problem. He warned that if Egypt or any other nation makes a move in the holy war which muezzins have been preaching throughout the Arab world this week, ''Israel will take what measures are indicated.'' He did not rule out the use of tactical nuclear weapons, which he revealed his country possesses. Defense Minister Rachmael Hertz stated bluntly, "Last week, after three thousand years, again the Lord God of Hosts made Himself known to us.")

"What can we do?" Helen Habib implored. "Tell me what we can do."

Gail Donaldson was quiet a while. They were, for once, alone in the apartment. Their husbands were in conference and the Habib children had been allowed a picnic, under supervision. *Mine are in care of my parents,* passed through her awareness. *Why have they been spared when these were not?*

On one side of the room, a window gave on a view of the bevatron building. Occasionally someone passed by. Work was resuming, an incredible business as usual. The sun was harshly bright, the air still and hot, but Helen refused to turn the conditioner on, though sweat ran over both their skins. "I've got to have that much natural," she had said.

At length Gail, who was seated, gave a direct look to the other woman, who paced back and forth before her. "I really have no right to counsel you," she murmured. "You're older. No, I don't mean calendar ages. They aren't important. But I suspect you've seen more of life than I have."

"Well, I can tell you about making a way from field work in the Central Valley to lower middle class in Oakland," Helen replied. "No information about how to be famous in that, is there? You're the only person I trust who might know." Her lips drew back, her voice rose. "Oh, help me!" Echoes bounced flatly off bare walls.

"Well." Gail decided she could be more soothing if she leaned back and pretended to be at ease. Damn, how the chair stuck to blouse and shorts and thighs! "Simon has a method of standing off from a problem to study it."

"He hasn't seemed any too calm either," Helen flung at her.

Gail winced. "No. Your man has no monopoly on troubles." She gathered will and words. "I'll try the system anyhow. First you spell the whole business out, item by item. Most seem too obvious to be worth bothering with, but that's misleading. What we need is the relationship between them."

Helen stopped, raised crook-fingered hands, and nearly screamed, "Santa María, hasn't this analyzing any end?"

"You asked for my help." Gail hoped she sounded as humble as she felt. "I'm doing my poor best."

"I'm sorry." Helen sat down on the edge of another chair. "Please go on."

"M-m-m. Because Lou is . . . associated . . . with what happened, everybody assumes he must have special talents or a direct line to God or something. Everybody except him."

"And me. I've told you that. I haven't seen a halo over him or . . . or any change, except that he's tired and worried and sorry. Why, I was the one who pushed him to write that letter and afterward go on that show. And I'm in no state of grace."

"What do the children think?"

"I can't tell. Who can tell about children? Maybe they don't know themselves. Dick prays a lot, Jimmy sulks a lot, and I think poor Steffie daydreams about how she'll be sought after when she returns to college."

"Okay," Gail said. "An officialdom that couldn't imagine what else to do hustled you here. Maybe that was unwise. Yet what can police, civil service, elected politicians do about a miracle? Play cautious; and, as long as Lou was sequestrated, make the effort to find out if there was in fact anything unique about him. A foolish, futile effort, seen by hindsight. Like quarantining the original lunar astronauts. But the stakes being what they were in either case, how could you not take every possible niggling precaution?"

"I know," Helen said. "He's made me understand and forgive, a little. We're lucky Simon was put in charge. We'd hoped, though—"

"Hoped you'd soon be released?" Gail shook her head. "Dear, Lou can no more escape being the first man who told us to ask for a sign than Neil Armstrong can escape, ever, being the first man on the moon. So don't fight it. Use it."

"That's what we can't," Helen whispered. "I'm afraid, I'm afraid."

"Let's keep on laying out the facts," Gail said. "Obviously your detention here is temporary. Half of humanity is aclamor to know what's become of you. President Reisner *must* be seen on television with Lou."

"That horrible woman—"

"Never mind her. I find her rather pathetic. Lou has incomparably more power, if only he can use it right. Which is what I'm getting at. Not simply that the Habibs can better themselves in a material way. Though what harm if you do? Mainly, however, think what an influence for good he can be. Suppose—oh, suppose he called for real, enforceable universal disarmament and real, meaningful justice for the poor and oppressed. He doesn't have to parrot what some scriptwriter hands him you know.''

"I'm afraid he will." Helen's fingers writhed in her lap. "Gail, he's—he's innocent. He never went to college. He did most of his Army hitch in Iceland, of all forsaken places. Afterward he met me and we got married, and ever since, it's been work, first in a filling station—night school to become a mechanic—then in a garage, then to make his own business go. He's never had any enemies. When somebody pushed him, he'd just go quiet and immovable, the person couldn't get angry. He doesn't read much; a bit of popular history has been the most intellectual stuff he's ever gotten through. What he likes best on television is pro football. He goes bowling and fishing with his friends. Vacations, we usually go . . . went . . . go auto camping." She bit her lip. "Never mind the rest. Ordinary too." Louder: "Put him in Washington among important fast-talking people and what can he do?"

"To a large extent," Gail said softly, "that will depend on you, Helen."

"Who am I?" Both rose to their feet. Helen was crying. "I told you I'm no saint. I'm not even bright."

"Between us, dear, I think you're considerably more bright than your husband."

"M-m-maybe. But—Gail, there's been nothing between us since . . . since before. . . . It's been like living with a shadow. And everybody back east, waiting for him, wanting him to use. . . . Yes, women, why not admit I . . . I . . . I'm scared of them? I shouldn't be, but I am." Helen sought her companion's arms. "I miss him, I miss him."

Gail stroked the dark hair while tears mingled with the sweat on her shoulder. "You'll have to fight, Helen," she said. "I'll try to help you plan. In the end, though, nobody but you can fight on your side. Not even God."

Thursday 30 June

(The vote of no confidence which toppled the government of India has ominous implications, according to knowledgeable observers. The new parliament is sure to contain a number of the Kali worshipers, who are making converts at a wildfire rate. Their truculence may well cause a reaction in Pakistan, already alight with Moslem fervor kindled by the "night of Allah" and fanned to a blaze by the Middle Eastern war. Other experts, while hoping conflict can be averted, foresee a turning away from what one called "rational-technological civilization" toward more traditional modes throughout southern Asia.)

"Well," Donaldson said, and knew how inanely he spoke, "soon you're off."

"Yeah." Louis Habib reached in his shirt pocket for a fresh cigar. The office smelled stale from those whose stubs overflowed the ashtray. But dusk blew in a window, cool and quiet. Early stars twinkled forth. They could be seen above darkened buildings, because Donaldson had only one small lamp lit on his desk.

Its glow was lost in the lines and hollows lately carved over his countenance. "Don't worry about Dick, Jim, Steffie," he said, still repeating himself. "We're glad to have them stay with us till you and Helen get back. And I don't think they'll meet any trouble. A lot of nuisance, yes, but nothing serious."

Habib's own gaze was dull. "You're too kind."

"Not in the least." Donaldson became busy polishing his glasses. "We like them. And . . . to tell the truth, Dick's in a position to help me."

"A boy?"

"Wiser than me, in the area where I most need wisdom. You, uh, you can't have failed to notice, I'm a shaken man these days."

Habib squinted at Donaldson, lit his cigar, and blew a couple of smoke rings before he said slowly, "I have noticed. Your religion fell apart last week, didn't it?"

"I've about decided that it did."

"Think Dick's church has the answer?"

"No. Or, at any rate, I can't bring myself to make the . . . the commitment. Too much seems to fly straight upwind of reason. And, without the creed, what use the rites?" Donaldson hesitated. "Your son told me the same. He believes, now. But he said to me, God wouldn't be honored by an act of autohypnosis on my part."

"What's he doing for you, then?"

"O-oh, listening, mainly. Like my wife. Dick, though, Dick knows the books. He can point out where these questions have been raised before, century after century. I . . . My problem is, Lou, and I'm surely far from unique—I have to make sense out of a universe which somehow contains both the data of science and the fact of what took place. I can't accept the Russian spacemen or the Chinese psionics. They're too *ad hoc*. Dick's helping me reconcile myself to the idea of a sentient, supernatural order of creation."

"Good." Habib's voice turned harsh. "But he'd better do some explaining away of his own."

"Hm?"

"Let him figure out how the same world can hold a God who's a loving Father, and what we see on every newscast or in every cancer ward."

"That problem is as old as Akhnaton."

"Who? Never mind. We have to live it today." Habib slammed fist into palm. In anguish: "What'm I supposed to do?"

Friday 1 July

(British and Irish troops are waging a vain struggle against fanatical Christian Liberation Front gangs rising throughout Northern Ireland and invading from the south. "Untrained and poorly armed though they are, barriers and tear gas are not stopping them," admitted Eire Premier John Ward. "Yet if we open fire, it will be a political as well as a moral catastrophe." In a statement issued from secret headquarters, CLF leaders scorned Pope Benedict's demand that they order an end to terrorism on pain of excommunication. "Irish Christianity was Celtic before it was Catholic," they maintained. "It will be Celtic anew. God's purpose is clear.")

Nobody knew whence the preacher had come, nor even his full name. He called himself simply Ivan, a simple worker on a nearby kolkhoz until an insight, which he dared not believe was divine, came to send him forth. He had been addressing the regiment at sunset for the past three days. The first time, a political officer had tried to arrest him, and was hauled away by a score of hands. Ivan told the men to show mercy. He reproached them next evening when he learned the political officer had been found dead of a dozen bayonet stabs. Then Colonel Kuprin decreed that every law-abiding Soviet citizen had a right to be heard and every soldier not on duty a right to listen; and he came too, with his staff.

Mikhail Grigorovitch Saltykov had to strain to hear. Ivan spoke softly, though his voice carried, and a wind had sprung up, chill and murmurous across the mournful plain. Mikhail, who was only a private and a small man, stood well back in the mass of his comrades. He was glad of that. It was a warmth amidst the blowing bleakness, and a comfort to feel human bodies around one at this hour when the sun slipped from sight.

Bearded, unkempt, raggedly clad, Ivan stood on a tank. The waning light cast him dark across a greenish western sky. Eastward a few stars appeared in gray-purple heaven. Mikhail shivered. He had been in his home village on furlough when it happened. Throughout that night without end the stars had stood unmoving, numberless, keen and terrible over the fields, and poor old Nikolai Ilyitch had gone mad.

Ivan pointed beyond camp, to the river, which shone like polished metal, broken by sandbars, and to the murky mass of the Chinese camp on the far side, where lanterns began to glow.

"—our brothers," he said. "All men are our brothers. Have you not heard the word of Jesus Christ? He damns himself like Cain who hates and slays his brother. Could our Lord not have called down the hosts of the angels to avenge His wounds? Instead, he reproved Peter for drawing a sword upon one man. For that man was a common soldier, and so was very precious to God.

"Our leaders have explained to us that the Earth was stopped in its course upon the great day by wise and kindly beings from yonder." He pointed aloft, and Mikhail discovered those lights were not really inhuman, they were almost like the lanterns over the river. "These beings would rescue us from our sinful folly. The Party has made it quite plain. I, a common man, a simpleton, have nothing to add except this: That those good guardians must have been here before. Our Lord Jesus Christ must have been chief among them. The Resurrection was no less real because it was done by scientific means, nor was our Lord less holy because he descended from a planet and returned thence."

Ivan laid a hand on the cannon that jutted forth beside him. "Well, comrades," he said, "I explained this much yesterday, and you, who are more learned than me, seemed to feel it is reasonable. Now I wish to ask a further question. If the masters from the stars are here again, *is this not the Second Coming of Jesus Christ which was foretold?*"

A gasp went into the wind.

"And if that be true," Ivan's patient sentences continued, "what is required of us? What except repentance for evil deeds, resolution to do better, and that love for our fellows which God and the Party alike tell us is our duty as well as our joy?

"Comrades, do not fear wrath and burning. It is unthinkable that the star masters would ravage a helpless Earth. We ourselves were about to do that, before we were stopped. Therefore, what need to fear other men? They too are stopped from drawing the sword. The motherland now needs something else than defense.

"What Jesus Christ Returned wants is simple. Lay down your arms. Go home to your dear ones. Work until our Russia has been made a temple fit for the Lord."

If we did! flashed through Mikhail. *If we did! A long march back, but singing all the way; and at the end, Marina, you!*

Saturday 2 July

(The junta which has seized power in Argentina is extending its control from Buenos Aires to the hinterland with little difficulty. Its pledge to "restore order and the holy Catholic faith" is popular. The situations in Brazil and Chile remain confused.)

Outside, the White House lawn was ringed by soldiers. Beyond its high iron fence, the crowd had become inhuman through sheer mass. William Reisner wondered how many would die today, packed like that in the suffocating Washington summer. Every once in a while a trooper fainted, was borne off and replaced. The mass was orderly—thus far—unlike too many elsewhere. It made noise, a scraping mumble which penetrated the whir of the air conditioner.

He released the hand of Helen Habib. "Do be seated," he told her and her husband.

"Thanks . . . uh . . . thank you, Mr. President," the man said. They obeyed stiffly.

Reisner settled down too, more at ease. It occurred to him that to them the aides and Secret Service men were not part of the Georgian decor. Their eyes, flickering about, reminded him of a wounded deer he'd once found and dispatched. (A quarter century ago? Impossible.) "I hope you had a pleasant trip," he said.

"Yes, thank you, Mr. President." Louis Habib was barely audible.

His wife showed more animation: "I'd never been on a plane before. To start out on Air Force One! And afterward a helicopter!"

No way to get you from National to here except by chopper, the President thought. He donned a smile. "We aim to please. I hope you'll be satisfied with your guest apartment. Whatever you need, tell the gentleman who'll conduct you there shortly." He paused. "I know you're tired. I've been through time-zone changes myself. But I did want a quiet, private chat, as private as one can be in this job, before the VIP storm breaks."

"The what?" Habib coughed. "Oh, yes. VIP." His tone lifted in pitch. "We're not, sir. Isn't there any way to convince people of what's true? I'm not holy, not smart, nothing."

"As a matter of fact," Reisner said, "I am convinced." That caught them. He laughed; a politician learns how to do so at need. "If you tell me you had no miraculous visions, no flash of inspiration, merely an idea that others may well also have had, I believe you."

"Well, tell them!" exploded from the wife.

Reisner sighed. "I'm afraid you're wrong on one detail, Mr. Habib. You're not 'nothing.' For better or worse, you're identified with the miracle. Let's try to make it for better."

"How?"

"It won't be too rough. After we finish here, I'd like

63

you to appear briefly on a balcony, just wave and accept the cheers. As for your scheduled press conference, we've screened the reporters very carefully. You'll be asked nothing embarrassing, nothing that will commit you to any particular position.''

"But Tuesday night—'' Habib gulped.

Reisner nodded. "Yes. Your televised speech. That's the payoff. You're bound to have the largest audience in history, and the most desperately anxious to follow any lead you give.''

"I haven't got anything.''

"Haven't you? It can be supplied. I hear that Senator Prescott has, ah, kindly volunteered assistance.''

Blood beat in Helen's Indian visage. "I read that 'draft speech' his wife gave Lou,'' she snapped.

"And?'' Reisner hinted.

"It's not a bad speech,'' Louis Habib said lamely.

Helen fleered. "It's a damn clever speech, if you think you ought to give God's personal endorsement to Senator Prescott's being elected the next President.''

"Uh, honey, I didn't see—'' The words trailed off. "Well, I'm only a knucklehead.''

"I wouldn't agree,'' Reisner lied. "You get the point, I'm sure. Inevitably, everyone wants your prestige to serve his personal or partisan ends.''

Habib ceased squirming. His eyes said, *You too*.

"Yes,'' Reisner confessed. "Of course I'd like to be reelected. I hope to do it on my merits, not on the cheap. The future of the United States is rather more important than the future of my career.''

They waited.

"I needn't remind you how difficult and dangerous this period is for the country," he said. "At the same time, we've never had more dazzling opportunities. Suddenly the morale, the entire organization of our rivals is disintegrating. Abroad. At home—that's another story." Reisner bridged his fingers and proceeded in his most judicious manner: "You can stand before the cameras Tuesday, Mr. Habib, and utter platitudes like 'Love thy neighbor.' Nice, safe, noncontroversial, and empty. Or you can come out for or against specific things that specific persons are trying to do. That will make you enemies as well as friends. But it might bring about the survival of your country.

"We'll discuss this in more detail tomorrow, after you've caught your breath. Meanwhile, you'll find a typescript in your suite. It's rather thick, I'm afraid, and heavy going— because it has the facts, the statistics, hard information rather than pious generalities—but I'll be grateful, America will be grateful, if you'll study it and let me know your reaction."

Sunday 3 July

(South African authorities admitted they were helpless in the face of the general strike by nonwhite workers which has paralyzed the nation. Native leader Bastiaan Ingwamza told correspondents: "That night under the unmoving stars, we heard God say, 'Enough.' Now, His will be done. Whether they shoot us down or let us starve or give us our ordinary rights as we ask, an end will come to the evil." Prime Minister Marcus de Smet declared in an official statement: "The government is willing to negotiate and to right wrongs as fast as possible. However, this cannot happen quickly. An industrial economy cannot function when the uneducated are set equal to the educated or when a separation which many hold to be divinely ordained is struck down. Collapse would be inevitable. Certain orators who have helped bring on the strike have openly said collapse is desirable.'')

The head of the political police cried, "But we have some loyal troops left! And the missiles! Now, to lose this very moment when the American fleet is departing and the Russian armies are melting away—"

Chairman Wu Yuan answered lifelessly, "We cannot afford a victory."

"What? Honored leader, I fail to grasp your thought."

"When every day more units mutiny, when at home more millions every day reject—or, worse, ignore or laugh at—official orders . . . do you seriously propose we spend what strength we have in Korea? No. I am recalling those brigades. The Koreans will have to liberate themselves." Wu sagged back. "I doubt they will. If reports of what is going on among them are to be trusted."

"Is anything to be trusted any longer?" the other man asked out of his despair.

"I do not know," Wu sighed. "I do not know. I was quite sincere in my idea, my dream, that man had moved the planet, man stood on the threshold of transcendence. Who would have guessed that . . . the thing . . . would turn the people to the past? Would make them serve their ancestors and read the *Tao-te-ching* and the *Analects* aloud to eager thousands, and divide the collectives up among

66

families where once more Grandfather is lord—and this within less than a month—?''

''Mere panic. They will come to their senses.''

''I doubt it.''

''They can be led.''

''Can they? How shall we even reach them?''

The police head gave the chairman a narrow look. His own courage was returning. ''You seem to feel this government will not endure,'' he said.

''Oh, it will, I suppose. We can limp along in a fashion, as one more set of warlords among the many who will soon rip our land apart. . . . China, China! What has Heaven done to you?''

The chairman covered his face and wept. The police head fingered his sidearm. It might prove necessary to replace the chairman. That was a gamble, however; it risked a struggle for succession which could, indeed, bring the state down in ruin.

Night thickened beyond the windows.

Monday 4 July

(In a grisly parody of Independence Day celebrations, fires in Baltimore, Newark, and Cincinnati raged out of control as firemen were checked by rioters. Street battles in Chicago, between extremists of the right and left convinced God is on their sides, mounted in frequency and ferocity. To date, the armored division which rings Washington against the People's Crusade converging on it has not suffered serious attack. But tension increases.)

*　　*　　*

They lay in each other's arms, in darkness, and whispered.

"Helen, what'm I going to say?"

Her breath touched his ear, her warmth enfolded him. "What's right, Lou. You're that kind of guy."

"What is right? How can I know? God, God, whatever I say, human beings'll die because of it."

Her voice turned dry. "Well, read your speech."

"Which speech?—I guess I forgot to tell you. After the reception today, I found two more slipped into my coat."

"No surprise." She stroked his hair a while, until she had the strength to give him strength. "I think you should scrap them all."

"What can *I* say?" He shuddered.

"You'll know."

"Huh? God's not with me!"

"You're with yourself, Lou. Let them hear a good man. You are one." Helen chuckled most softly. "I'm sure of that. I have experience."

"You. You." He clung to her as the children had done when they were small and hurt. "I love you."

"Regardless of what happens tomorrow," she said, "they've been wonderful years. Thanks for them, darling."

Tuesday 5 July

(Distinguished Harvard economist Martin Bielawski warns of possible national collapse. "Spreading lawlessness is only a symptom," he stated in a public lecture. "True, it may destroy us, as fever may destroy a sick person. Yet fever is not the sole symptom of a disease, nor are any symptoms its cause. What appears to be happening is this. Across the whole world, a God-starved generation has encountered the supernatural and become, overnight, God-intoxicated. Fanaticism is an ugly manifestation. It can be countered. What cannot be controlled is the seemingly benign, peaceful absorption of millions in their newfound faith. The job, the state, the obligations and satisfactions of temporal existence no longer impress them as of any great importance. The exodus from the cities, in search of utopian rural simplicity, is high in the news. But more significant is the exodus within the cities. Thousands each day quit their work in favor of something less demanding, something that leaves them time and energy to explore their own souls. Intelligent, educated persons, in positions of responsibility, are especially prone to this change of heart, as might be expected. No doubt, in its fashion, it is commendable. But industrial society cannot survive much of it. Consider the power blackouts, the stock-market nosedive, and the virtual breakdown of banking and credit systems this past week. Such disintegration feeds upon itself; those who had not intended to resign from their jobs will soon lose them. We rejoice to see hostile governments turning impotent. We forget that our own is equally mortal.'')

Louis Habib's talk was set for nine P.M., which was six on the West Coast. His children and the Donaldsons ate an early dinner. It was interrupted by a reporter who wanted to watch them watching the screen. Gail had to be downright nasty before they were rid of him.

She drew the curtains so that the image would be brighter. Because of sparse auto traffic and the shutdown of most factories, the air above the streets was clear. Fog rolled in

69

through the Gate and across the Bay, which at sunset would become a bowl of molten gold.

The young Habibs poised mute, altogether vulnerable. Her own boys sprawled bottoms up on the floor, eagerly awaiting whatever they were to see. *Your future lives, perhaps,* she thought. The uselessness of her wish to guard them made a pain in her throat. Simon sat chain-smoking but otherwise calm. She switched on the set, adjusted the color, and lowered herself to a chair beside his.

"—the new, new, new product—"

Her older son made an obscene comment.

"John!" she exclaimed. "Where'd you learn such language?"

He grinned. "From my father." In chilling scorn, he jerked a thumb at the commercial and said, "Big, grown men still think that garbage matters."

She wanted to send him out, but the station break ended. "—Ladies and gentlemen, the President of the United States."

Through all the makeup and mannerism, Reisner looked weary unto death, Gail thought. His introduction was good: brief, reasonably free of clichés, frank about the fact that the speaker disavowed prophethood. "Nevertheless, his modesty cannot conceal his wisdom. Though he may disagree, it is my honest belief, shared by millions, that he is at least partly responsible for the tremendous event of two weeks ago. Mankind waits to hear him. To his country, to humanity, I have the honor of presenting Louis Habib."

A camera swung about. For a moment the man stood small and alone at a lectern. Then the zoom lens brought him in, as if he were shoved through a tunnel, until his face filled the screen. It was also a tired face; but the nervousness, the near-terror that Gail remembered were gone.

"Good evening," he said.

He lifted a sheaf of papers. The optics hastily backed up to give a wider view. "Here's the speech I was supposed to read," he went on. He strewed it across the floor. "Sorry."

"Good for you, dad!" yelped his younger son.

"Oh, no." His daughter shrank into herself.

His older son drew the sign of the cross. Gail's hand sought her husband's, found it and clung.

"Never mind who wrote those pages," Habib was saying. "I had quite a few scripts given me. Pretty well done, too. Any of 'em would've sounded better than I will. I decided, though, if you figured you'd be hearing me, the only fair thing to do was speak my own piece."

The picture blanked. PLEASE STAND BY flashed on the screen. "They can't!" Gail protested.

"They'll realize that in a minute," Simon Donaldson said grimly.

Sight and sound returned: "—trouble is, I haven't got any real piece to speak. No message from on high. No solutions to your problems. No comfort for your griefs.

"Look," said the plodding voice, "the men who wanted to use me for a mouthpiece are a lot smarter than me. And I suppose they mostly are decent. They want me to, uh, endorse platforms or candidates or ideas . . . whatever . . . whatever they think is best for the country, for the world. Maybe they're right, some of them. But they can't all be right.

71

"For instance, well, President Reisner, who's been very kind, President Reisner has a program which amounts to, uh, restoring the same old rickety balance of power." The camera panned to the introducer, seated behind the speaker, and caught him appalled. Habib smiled. "Understand, he means well. And maybe we should stick with the devil we maybe know. But a big publisher, a gentleman named Link, wants the United States to make itself world boss. Senator Leverett feels that God wants us to put ourselves under the command of the United Nations. Senator Prescott says we have to, uh, institute a consortium. I'm not sure what that means. Congressman Lippert says we've got to drop everything else and go to the aid of Israel. Congressman Flaherty says we have a sacred mission to liberate Northern Ireland. Congressman Bradford says we have to guarantee every citizen five thousand dollars a year. And so on and so on, including those who didn't get a chance to approach me.

"Well, like I said, none of these gentlemen are crooks, and could be one of them is right. Only how can I tell which? How can you?"

Habib stuck hands in pockets of the suit that, tailored for him, had instantly lost its superb fit. Between thin strands of hair his scalp caught a highlight. "Now I'll tell you what I think," he said, "if you'll please bear in mind it's just me thinking, an ordinary guy who's probably dead wrong. I think we must've been mighty close to wrecking the world. Else why did God pass a miracle? He sure didn't for the Ukrainians under Stalin or the Jews under Hitler or the Tibetans under Mao. Maybe He gives us a leg up now and then, like the Bible says, and this was the latest. Or maybe He had to save this beautiful planet from us. And you know, it could be He's not saving it for us. Get the difference? We could be a kind of dinosaur, or become one if we don't take care.''

He drew breath. ''I wonder if maybe it isn't the world that God loves,'' he said. ''The whole of it. Everything that is. Mountains, bugs, and trees the same as people. I wonder if maybe we shouldn't stop supposing we're the center and, uh, the purpose of everything. If maybe we shouldn't stop hiding God behind a mask shaped like a human face.''

He stood silent for a space, took his hands out, shrugged, and smiled. ''I don't know,'' he said. ''I can't tell you what to do. Can anybody? Thanks and good night.''

The cameras followed him as he stumped offstage.

Wednesday 6 July

(The Salvation Army today announced plans for monastery-like communities. A statement issued at national headquarters said: ''Our recruits are so fantastically numerous since God last manifested Himself that we have no place for most of them in our usual work among the urban needy. At the same time, the number of those needy is growing as the current financial panic deepens into a depression. Federal and state governments are in such difficulties that we dare not assume they can cope much longer with the problem. Therefore men must turn from impersonal 'welfare' and 'charity' to that *caritas,* love of man within the love of God, enjoined by Scripture. We plan to use the added personnel whom divine grace has brought us on large farms—since land is being deeded and

73

willed us all over North America—to produce necessities for distribution among the poor. It is hoped that many of the poor, in turn, will wish to join this effort.'')

"Okay," the Secret Service agent said. "End of the line."

Habib rose. The airplane enclosed him and Helen; beyond, the airport was bare concrete. "Uh, I thought—" he began.

The agent grinned. "Thought a limousine 'ud chauffeur you to your house? Sorry. The President said return you to Oakland."

The President had said little more than that.

Sweat studded the agent's forehead. "I oughtn't to blab this," rasped from him. "But I will. I'm probably going to quit my job anyway. Habib, you had your chance to save the country, and you flushed it down the drain. Do you really expect any more red carpets? I have three small kids of my own, Habib."

"But . . . what could I do . . . how could I know . . . ? And we *weren't* looking for a limousine!"

"Come." Helen took her man's arm. "Thanks for the ride, sir."

When they were outside, she remarked, "People don't like being told they have to make their own lives and success isn't guaranteed. But you were right to tell them."

They trudged across hardness, beneath an empty sky. Two stood at the fence behind the terminal. Recognition startled Habib. "Hey, Si and Gail! Let's go!" He jogged. Passing the gate, he hugged them both.

It had taken repeated attempts to telephone them from Washington. Connections were scatty.

It was worth the trouble. A clean wind blew and the hills lifted lion-colored.

Gail Donaldson said unevenly, "I'm afraid we have bad news. The police guard on your home was withdrawn last night. Nothing's left. Looted and burned."

Habib and his wife regarded each other. She managed a smile. "Well, we have insurance."

"I hope your insurance company isn't one of those that've filed bankruptcy." Simon Donaldson blinked hard behind his glasses. "Whatever happens, we'll always have an extra potato in the pot."

Habib wrung his hand for a moment before, again, clasping Helen's. Gail explained, "There're quite a few onlookers around our own place. They don't know when or how you were due back, but figure it must be soon. That's why Simon and I left everybody else behind and went off by ourselves as if to go shopping. At that, we were followed, but shook those cars by ducking around an Army convoy."

"Are they mad at us?" Helen asked quickly.

"No," Donaldson said. "Contrariwise. Expectant. Hopeful. Big 'Welcome Back' signs. Doubtless you will have to beware of the embittered disillusioned. But some faiths are unshaken."

"I tried to tell them—" Habib slumped. They walked to the car in silence. It stood almost alone in the parking lot. On the freeway he stirred and said, "Maybe God was also trying to get a simple message across. Maybe He's always been trying."

Helen stroked his cheek.

Donaldson took the Gilman Street exit into Berkeley.

Though other automobiles were few, he found the way crowded. From the campus area had overflowed processions of candle-bearing Christian penitents and yellow-robed, shaven-headed, joyfully chanting and dancing Krishna worshipers. Householders stood at their doors and watched. Some joined in.

When the ground began to climb, the pavement grew clear and they drove among rose gardens. Habib gusted a sigh. "Good to be home," he said.

"What are your plans?" Gail inquired.

"Oh . . . to rebuild. House and business both."

"Frankly," Donaldson said, "I'm not sure a garage is a sound investment any longer. I wouldn't be surprised but what I finish my life as a teacher in a one-room country school."

"No odds to me," Habib said. "Any area needs men who can make machinery behave. A pity for you."

"Not necessarily," Donaldson replied. "It could beat designing weapons—a job I'll gladly drop when everybody else does. I don't want to sound Pollyanna. Still, I could perhaps even do some research. The end of huge apparatus and huge organization, if it comes, doesn't have to spell the end of discovery."

Louis Habib laid an arm around Helen. "Nor the end of being happy," she said.

They rounded a curve. Donaldson cursed and stamped on the brakes. Gail choked off a yell. "That many—that fast? Who told them? Get away from here!"

He threw the gears into reverse and backed. He was too late. The fringes of those ten thousand human beings who surrounded his place had seen him, and called to the rest.

They engulfed the car. The doors came off beneath their reaching. The faces were only eyeballs and mouths, the voices mostly a shriek through stench. Here and there a word slashed past.

"Help."

"Tell us what God wants."

"Why won't you?"

"Get the Jews out of Palestine."

"What should we pray for next?"

"Listen, I got this great idea."

"Help."

"I have the secret of the ages."

"I am chosen to bear your son."

"Get the Jews out of Russia."

"I understood what your sermon really meant."

"Lead us against the missile bases."

"Help."

"I'm starving."

"I'm blind."

"I'm afraid."

"I'm alone."

"My little girl has leukemia."

"Help."

The hands laid hold on Louis Habib, dragged him forth and plucked, while the bodies closed in. Donaldson broke a jaw with his fist, a rib with his shoe, and somehow got Gail and Helen down under the car. It rocked beneath surging impacts. The one man's screams were soon over. Then the mob stampeded, as a herd of bison stampedes. Belated police vehicles arrived to halt the damage, succor the wounded, and bear away the trampled, unrecognizable dead.

Thursday 7 July

(David Greenfeather, president of the newly formed American Council, today explained its purposes in a broadcast from Santa Fe, N.M. "We are by no means an exclusively Indian group, nor are we romantics trying to raise from the dust a past that never was," he said. "No, we welcome everyone of every race, color, or creed. We hope to make use of advanced scientific knowledge, for example in plant genetics, if not of an elaborate technology that is doomed to crumble. We do seek to regain the values of our forebears, values we believe are necessities of survival in the coming era. They include renunciation of lust for the merely material—there will not be many material goods for a long time to come; a readiness to suffer and die when needful—it often will be; a sense of intimate community with a few dear neighbors—megalopolis is a dry husk; at the same time, a oneness with the entire living world and the living God." His speech, which had been widely looked forward to, went unheard in numerous areas because of power failures and civil disturbances. But it is expected that mimeographed or hand-copied pamphlets will be made available.)

Near sunset, Donaldson parked his new station wagon. "This looks ideal," he said.

They were well into the Sierra, well off the highway on a deserted dirt road. The site was a meadow among pine trees, dropping sharply down to a valley. Someone must formerly, lovingly have dwelt here, for water trickled from an iron pipe out of the hillside into a moss-grown trough. It tasted of earth and purity.

"How long do we stay?" Helen Habib asked.

"As long as seems prudent," Donaldson told her. "Couple weeks, maybe. We've supplies for that. Afterward, if the radio says things haven't calmed down, we search for a pleasant village."

"You shouldn't do this much for us."

"It's also for ourselves, Helen. I don't think the future lies in the cities."

She went off for a while, alone, walking like an old woman. But later she insisted on helping pitch camp, cook dinner, and clean up. Her oldest son was much beside her; Jimmy and Steffie hung back, awkward. John and Mike rollicked, of course, under the eyes of Gail's parents.

Only once did Helen speak of the day before. She was scrubbing a pot when, apropos of nothing but silence, she said, "Dick, you're educated about these things. Did he have to die?"

"Everyone must," the young man answered. He paused. "If you mean, did he have to be martyred, I think not. Most prophets, in most faiths, lived to a ripe age. Today's people . . . couldn't understand. Let's hope later generations will be able to." He squeezed her shoulder. "He is, mother."

"He was, anyway." She raised her head. "I can live on that."

Tired from their journey, all but Donaldson and Gail were soon in the tents and asleep. Those two walked about.

"Do you really believe, Si," she wondered, "we're in for a new Dark Age?"

"No," he said. "It's not predestined, at least. Nothing

79

is. For all I know, we're coming out of one. I do expect the great empires to fall, ours among them. Whatever civilization rises on the ruins won't be like any the world has seen before. And that, however painful, may show us a new side of our souls.''

They reached the cliff edge and stopped. The moon had risen, bright enough that only a few stars appeared. The pines were tall shadows with sweet breath; the spring murmured and chimed; underfoot, the valley fell away in tremendous distances which upheaved themselves on the farther side to a snowpeak that seemed afloat in the violet night. The air was cold. Gail leaned against her man, seeking warmth.

"After all," he said, "changes are bound to follow a miracle."

She replied slowly, "When will we see that we've always lived in a miracle?"

Sister Planet

Long afterward they found a dead man in shabby clothes adrift near San Francisco. The police decided he must have jumped from the Golden Gate Bridge one misty day. That was an oddly clean and lonesome place for some obscure wino to die, but no one was very much interested. Beneath his shirt he carried a Bible with a bookmark indicating a certain passage which had been underlined. Idly curious, a member of the Homicide Squad studied the waterlogged pulp until he deduced the section: Ezekiel vii, 3-4.

I

A squall hit when Shorty McClellan had almost set down. He yanked back the stick; jets snorted and the ferry stood on her tail and reached for heaven. An eyeblink later she was whipping about like a wind-tossed leaf. The viewports showed blackness. Above the wind there was a bongo beat of rain. Then lightning blazed and thunder followed and Nat Hawthorne closed off smitten sense channels.

Welcome back! he thought. Or did he say it aloud? The thunder rolled off, monster wheels if it was not laughter. He felt the vessel steady around him. When the dazzle had cleared from his eyes, he saw clouds and calm. A smoky blueness in the air told him that it was near sunset. What answered to sunset on Venus, he reminded himself. The daylight would linger on for hours, and the night never got truly dark.

"That was a near one," said Shorty McClellan.

"I thought these craft were designed to ride out storms," said Hawthorne.

"Sure. But not to double as submarines. We were pretty close to the surface when that one sneaked up on us. We could'a got dunked, and then—" McClellan shrugged.

"No real danger," Hawthorne answered. "We could get out the airlock, I'm sure, with masks, and stay afloat till they picked us up from the station. If Oscar and company didn't rescue us first. You realize there's no trouble from any native life-form. They find us every bit as poisonous as we find them."

"No danger, he says," groaned McClellan. "Well, you wouldn't have to account for five million bucks' worth of boat!"

He began whistling tunelessly as he spiraled down for another approach. He was a small, heavy-set, quick-moving man with a freckled face and sandy hair. For years Hawthorne had only known him casually, as one of the pilots who took cargo between orbiting spaceships and Venus Station: a cocky sort, given to bawdy limericks and improbable narratives about himself and what he called the female race. But on the voyage from Earth, he had ended with shyly passing around stereos of his children and describing plans for opening a little resort on Great Bear Lake when he reached retirement age.

I thank the nonexistent Lord that I am a biologist, thought Hawthorne. *The farcical choice of quitting or accepting a desk job at thirty-five has not yet reached my line of work. I hope I'll still be tracing ecological chains and watching auroras over the Phosphor Sea at eighty.*

As the boat tilted forward, he saw Venus below him. One would never have expected a landless, planet-wide ocean to be so alive. But there were climatic zones, each with its own million restless hues—the color of light, the quality of living organisms, nowhere the same, so that a sea on Venus was not an arbitrary section of water but an iridescent belt around the world. And then there was the angle of the sun, night-lighting, breezes and gales and typhoons, seasons, solar tides which had no barrier to their 20,000 mile march, and the great biological rhythms which men did not yet understand. No, you could sit for a hundred years in one place, watching, and never see the same thing twice. And all that you saw would be beautiful.

The Phosphor Sea girdled the planet between 55 and 63 degrees north latitude. Now from above, at evening, it had grown indigo, streaked with white; but on the world's very edge it shaded to black in the north and an infinitely clear green in the south. Here and there beneath the surface twined scarlet veins. A floating island, a jungle twisted over giant bladderweeds, upbore flame yellows and a private mistiness. Eastward walked the squall, blue-black and lightning, the water roaring in its track. The lower western clouds were tinged rose and copper. The permanent sky-layer above ranged from pearl gray in the east to a still blinding white in the west, where the invisible sun burned. A double rainbow arched the horizon.

Hawthorne sighed. It was good to be back.

Air whistled under the ferry's glider wings. Then it touched pontoons to water, bounced, came down again, and taxied for the station. A bow wave broke among those caissons and spouted toward the upper deck and the buildings which, gyro-stabilized, ignored such disturbances. As usual, the whole station crew had turned out to greet the vessel. Spaceship arrivals were months apart.

"End of the line." McClellan came to a halt, unbuckled himself, stood up and struggled into his air harness. "You know," he remarked, "I've never felt easy in one of these gizmos."

"Why not?" Hawthorne, hanging the tank on his own shoulders, looked in surprise at the pilot.

McClellan adjusted his mask. It covered nose and mouth with a tight airseal of celluplastic gasketing. Both men had already slipped ultraviolet-filtering contact lenses over their eyeballs. "I keep remembering that there isn't any oxygen molecule that's not man-made for twenty-five million miles," he confessed. The airhose muffled his voice, giving it for Hawthorne a homelike accent. "I'd feel safer with a space suit."

"De gustibus non disputandum est," said Hawthorne, "which has been translated as, 'There is no disputing that

Gus is in the east.' Me, I was never yet in a space suit that didn't squeak and smell of somebody else's garlic.''

Through the port he saw a long blue back swirl in the water and thresh impatient foam. A grin tugged at his lips. ''Why, I'll bet Oscar knows I'm here,'' he said.

''Yeah. Soul mates,'' grunted McClellan.

They went out the airlock. Ears popped, adjusting to a slight pressure difference. The masks strained out some water vapor for reasons of comfort, and virtually all the carbon dioxide, for there was enough to kill a man in three gulps. Nitrogen, argon, and trace gases passed on, to be blent with oxygen from the harness tank and breathed. Units existed which electrolyzed the Earth-vital element directly from water, but so far they were cumbersome.

A man on Venus did best to keep such an engine handy in his boat or on the dock, for recharging the bottle on his back every few hours. Newcomers from Earth always found that an infernal nuisance, but after a while at Venus Station you fell into a calmer pattern.

A saner one? Hawthorne had often wondered. His latest visit to Earth had about convinced him.

The heat struck like a fist. He had already donned the local costume: loose, flowing garments of synthetic, designed to ward ultraviolet radiation off his skin and not absorb water. Now he paused for a moment, reminded himself that Man was a mammal able to get along quite well at even higher temperatures, and relaxed. The sea lapped his bare feet where he stood on a pontoon. It felt cool. Suddenly he stopped minding the heat; he forgot it entirely.

Oscar frisked up. Yes, of course it was Oscar. The other

cetoids, a dozen or so, were more interested in the ferry, nosing it, rubbing their sleek flanks against the metal, holding their calves up in their foreflippers for a good look.

Oscar paid attention only to Hawthorne. He lifted his blunt bulky head, nuzzled the biologist's toes, and slapped flukes on water twenty feet away.

Hawthorne squatted. "Hi, Oscar," he said. "Didn't think I'd make it back, did you?" He chucked the beast under the chin. Be damned if the cetoids didn't have true chins. Oscar rolled belly-up and snorted.

"Thought I'd pick up some dame Earthside and forget all about you, huh?" murmured Hawthorne. "Why, bless your ugly puss, I wouldn't dream of it! Certainly not. I wouldn't waste Earthside time dreaming of abandoning you for a woman. I'd do it! C'mere, creature."

He scratched the rubbery skin just behind the blow-hole. Oscar bumped against the pontoon and wriggled.

"Cut that out, will you?" asked McClellan. "I don't want a bath just yet." He threw a hawser. Wim Dykstra caught it, snubbed it around a bollard, and began to haul. The ferry moved slowly to the dock.

"Okay, Oscar, okay, okay," said Hawthorne. "I'm home. Let's not get sickening about it." He was a tall, rather bony man, with dark-blond hair and a prematurely creased face. "Yes, I've got a present for you too, same as the rest of the station, but let me get unpacked first. I got you a celluloid duck. Leggo there!"

The cetoid sounded. Hawthorne was about to step off onto the dock ladder when Oscar came back. With great care, the swimmer nudged the man's ankles and then, awkwardly, because this was not the regular trading pier, pushed something out of his mouth to lay at Hawthorne's feet. After which Oscar sounded again and Hawthorne muttered total, profane astonishment and felt his eyes sting a little.

He had just been presented with one of the finest firegems on record.

II

After dark, the aurora became visible. The sun was so close, and the Venusian magnetic field so weak, that even in the equator the sky became criss-crossed at times with great banners of light. Here in the Phosphor Sea, the night was royal blue, with rosy curtains and silent white shuddering streamers. And the water itself shone, bioluminescence, each wave laced by cold fires. Where droplets struck the station deck, they glowed for minutes before evaporating, as if gold coals had been strewn at random over its gleaming circumference.

Hawthorne looked out the transparent wall of the wardroom. "It's good to be back," he said.

"Get that," said Shorty McClellan. "From wine and women competing in droves for the company of a glamorous interplanetary explorer, it is good to be back. This man is crazy."

The geophysicist, Wim Dykstra, nodded with seriousness. He was the tall swarthy breed of Dutchman, whose ancestral memories are of Castilian uplands. Perhaps that is why so many of them feel forever homeless.

"I think I understand, Nat," he said. "I read between the lines of my mail. Is it that bad on Earth?"

"In some ways." Hawthorne leaned against the wall, staring into Venus' night.

The cetoids were playing about the station. Joyous torpedo shapes would hurtle from the water, streaming liquid radiance, arch over and come down in a fountain that burned. And then they threshed the sea and were off around a mile-wide circle, rolling and tumbling. The cannon-crack of bodies and flukes could be heard this far up.

"I was afraid of that. I do not know if I want to take my next furlough when it comes," said Dykstra.

McClellan looked bewildered. "What're you fellows talking about?" he asked. "What's wrong?"

Hawthorne sighed. "I don't know where to begin," he said. "The trouble is, Shorty, you see Earth continually. Get back from a voyage and you're there for weeks or months before taking off again. But we . . . we're gone three, four, five years at a stretch. We notice the changes."

"Oh, sure." McClellan shifted his weight uneasily in his chair. "Sure, I suppose you aren't used to—well, the gangs, or the corvées, or the fact that they've begun to ration dwelling space in America since the last time you were there. But still, you guys are well paid, and your job has prestige. You rate special privileges. What are *you* complaining about?"

"Call it the atmosphere," said Hawthorne. He sketched a smile. "If God existed, which thank God He doesn't, I'd say He has forgotten Earth."

Dykstra flushed. "God does not forget," he said. "Men do."

"Sorry, Wim," said Hawthorne. "But I've seen—not just Earth. Earth is too big to be anything but statistics. I visited my own country, the place where I grew up. And the lake where I went fishing as a kid is an alga farm and my mother has to share one miserable room with a yattering old biddy she can't stand the sight of.

"What's worse, they've cut down Bobolink Grove to put up still another slum mislabeled a housing project, and the gangs are operating in open daylight now. Armed escort has become a major industry. I walk into a bar and not a face is happy. They're just staring stupefied at a telescreen, and—" He pulled up short. "Never mind. I probably exaggerate."

"I'll say you do," said McClellan. "Why, I can show you places where no man has been since the Indians left—if it's nature you want. You've never been to San Francisco, have you? Well, come with me to a pub I know in North Beach, and I'll show you the time of your life."

"Sure," said Hawthorne. "What I wonder is, how much longer will those fragments survive?"

"Some of them, indefinitely," said McClellan. "They're corporate property. These days C. P. means private estates."

Wim Dykstra nodded. "The rich get richer," he said, "and the poor get poorer, and the middle class vanishes. Eventually there is the fossilized Empire. I have read history."

He regarded Hawthorne out of dark, thoughtful eyes. "Medieval feudalism and monasticism evolved *within* the Roman domain: they were there when it fell apart. I wonder if a parallel development may not already be taking place. The feudalism of the large organizations on Earth; the monasticism of planetary stations like this."

"Complete with celibacy," grimaced McClellan. "Me, I'll take the feudalism!"

Hawthorne sighed again. There was always a price. Sex-suppressive pills, and the memory of fervent lips and clinging arms on Earth, were often poor comfort.

"We're not a very good analogy, Wim," he argued. "In the first place, we live entirely off the jewel trade. Because it's profitable, we're allowed to carry on the scientific work which interests us personally: that's part of our wage, in effect. But if the cetoids stopped bringing gems, we'd be hauled home so fast we'd meet ourselves coming back. You know nobody will pay the fabulous cost of interplanetary freight for pure knowledge—only for luxuries."

Dykstra shrugged. "What of it? The economics is irrelevant to our monasticism. Have you ever drunk Benedictine?"

"Uh . . . yeah, I get it. But also, we're only celibate by necessity. Our big hope is that eventually we have our own women."

Dykstra smiled. "I am not pressing the analogy too close," he said. "My point is that we feel ourselves serving a larger purpose, a cultural purpose. Science, in our case, rather than religion, but still a purpose worth all the isolation and other sacrifice. If, in our hearts, we really consider the isolation a sacrifice."

Hawthorne winced. Sometimes Dykstra was too analytical. Indeed, thought Hawthorne, the station personnel were monks. Wim himself—but he was a passionate man, fortunate enough to be single-minded. Hawthorne, less lucky, had spent fifteen years shaking off a Puritan upbringing, and finally realized that he never would. He had killed his father's unmerciful God, but the ghost would always haunt him.

He could now try to make up for long self-denial by an Earthside leave which was one continuous orgy, but the sense of sin plagued him notwithstanding, disguised as bitterness. I have been iniquitous upon Terra. Ergo, Terra is a sink of evil.

Dykstra continued, with a sudden unwonted tension in his voice: "The analogy with medieval monasteries holds good in another respect too. They thought they were retreating from the world. Instead, they became the nucleus of its next stage. And we too, unwittingly until now, may have changed history."

"Uh-uh," denied McClellan. "You can't have a history without a next generation, can you? And there's not a woman on all Venus."

Hawthorne said, quickly, to get away from his own thoughts: "There was talk in the Company offices about that. They'd like to arrange it, if they can, to give all of us more incentive to stay. They think maybe it'll be possible. If trade continues to expand, the Station will have to be enlarged, and the new people could just as well be female technicians and scientists."

"That could lead to trouble," said McClellan.

"Not if there were enough to go around," said Hawthorne. "And nobody signs on here who hasn't long ago given up any hope of enriching their lives with romantic love, or fatherhood."

"They could have that," murmured Dykstra. "Fatherhood, I mean."

Poul Anderson

"Kids?" Hawthorne was startled. "On Venus?"

A look of exultant triumph flickered across Dykstra's face. Hawthorne, reverting to the sensitivity of intimate years, knew that Dykstra had a secret, which he wanted to shout to the universe, but could not yet. Dykstra had discovered something wonderful.

To give him a lead, Hawthorne said: "I've been so busy swapping gossip, I've had no time for shop talk. What have you learned about this planet since I left?"

"Some promising things," said Dykstra, evasively. His tone was still not altogether steady.

"Found how the firegems are created?"

"Heavens, no. That would scuttle us, wouldn't it—if they could be synthesized? No . . . you can talk to Chris, if you wish. But I know he has only established that they are a biological product, like pearls. Apparently several strains of bacteroids are involved, which exist only under Venusian deep-sea conditions."

"Learn more about the life cycle?" asked McClellan. He had a spaceman's somewhat morbid fascination with any organisms that got along without oxygen.

"Yes, Chris and Mamoru and their co-workers have developed quite a lot of the detailed chemistry," said Dykstra. "It is over my head, Nat. But you will want to study it, and they have been anxious for your help as an ecologist. You know this business of the plants, if one may call them that, using solar energy to build up unsaturated compounds, which the creatures we call animals then oxidize? Oxidation need not involve oxygen, Shorty."

"I know that much chemistry," said McClellan, looking hurt.

"Well, in a general way the reactions involved did not seem energetic enough to power animals the size of Oscar. No enzymes could be identified which—" He paused, frowning a little. "Anyhow, Mamoru got to thinking about fermentation, the closest Terrestrial analogy. And it seems that micro-organisms really *are* involved. The Venusian enzymes are indistinguishable from . . . shall we call them viruses, for lack of a better name? Certain forms even seem to function like genes. How is that for a symbiosis, eh? Puts the classical examples in the shade."

Hawthorne whistled.

"I daresay it's a very fascinating new concept," said McClellan. "As for myself, I wish you'd hurry up and give us our cargo, so we can go home. Not that I don't like you guys, but you're not exactly my type."

"It will take a few days," said Dykstra. "It always does."

"Well, just so they're Earth days, not Venusian."

"I may have a most important letter for you to deliver," said Dykstra. "I have not yet gathered the crucial data, but you must wait for that if nothing else."

Suddenly he shivered with excitement.

III

The long nights were devoted to study of material gathered in the daytime. When Hawthorne emerged into sunrise, where mists smoked along purple waters under a sky like nacre, the whole station seemed to explode outward around him. Wim Dykstra had already scooted off with his new assistant, little Jimmy Cheng-tung of the hopeful grin, and their two-man sub was over the horizon, picking up

93

data-recording units off the sea bottom. Now boats left the wharf in every direction: Diehl and Matsumoto to gather pseudo-plankton, Vassiliev after some of the beautiful coralite on Erebus Bank, Lafarge continuing his mapping of the currents, Glass heading straight up to investigate the clouds a bit more . . .

The space ferry had been given its first loading during the night. Shorty McClellan walked across a bare deck with Hawthorne and Captain Jevons. "Expect me back again about local sundown," he said. "No use coming before then, with everyone out fossicking."

"I imagine not." Jevons, white-haired and dignified, looked wistfully at Lafarge's retreating craft.

Five cetoids frisked in its wake, leaping and spouting and gaily swimming rings around it. Nobody had invited them, but by now few men would have ventured out of station view without such an escort.

More than once, when accidents happened—and they happened often on an entire planet as big and varied as Earth—the cetoids had saved lives. A man could ride on the back of one, if worst came to worst, but more often several would labor to keep a damaged vessel afloat, as if they knew the cost of hauling even a rowboat across space.

"I'd like to go fossicking myself," said Jevons. He chuckled. "But someone has to mind the store."

"Uh, how did the Veenies go for that last lot of stuff?" asked McClellan. "The plastic jewelry?"

"They didn't," said Jevons. "They simply ignored it. Proving, at least, that they have good taste. Do you want the beads back?"

"Lord, no! Chuck 'em in the ocean. Can you recommend any other novelties? Anything you think they might like?''

"Well," said Hawthorne, "I've speculated about tools such as they could use, designed to be held in the mouth and—"

"We'd better experiment with that right here, before getting samples from Earth," said Jevons. "I'm skeptical, myself. What use would a hammer or a knife be to a cetoid?"

"Actually," said Hawthorne, "I was thinking about a saw. To cut coralite blocks and make shelters on the sea bottom.''

"Whatever for?" asked McClellan, astonished.

"I don't know," said Hawthorne. "There's so little we know. Probably not shelters against undersea weather— though that might not be absolutely fantastic, either. There are cold currents in the depths, I'm sure. What I had in mind, was—I've seen scars on many cetoids, like teeth marks, but left by something gigantic.''

"It's an idea." Jevons smiled. "It's good to have you back ideating, Nat. And it's decent of you to volunteer to take your station watch the first thing, right after your return. That wasn't expected of you.''

"Ah, he's got memories to soften the monotony," said McClellan. "I saw him in a hostess joint in Chicago. Brother, was he making time!"

The air masks hid most expression, but Hawthorne felt his ears redden. Jevons minded his own business, but he was old-fashioned, and more like a father than the implacable man in black whom Hawthorne dimly remembered.

One did not boast of Earthside escapades in Jevons' presence.

"I want to mull over the new biochemical data and sketch out a research program in the light of it," said the ecologist hastily. "And, too, renew my acquaintance with Oscar. I was really touched when he gave me that gem. I felt like a louse, handing it over to the Company."

"At the price it'll command, I'd feel lousy too," said McClellan.

"No, I don't mean that. I mean— Oh, run along jetboy!"

Hawthorne and Jevons stood watching the spacecraft taxi off across the water. Its rise was slow at first—much fire and noise, then a gradual acceleration. But by the time it had pierced the clouds, it was a meteor in reverse flight. And still it moved faster, streaking through the planet's thick permanent overcast until it was high in the sky and the clouds to the man inside did not show as gray but as blinding white.

So many miles high, even the air of Venus grew thin and piercingly cold, and water vapor was frozen out. Thus absorption spectra had not revealed to Earthbound astronomers that this planet was one vast ocean. The first explorers had expected desert and instead they had found water. But still McClellan rode his lightning horse, faster and higher, into a blaze of constellations.

When the rocket noise had faded, Hawthorne came out of his reverie and said: "At least we've created one beautiful thing with all our ingenuity—just one, space travel. I'm not sure how much destruction and ugliness that makes up for."

"Don't be so cynical," said Jevons. "We've also done

Beethoven sonatas, Rembrandt portraits, Shakespearean drama . . . and you, of all people, should be able to rhapsodize on the beauty of science itself.''

"But not of technology," said Hawthorne. "Science, pure ordered knowledge, yes. I'll rank that beside anything your Beethovens and Rembrandts ever made. But this machinery business, gouging a planet so that more people can pullulate—" It was good to be back with Jevons, he thought. You could dare be serious talking to the captain.

"You've been saddened by your furlough," said the old man. "It should be the other way around. You're too young for sadness."

"New England ancestors." Hawthorne tried to grin. "My chromosomes insist that I disapprove of something."

"I am luckier," said Jevons. "Like Pastor Grundtvig, a couple of centuries back, I have made a marvelous discovery. God is *good*."

"If one can believe in God. You know I can't. The concept just doesn't square with the mess humanity has made of things on Earth."

"God has to leave us free, Nat. Would you rather be an efficient, will-less puppet?"

"Or He may not care," said Hawthorne. "Assuming He does exist, have we any strong empirical grounds for thinking we're His particular favorites? Man may be just another discarded experiment, like the dinosaurs, set aside to gather dust and die. How do you know Oscar's breed don't have souls? And how do you know we do?"

"It's unwise to romanticize the cetoids," said Jevons. "They show a degree of intelligence, I'll concede. But—"

"I know. But they don't build spaceships. They haven't

got hands, and of course fire is impossible for them. I've heard all that before, Cap. I've argued it a hundred times, here and on Earth. But how can we tell what the cetoids do and don't do on the sea floor? They can stay underwater for days at a time, remember. And even here, I've watched those games of 'tag' they play. They are very remarkable games in some respects.

"I swear I can see a pattern, too intricate to make much sense to me, but a distant pattern notwithstanding. An art form, like our ballet, but using the wind and currents and waves to dance to. And how do you account for their display of taste and discrimination in music, individual taste, so that Oscar goes for those old jazz numbers, and Sambo won't come near them but will pay you carat for carat if you give him some Buxtehude? Why trade at all?"

"Pack rats trade on Earth," said Jevons.

"Now you're being unfair. The first expedition rafting here thought it was pack rat psychology, too—cetoids snatching oddments off the lower deck and leaving bits of shell, coralite, finally jewels. Sure, I know all that. But by now it's developed into too intricate a price system. The cetoids are shrewd about it—honest, but shrewd. They've got our scale of values figured to an inch: everything from a conchoidal shell to a firegem. Completely to the inch— keep that in mind.

"And why should mere animals go for music tapes, sealed in plastic and run off a thermionic cell? Or for waterproof reproductions of our great art? As for tools? They're often seen helped by schools of specialized fish, rounding up sea creatures, slaughtering and flensing, harvesting pseudo-kelp. They don't need hands, Cap! They use *live* tools!''

"I have been here a good many years," said Jevons dryly.

Hawthorne flushed. "Sorry. I gave that lecture so often Earthside, to people who didn't even have the data, that it's become a reflex."

"I don't mean to down-grade our damp friends," said the captain. "But you know as well as I do that all the years of trying to establish communication with them, symbols, signals—everything has failed."

"Are you sure?" asked Hawthorne.

"What?"

"How do you know the cetoids have not learned our alphabet off those slates?"

"Well . . . after all—"

"They might have good reasons for not wanting to take a grease pencil in their jaws and scribble messages back to us. A degree of wariness, perhaps. Let's face it, Cap. We're the aliens here, the monsters. Or maybe they simply aren't interested: our vessels are fun to play with, our goods amusing enough to be worth trading for, but we ourselves seem drab. Or, of course—and I think this is the most probable explanation—our minds are too strange. Consider the two planets, how different they are. How alike would you expect the thinking of two wholly different races to be?"

"An interesting speculation," said Jevons. "Not new, of course."

"Well, I'll go set out the latest gadgets for them," said

Hawthorne. He walked a few paces, then stopped and turned around.

"You know," he said, "I'm being a fool. Oscar did communicate with us, only last evening. A perfectly unambiguous message, in the form of a firegem."

IV

Hawthorne went past a heavy machine gun, loaded with explosive slugs. He despised the rule that an entire arsenal must always be kept ready. When had Venus ever threatened men with anything but the impersonal consequences of ignorance?

He continued on along the trading pier. Its metal gleamed, nearly awash. Basketlike containers had been lowered overnight, with standard goods. These included recordings and pictures the cetoids already knew, but always seemed to want more of. Did each individual desire some, or did they distribute these things around their world, in the undersea equivalent of museums or libraries?

Then there were the little plastic containers of sodium chloride, aqua ammonia, and other materials, whose taste the cetoids apparently enjoyed. Lacking continents to leach out, the Venusian ocean was less mineralized than Earth's, and these chemicals were exotic. Nevertheless the cetoids had refused plastibulbs of certain compounds, such as the permanganates—and later biochemical research had shown that these were poisonous to Venusian life.

But how had the cetoids known that, without ever crushing a bulb between teeth? They just knew, that was all. Human senses and human science didn't exhaust all the information in the cosmos. The standard list of goods had come to include a few toys, like floating balls, which the cetoids used for some appallingly rough games; and specially devised dressings, to put on injuries . . .

Oh, nobody doubted that Oscar was much more intelligent than a chimpanzee, thought Hawthorne. The problem had always been, was he as highly intelligent as a man?

He pulled up the baskets and took out the equally standardized payments which had been left in them. There were firegems, small and perfect or large and flawed. One was both big and faultless, like a round drop of rainbow. There were particularly beautiful specimens of coralite, which would be made into ornaments on Earth, and several kinds of exquisite shell.

There were specimens of marine life for study, most of them never before seen by Man. How many million species would an entire planet hold? There were a few tools, lost overboard, and only now freed of ooze by shifting currents; a lump of something unidentifiable, light and yellow and greasy to the touch, perhaps a biological product like ambergris, possibly only of slight interest and possibly offering a clue to an entire new field of chemistry. The plunder of a world rattled into Hawthorne's collection boxes.

All novelties had a fixed, rather small value. If the humans took the next such offering, its price would go up, and so on until a stable fee was reached, not too steep for the Earthmen or too low to be worth the cetoids' trouble. It was amazing how detailed a bargain you could strike without language.

Hawthorne looked down at Oscar. The big fellow had

nosed up close to the pier and now lay idly swinging his tail. The blue sheen along his upcurved back was lovely to watch.

"You know," murmured Hawthorne, "for years all Earth has been chortling over your giving us such nearly priceless stuff for a few cheaply made geegaws. But I've begun to wonder if it isn't reciprocal. Just how rare are firegems on Venus?"

Oscar spouted a little and rolled a wickedly gleaming eye. A curious expression crossed his face. Doubtless one would be very unscientific to call it a grin. But Hawthorne felt sure that a grin was what Oscar intended.

"Okay," he said. "Okay. Now let's see what you think of our gr-r-reat new products, brought to you after years of research for better living. Each and every one of these products, ladies and gentle-cetoids, has been tested in our spotless laboratories, and don't think it was easy to test the patent spot remover in particular. Now—"

The music bubbles of Schonberg had been rejected. Perhaps other atonalists would be liked, but with spaceship mass ratios what they were, the experiment wasn't going to be done for a long time. On the other hand, a tape of traditional Japanese songs was gone and a two-carat gem had been left, twice the standard price for a novelty: in effect, some cetoid was asking for more of the same.

As usual, every contemporary pictorial artist was refused, but then, Hawthorne agreed they were not to his taste either. Nor did any cetoid want Picasso (middle period), but Mondrian and Matisse had gone well. A doll had been accepted at low valuation, a mere bit of mineral: "Okay, we (I?) will take just this one sample, but don't bother bringing any more."

Once again, the waterproof illustrated books had been rejected; the cetoids had never bought books, after the first few. It was an idiosyncrasy, among others, which had led many researchers to doubt their essential basic intelligence and perception.

That doesn't follow, thought Hawthorne. *They haven't got hands, so a printed text isn't natural for them. Because of sheer beauty—or interest, or humor, or whatever they get out of it—some of our best art is worth the trouble of carrying underwater and preserving. But if they're looking for a factual record, they may well have more suitable methods. Such as what? God knows. Maybe they have perfect memories. Maybe, by sheer telepathy or something, they build their messages into the crystal structure of stones on the ocean bed.*

Oscar bustled along the pier, following the man. Hawthorne squatted down and rubbed the cetoid's smooth wet brow. "Hey, what do you think about me?" he asked aloud. "Do you wonder if *I* think? All right. All right. My breed came down from the sky and built floating metal settlements and brought all sorts of curious goodies. But ants and termites have pretty intricate behavior patterns, and you've got similar things on Venus."

Oscar snorted and nosed Hawthorne's ankles. Out in the water, his people were playing, and foam burned white against purple where they arched skyward and came down again. Still further out, on the hazy edge of vision, a few adults were at work, rounding up a school of "fish" with the help of three tame (?) species. They seemed to be enjoying the task.

"You have no right to be as smart as you are, Oscar," said Hawthorne. "Intelligence is supposed to evolve in response to a rapidly changing environment, and the sea isn't supposed to be changeable enough. Well, maybe the Terrestrial sea isn't. But this is Venus, and what do we know about Venus? Tell me, Oscar, are your dog-type and cattle-type fish just dull-witted animal slaves like the aphids kept by ants, or are they real domestic animals, consciously trained? It's got to be the latter. I'll continue to insist it is, until ants develop a fondness for van Gogh and Beiderbecke."

Oscar sounded, drenching Hawthorne with carbonated sea water. It foamed spectacularly, and tingled on his skin. A small wind crossed the world, puffing the wetness out of his garments. He sighed. The cetoids were like children, never staying put—another reason why so many psychologists rated them only a cut above Terrestrial apes.

A logically unwarranted conclusion, to say the least. At the quick pace of Venusian life, urgent business might well arise on a second's notice. Or, even if the cetoids were merely being capricious, were they stupid on that account? Man was a heavy-footed beast, who forgot how to play if he was not always being reminded. Here on Venus there might just naturally be more joy in living.

I shouldn't run down my own species the way I do, thought Hawthorne. *"All centuries but this and every country but his own." We're different from Oscar, that's all. But by the same token, is he any worse than us?*

He turned his mind to the problem of designing a saw

which a cetoid could handle. Handle? Manipulate? Not when a mouth was all you had! If the species accepted such tools in trade, it would go a long way toward proving them comparable to man. And if they didn't, it would only show that they had other desires, not necessarily inferior ones.

Quite conceivably, Oscar's race was more intellectual than mankind. Why not? Their bodies and their environment debarred them from such material helps as fire, chipped stone, forged metal, or pictograms. But might this not force their minds into subtler channels? A race of philosophers, unable to talk to Man because it had long ago forgotten baby talk . . .

Sure, it was a far-fetched hypothesis. But the indisputable fact remained, Oscar was far more than a clever animal, even if he was not on a level with Man.

Yet, if Oscar's people had evolved to, say, the equivalent of Pithecanthropus, they had done so because something in Venusian conditions had put a premium on intelligence. The same factor should continue to operate. In another half-million years or so, almost certainly, the cetoids would have as much brain and soul as Man today. (And Man himself might be extinct, or degraded.) Maybe more soul—more sense of beauty and mercy and laughter—if you extrapolated their present behavior.

In short, Oscar was (a) already equal to Man, or (b) already beyond Man, or (c) on the way up, and his descendants would in time achieve (a) and then (b). Welcome, my brother!

The pier quivered. Hawthorne glanced down again. Oscar had returned. He was nosing the metal impatiently and making gestures with his foreflipper. Hawthorne went over and looked at him. Oscar curved up his tail and whacked his own back, all the time beckoning.

"Hey, wait!" Hawthorne got the idea. He hoped. "Wait, do you want me to come for a ride?" he asked.

The cetoid blinked both eyes. Was the blink the counterpart of a nod? And if so, had Oscar actually understood the English words?

Hawthorne hurried off to the oxygen electrolyzer. Skindiving equipment was stored in the locker beside it. He wriggled into the flexible, heat-retaining Long John. Holding his breath, he unclipped his mask from the tank and air mixer he wore, and put on a couple of oxynitro flasks instead, thus converting it to an aqualung.

For a moment he hesitated. Should he inform Jevons, or at least take the collection boxes inside? No, to hell with it! This wasn't Earth, where you couldn't leave an empty beer bottle unwatched without having it stolen. Oscar might lose patience. The Venusians—damn it, he *would* call them that, and the devil take scientific caution!—had rescued distressed humans, but never before had offered a ride without utilitarian purpose. Hawthorne's pulse beat loudly.

He ran back. Oscar lay level with the pier. Hawthorne straddled him, grasping a small cervical fin and leaning back against the muscular dorsal. The long body glided from the station. Water rippled sensuously around Hawthorne's bare feet. Where his face was not masked, the wind was fresh upon it. Oscar's flukes churned up foam like a snowstorm.

Low overhead there scudded rainclouds, and lightning

veined the west. A small polypoid went by, its keelfin submerged, its iridescent membrane-sail driving it on a broad reach. A nearby cetoid slapped the water with his tail in a greeting.

The motion was so smooth that Hawthorne was finally startled to glance behind and see the station five miles off. Then Oscar submerged.

Hawthorne had done a lot of skin-diving, as well as more extensive work in submarines or armor. He was not surprised by the violet clarity of the first yards, nor the rich darkening as he went on down. The glowfish which passed him like rainbow comets were familiar. But he had never before felt the living play of muscles between his thighs; suddenly he knew why a few wealthy men on Earth still kept horses.

When he was in cool, silent, absolute blackness, he felt Oscar begin to travel. Almost, he was torn off by the stream; he lost himself in the sheer exhilaration of hanging on. With other senses than vision he was aware how they twisted through caves and canyons in buried mountains. An hour had passed when light glowed before him, a spark. It took another half hour to reach its source.

He had often seen luminous coralite banks. But never this one. It lay not far from the station as Venusian distances went, but even a twenty-mile radius sweeps out a big territory and men had not chanced by here. And the usual reef was a good bit like its Terrestrial counterpart, a ragged jumble of spires, bluffs, and grottos, eerie but unorganized beauty.

Here, the coralite was shaped. A city of merfolk opened up before Hawthorne.

Afterward he did not remember just how it looked. The patterns were so strange that his mind was not trained to register them. He knew there were delicate fluted columns, arched chambers with arabesque walls, a piling of clean masses at one spot and a Gothic humoresque elsewhere. He saw towers enspiraled like a narwhal's tusk, arches and buttresses of fragile filigree, an overall unity of pattern at once as light as spindrift and as strong as the world-circling tide, immense, complex, and serene.

A hundred species of coralite, each with its own distinctive glow, were blended to make the place, so that there was a subtle play of color, hot reds and icy blues and living greens and yellows, against ocean black. And from some source, he never knew what, came a thin crystal sound, a continuous contrapuntal symphony which he did not understand but which recalled to him frost flowers on the windows of his childhood home.

Oscar let him swim about freely and look. He saw a few other cetoids, also drifting along, often accompanied by young. But plainly, they didn't live here. Was this a memorial, an art gallery, or—Hawthorne didn't know. The place was huge, it reached farther downward than he could see, farther than he could go before pressure killed him, at least half a mile straight down to the sea bottom. Yet this miraculous place had never been fashioned for any "practical" reason. Or had it? Perhaps the Venusians recognized what Earth had forgotten, though the ancient Greeks had known it—that the contemplation of beauty is essential to thinking life.

The underwater blending of so much that was constructively beautiful could not be a freak of nature. But neither had it been carved out of some pre-existing mountain. No matter how closely he looked, and the flameless fire was adequate to see by, Hawthorne found no trace of chisel or mould. He could only decide that in some unknown way, Oscar's people had grown this thing.

He lost himself. It was Oscar who finally nudged him—a reminder that he had better go back before he ran out of air. When they reached the pier and Hawthorne had stepped off, Oscar nuzzled the man's foot, very briefly, like a kiss, and then he sounded in a tremendous splash.

V

Toward the close of the forty-three-hour daylight period, the boats came straggling in. For most it had been a routine shift, a few dozen discoveries, books and instruments filled with data to be wrestled with and perhaps understood. The men landed wearily, unloaded their craft, stashed their findings and went off for food and rest. Later would come the bull sessions.

Wim Dykstra and Jimmy Cheng-tung had returned earlier than most, with armfuls of recording meters. Hawthorne knew in a general way what they were doing. By seismographs, sonic probes, core studies, mineral analyses, measurements of temperature and radioactivity and a hundred other facets, they tried to understand the planet's inner structure. It was part of an old enigma. Venus had 80% of Earth's mass, and the chemical composition was nearly identical.

The two planets should have been sisters. Instead, the Venusian magnetic field was so weak that iron compasses were useless; the surface was so nearly smooth that no land rose above the water; volcanic and seismic activity were not only less, but showed unaccountably different patterns, lava flows and shock waves here had their own laws; the rocks were of odd types and distributions. And there was a galaxy of other technicalities which Hawthorne did not pretend to follow.

Jevons had remarked that in the past weeks Dykstra had been getting more and more excited about something. The Dutchman was the cautious type of scientist, who said never a word about his results until they were nailed down past argument. He had been spending Earthdays on end in calculations. When someone finally insisted on a turn at the computer, Dykstra often continued figuring with a pencil. One gathered he was well on the way to solving the geological problem of Venus.

"Or aphroditological?" Jevons had murmured. "But I know Wim. There's more behind this than curiosity, or a chance at glory. Wim has something very big afoot, and very close to his heart. I hope it won't take him too long!"

Today Dykstra had rushed downstairs and sworn nobody would get at the computer until he was through. Cheng-tung hung around for a while, brought him sandwiches, and finally wandered up on deck with the rest of the station to watch Shorty McClellan come in again.

Hawthorne sought him out. "Hey, Jimmy," he said. "You don't have to keep up that mysterious act. You're among friends."

The Chinese grinned. "I have not the right to speak," he said. "I am only the apprentice. When I have my own

110

doctorate, then you will hear me chatter till you wish I'd learn some Oriental inscrutability.''

"Yes, but hell, it's obvious what you're doing in general outline," said Hawthorne. "I understand Wim has been calculating in advance what sort of data he ought to get if his theory is sound. Now he's reducing those speculative assumptions for comparison. So okay, what *is* his theory?"

"There is nothing secret about its essence," said Cheng-tung. "It is only a confirmation of a hypothesis made more than a hundred years ago, before anyone had even left Earth. The idea is that Venus has a core unlike our planet's, and that this accounts for the gross differences we've observed.

"Dr. Dykstra has been elaborating it, and data so far have confirmed his beliefs. Today we brought in what may be the crucial measurements—chiefly seismic echoes from depth bombs exploded in undersea wells.''

"M-m-m, yeah, I do know something about it.'' Hawthorne stared across the ocean. No cetoids were in sight. Had they gone down to their beautiful city? And if so, why? *It's a good thing the questions aren't answered,* he thought. *If there were no more riddles on Venus, I don't know what I'd do with my life.*

"The core here is supposed to be considerably smaller and less dense than Earth's, isn't it?" he went on. His curiosity was actually no more than mild, but he wanted to make conversation while they waited for the spacecraft.

The young Chinese had arrived on the same ship which had taken Hawthorne home to furlough. Now they would be together for a long time, and it was well to show quick friendliness. He seemed a likeable little fellow anyhow.

"True," nodded Cheng-tung. "Though 'supposed' is the wrong word. The general assertion was proven quite satisfactorily quite some time ago. Since then Dr. Dykstra has been studying the details."

"I seem to have read somewhere that Venus ought by rights not to have a core at all," said Hawthorne. "Not enough mass to make enough pressure, or something of the sort. The planet ought to have a continuous rocky character right to the center, like Mars."

"Your memory is not quite correct," said Cheng-tung. His sarcasm was gentle and inoffensive. "But then, the situation is a trifle complex. You see, if you use quantum laws to calculate the curve of pressure at a planet's center, versus the planet's mass, you do not get a simple figure.

"Up to about eight-tenths of an Earth-mass it rises smoothly, but there is a change at what is called the Y-point. The curve doubles back, as if mass were decreasing with added pressure, and only after it has thus jogged back a certain amount—equivalent to about two percent of Earth's mass—does the curve resume a steady rise."

"What happens at this Y-point?" asked Hawthorne rather absently.

"The force becomes great enough to start collapsing the central matter. First crystals, which had already assumed their densest possible form, break down completely. Then, as more mass is added to the plant, the atoms themselves collapse. Not their nuclei, of course. That requires mass on the order of a star's.

"But the electron shells are squeezed into the smallest

112

possible compass. Only when this stage of quantum degeneracy has been reached—when the atoms will not yield any further, and there is a true core, with a specific gravity of better than ten—only thereafter will increased mass again mean a steady rise in internal pressure.''

"Uh . . . yes. I do remember Wim speaking of it, quite some time ago. But he never did like to talk shop, either, except to fellow specialists. Otherwise he'd rather debate history. I take it, then, that Venus has a core which is not collapsed as much as it might be?''

"Yes. At its present internal temperature, Venus is just past the Y-point. If more mass should somehow be added to this planet, its radius would actually decrease. This, not very incidentally, accounts rather well for the observed peculiarities. You can see how the accretion of material in the beginning, when the planets were formed, reached a point where Venus began to shrink—and then, as it happened, stopped, not going on to produce maximum core density and thereafter a steadily increasing size like Earth.

"This means a smooth planet, with no upthrust masses to reach above the hydrosphere and form continents. With no exposed rocks, there was nothing to take nearly all the CO_2 from the air. So life evolved for a different atmosphere. The relatively large mantle, as well as the low-density core, lead to a non-Terrestrial seismology, vulcanology, and mineralogy. The Venusian core is less conductive than Earth's—conductivity tends to increase with degeneracy—so the currents circulating in it are much smaller. Hence, the weak planetary magnetism.''

"Very interesting," said Hawthorne. "But why the big

113

secret? I mean, it's a good job of work, but all you've shown is that Venusian atoms obey quantum laws. That's hardly a surprise to spring on the universe.''

Cheng-tung's small body shivered a bare trifle. "It has been more difficult than one might suspect," he said. "But yes, it is true. Our data now reveal unequivocally that Venus has just the type of core which it could have under present conditions.''

Since Cheng-tung had during the night hours asked Hawthorne to correct any mistakes in his excellent English, the American said, "You mean, the type of core it should have.''

"I mean precisely what I said, and it is not a tautology." The grin was dazzling. Cheng-tung hugged himself and did a few dance steps. "But it is Dr. Dykstra's brain child. Let him midwife it." Abruptly he changed the conversation.

Hawthorne felt puzzled, but dismissed the emotion. And presently McClellan's ferry blazed out of the clouds and came to rest. It was a rather splendid sight, but Hawthorne found himself watching it with only half an eye. Mostly he was still down under the ocean, in the living temple of the Venusians.

Several hours past nightfall, Hawthorne laid the sheaf of reports down on his desk. Chris Diehl and Mamoru Matsumoto had done a superb task. Even in this earliest pioneering stage, their concept of enzymatic symbiosis offered possibilities beyond imagination. Here there was work for a century of science to come. And out of that work would be gotten a deeper insight into living processes, including those of Earth, than men had yet hoped for.

And who could tell practical benefits? The prospect was

heartcatching. Hawthorne had already realized a little of what he himself could do, and yes, in a hazy fashion he could even begin to see, if not understand, how the Venusians had created that lovely thing beneath the water . . . But a person can only concentrate so long at a time. Hawthorne left his cubbyhole office and wandered down a passageway toward the wardroom.

The station murmured around him. He saw a number of its fifty men at work. Some did their turn at routine chores, maintenance of apparatus, sorting and baling of trade goods, and the rest. Others puttered happily with test tubes, microscopes, spectroscopes, and less understandable equipment. Or they perched on lab benches, brewing coffee over a Bunsen burner while they argued, or sat feet on desk, pipe in mouth, hands behind head, and labored. Those who noticed Hawthorne hailed him as he passed. The station itself muttered familiarly, engines, ventilators, a faint quiver from the surrounding forever unrestful waters.

It was good to be home again.

Hawthorne went up a companionway, down another corridor, and into the wardroom. Jevons sat in a corner with his beloved Montaigne. McClellan and Cheng-tung were shooting dice. Otherwise the long room was deserted. Its transparent wall opened on seas which tonight were almost black, roiled and laced with gold luminosity.

The sky seemed made from infinite layerings of blue and gray, a low haze diffusing the aurora, and a rain-storm was approaching from the west with its blackness and lightning. The only sign of life was a forty-foot sea snake, quickly writhing from one horizon to another, its created jaws dripping phosphorescence.

McClellan looked up. "Hi, Nat," he said. "Want to sit in?"

"Right after Earth leave?" said Hawthorne. "What would I use for money?" He went over to the samovar and tapped himself a cup.

"Eighter from Decatur," chanted Jimmy Cheng-tung. "Come on, boys, let's see that good old Maxwell distribution."

Hawthorne sat down at the table. He was still wondering how to break his news about Oscar and the holy place. He should have reported it immediately to Jevons, but for hours after returning he had been dazed, and then the inadequacy of words had reared a barrier. He was too conditioned against showing emotion to want to speak about it at all.

He had, though, prepared some logical conclusions. The Venusians were at least as intelligent as the builders of the Taj Mahal; they had finally decided the biped strangers were fit to be shown something and would presumably have a whole planet's riches and mysteries to show on later occasions. Hawthorne scalded his tongue on red bitterness.

"Cap," he said.

"Yes?" Jevons lowered his dog-eared volume, patient as always at the interruption.

"Something happened today," said Hawthorne.

Jevons looked at him keenly. Cheng-tung finished a throw but did not move further, nor did McClellan. Outside there could be heard the heavy tread of waves and a rising wind.

"Go ahead," invited Jevons finally.

"I was on the trading pier and while I was standing there—"

Wim Dykstra entered. His shoes rang on the metal floor. Hawthorne's voice stumbled into silence. The Dutchman dropped fifty clipped-together sheets of paper on the table. It seemed they should have clashed, like a sword thrown in challenge, but only the wind spoke.

Dykstra's eyes blazed. "I have it," he said.

"By God!" exploded Cheng-tung.

"What on Earth?" said Jevons' mild old voice.

"You mean off Earth," said McClellan. But tightness grew in him as he regarded Dykstra.

The geophysicist looked at them all for several seconds. He laughed curtly. "I was trying to think of a suitable dramatic phrase," he said. "None came to mind. So much for historic moments."

McClellan picked up the papers, shuddered, and dropped them again. "Look, math is okay, but let's keep it within reason," he said. "What do those squiggles mean?"

Dykstra took out a cigaret and made a ceremony of lighting it. When smoke was in his lungs, he said shakily: "I have spent the past weeks working out the details of an old and little-known hypothesis, first made by Ramsey in nineteen fifty-one, and applying it to Venusian conditions. The data obtained here have just revealed themselves as final proof of my beliefs."

"There isn't a man on this planet who doesn't hope for a Nobel Prize," said Jevons.

His trick of soothing dryness didn't work this time. Dykstra pointed the glowing cigaret like a weapon and answered: "I do not care about that. I am interested in the largest and most significant engineering project of history."

They waited. Hawthorne began for no good reason to feel cold.

"The colonization of Venus," said Dykstra.

VI

Dykstra's words fell into silence as if into a well. And then, like the splash, Shorty McClellan said, "Huh? Isn't the Mindanao Deep closer to home?"

But Hawthorne spilled hot tea over his own fingers.

Dykstra began to pace, up and down, smoking in short nervous drags. His words rattled out: "The basic reason for the steady decay of Terrestrial civilization is what one may call crampedness. Every day we have more people and fewer resources. There are no longer any exotic foreigners to challenge and stimulate any frontier . . . no, we can only sit and brew an eventual, inevitable atomic civil war.

"If we had some place to go, what a difference! Oh, one could not relieve much population pressure by emigration to another planet—though an increased demand for such transportation would surely lead to better, more economical spaceships. But the fact that men could go, somehow, perhaps to hardship but surely to freedom and opportunity, that fact would make a difference even to the stay-at-homes. At worst, if civilization on Earth must die, its best elements would be on Venus, carrying forward what was good, forgetting what was evil. A second chance for humankind—do you see?"

"It's a pleasant theory, at least," said Jevons slowly, "but as for Venus. No, I don't believe a permanent colony forced to live on elaborated rafts and to wear masks every minute outdoors could be successful."

"Of course not," said Dykstra. "That is why I spoke of an engineering project. The transformation of Venus to another Earth."

"Now wait a minute!" cried Hawthorne, springing up.

No one noticed him. For them, in that moment, only the dark man who spoke like a prophet had reality. Hawthorne clenched his fists together and sat down, muscle by muscle, forcing himself.

Dykstra said through a veil of smoke: "Do you know the structure of this planet? Its mass puts it just beyond the Y-point—"

Even then, McClellan had to say, "No, I don't know. Tell me w'y point?"

But that was automatic, and ignored. Dykstra was watching Jevons, who nodded.

The geophysicist went on, rapidly, "Now in the region where the mass-pressure curve jogs back, it is not a single-valued function. A planet with the mass of Venus has three possible central pressures. There is the one it does actually have, corresponding to a small core of comparatively low density and a large rocky mantle. But there is also a higher-pressure situation, where the planet has a large degenerate core, hence a greater overall density and smaller radius. And, on the other side of the Y-point, there is the situation of lower central pressure. This means that the planet has no true core but, like Mars, is merely built in layers of rock and magma.

"Now such an ambiguous condition is unstable. It is possible for the small core which exists to change phase. This would not be true on Earth, which has too much mass, or on Mars, which does not have enough. But Venus is very near the critical point. If the lower mantle collapsed, to make a larger core and smaller total radius, the released energy would appear as vibrations and ultimately as heat."

He paused an instant, as if to give weight to his words. "If, on the other hand, the at-present collapsed atoms of the small core were to revert to a higher energy level, there would be blast waves traveling to the surface, disruption on a truly astronomical scale—and, when things had quieted down, Venus would be larger and less dense than at present, *without any core at all.*"

McClellan said, "Wait a bit, pal! Do you mean this damn golf ball is liable to explode under us at any minute?"

"Oh, no," said Dykstra more calmly. "Venus does have a mass somewhat above the critical for existing temperatures. Its core is in a metastable rather than unstable condition, and there would be no reason to worry for billions of years. Also, if temperature did increase enough to cause an expansion, it would not be quite as violent as Ramsey believed, because the Venusian mass *is* greater than his Y-point value. The explosion would not actually throw much material into space. But it would, of course, raise continents."

"Hey!" That was from Jevons. He jumped up. (Hawthorne sat slumped into nightmare. Outside, the wind lifted, and the storm moved closer across the sea.) "You mean . . .

increased planetary radius, magnifying surface irregularities—''

"And the upthrust of lighter rocks," added Dykstra, nodding. "It is all here in my calculations. I can even predict the approximate area of dry land resulting—about equal to that on Earth. The newly exposed rocks will consume carbon dioxide in huge amounts, to form carbonates. At the same time, specially developed strains of Terrestrial photosynthetic life—very like those now used to maintain the air on spaceships—can be sown.

"They will thrive, liberating oxygen in quantity, until a balance is struck. I can show that this balance can be made identical with the balance which now exists in Earth's atmosphere. The oxygen will form an ozone layer, thus blocking the now dangerous level of ultraviolet radiation. Eventually, another Earth. Warmer, of course—a milder climate, nowhere too hot for man—cloudy still, because of the closer sun—but nevertheless, New Earth!"

Hawthorne shook himself, trying to find a strength which seemed drained from him. He thought dully that one good practical objection would end it all, and then he could wake up.

"Hold on, there," he said in a stranger's voice. "It's a clever idea, but these processes you speak of—I mean, all right, perhaps continents could be raised in hours or days, but changing the atmosphere, that would take millions of years. Too long to do humans any good."

"Ah, no," said Dykstra. "This also I have investigated. There are such things as catalysts. Also, the growth of micro-organisms under favorable conditions, without any natural enemies, presents no difficulties. Using only known

121

techniques, I calculate that Venus could be made so a man can safely walk naked on its surface in fifty years.

"In fact, if we wanted to invest more effort, money, and research, it could be done faster. To be sure, then must come the grinding of stone into soil, the fertilizing and planting, the slow painful establishment of an ecology. But that, again, needs only to be started. The first settlers on Venus could make oases for themselves, miles wide, and thereafter expand these at their leisure. By using specialized plants, agriculture can even be practiced in the original desert.

"Oceanic life would expand much more rapidly, of course, without any human attentions. Hence the Venusians could soon carry on fishing and pelagiculture. I have good estimates to show that the development of the planet could even exceed the population growth. The firstcomers would have hope—their grandchildren will have wealth!"

Hawthorne sat back. "There are already Venusians," he mumbled.

Nobody heard him. "Say," objected McClellan, "how do you propose to blow up this balloon in the first place?"

"Is it not obvious?" said Dykstra. "Increased core temperature can supply the energy to push a few tons of matter into a higher quantum state. This would lower the pressure enough to trigger the rest. A single large hydrogen bomb at the very center of the planet would do it. Since this is unfortunately not attainable, we must tap several thousand deep wells in the ocean floor, and touch off a major nuclear explosion in all simultaneously.

"That would be no trick at all. Very little fallout would result, and what did get into the atmosphere would be gone again in a few years. The bombs are available. In fact, they exist already in far larger amounts than would be needed for this project. Would this not be a better use for them than using them as a stockpile to destroy human life?"

"Who would pay the bill?" asked Cheng-tung unexpectedly.

"Whatever government has the foresight—if all the governments on Earth cannot get together on it. I am not greatly concerned about that. Regimes and policies go, nations die, cultures are forgotten. But I want to be sure that *Man* will survive. The cost would not be great—comparable, at most, to one military satellite, and the rewards are enormous even on the crassest immediate terms. Consider what a wealth of uranium and other materials, now in short supply on Earth, would become accessible."

Dykstra turned to the transparent wall. The storm had reached them. Under the station caissons, the sea raged and struck and shattered in radiant foam. The deep, strong force of those blows traveled up through steel and concrete like the play of muscles in a giant's shoulders. Rain began to smash in great sheets on the deck. A continuous lightning flickered across Dykstra's lean countenance, and thunder toned.

"A world," he whispered.

Hawthorne stood up again. He leaned forward, his fingertips resting on the table. They were cold. His voice still came to him like someone else's. "No," he said. "Absolutely not."

"Eh?" Dykstra turned almost reluctantly from watching the storm. "What is wrong, Nat?"

"You'd sterilize a living planet," said Hawthorne.

"Well . . . true," admitted Dykstra. "Yes. Humanely, though. The first shock wave would destroy all organisms before they even had time to feel it."

"But that's murder!" cried Hawthorne.

"Come, now," said Dykstra. "Let us not get sentimental. I admit it will be a pity to destroy life so interesting, but when children starve and one nation after another is driven to despotism—" He shrugged and smiled.

Jevons, still seated, stroked a thin hand across his book, as if he wanted to recall a friend five hundred years dead. There was trouble on his face. "This is too sudden to digest, Wim," he said. "You must give us time."

"Oh, there will be time enough, years of it," said Dykstra. He laughed. "First my report must go to Earth, and be published, and debated, and publicized, and wrangled about, and then they will send elaborate expeditions to do my work all over again, and they will haggle and—have no fears, it will be at least a decade before anything is actually done. And thereafter we of the station, with our experience, will be quite vital to the project."

"Shucks," said McClellan, speaking lightly to conceal the way he felt, "I wanted to take a picnic lunch and watch the planet go up next Fourth of July."

"I don't know." Jevons stared into emptiness. "There's a question of . . . prudence? Call it what you will, but Venus can teach us so much as it is. A thousand years is not too long to study everything here. We may gain a few more continents at the price of understanding what life is

124

all about, or the means for immortality—if that's a goal to be desired—or perhaps a philosophy. I don't know.''

"Well, it is debatable," conceded Dykstra. "But let all mankind debate it, then."

Jimmy Cheng-tung smiled at Hawthorne. "I believe the captain is right," he said. "And I can see your standpoint, as a scientist. It is not fair to take your lifework away from you. I shall certainly argue in favor of waiting at least a hundred years."

"That may be too long," warned Dykstra. "Without some safety valve, technological civilization on Earth may not last another century."

"You don't understand!"

Hawthorne shouted it at them, as he looked into their eyes. Dykstra's gaze in particular caught the light in such a way that it seemed blank, Dykstra was a skull with two white circles for eyes. Hawthorne had the feeling that he was talking to deaf men. Or men already dead.

"You don't understand," he repeated. "It isn't my job, or science, or any such thing I'm worried about. It's the brutal fact of murder. The murder of an entire intelligent race. How would you like it if beings came from Jupiter and proposed to give Earth a hydrogen atmosphere? My God, what kind of monsters are we, that we can even think seriously about such a thing?"

"Oh, no!" muttered McClellan. "Here we go again. Lecture Twenty-eight-B. I listened to it all the way from Earth."

"Please," said Cheng-tung. "The issue is important."

"The cetoids do pose an embarrassing problem," conceded Jevons. "Though I don't believe any scientist has

125

ever objected to vivisection—even the use of close cousins like the apes—for human benefit.''

"The cetoids aren't apes!" protested Hawthorne, his lips whitening. "They're more human than you are!"

"Wait a minute," said Dykstra. He moved from his vision of lightning, toward Hawthorne. His face had lost its glory. It was concerned. "I realize you have opinions about this, Nat. But after all, you have no more evidence—"

"I do!" gasped Hawthorne. "I've got it at last. I've been wondering all day how to tell you, but now I must."

What Oscar had shown him came out in words, between peals of thunder.

At the end, even the gale seemed to pause, and for a while only rain, and the *brroom-brroom* of waves far below, continued to speak. McClellan stared at his hands, which twisted a die between the fingers. Cheng-tung rubbed his chin and smiled with scant mirth. Jevons, however, became serenely resolute. Dykstra was harder to read, his face flickered from one expression to the next. Finally he got very busy lighting a new cigaret.

When the silence had become too much, Hawthorne said, "Well?" in a cracked tone.

"This does indeed put another complexion on the matter," said Cheng-tung.

"It isn't proof," snapped Dykstra. "Look at what bees and bower birds do on Earth."

"Hey," said McClellan. "Be careful, Wim, or you'll prove that we're just glorified ants ourselves."

"Exactly," said Hawthorne. "I'll take you out in a submarine tomorrow and show you, if Oscar himself won't guide us. Add this discovery to all the other hints we've

126

had, and damn it, you can no longer deny that the cetoids are intelligent. They don't think precisely as we do, but they think at least as well.''

"And could doubtless teach us a great deal," said Cheng-tung. "Consider how much your people and mine learned from each other: and they were of the same species.''

Jevons nodded. "I wish you had told me this earlier, Nat," he said. "Of course there would have been no argument.''

"Oh, well," said McClellan, "guess I'll have to go back to blowing up squibs on the Fourth.''

The rain, wind-flung, hissed against the wall. Lightning still flickered, blue-white, but the thunder wagon was rolling off. The sea ran with wild frosty fires.

Hawthorne looked at Dykstra. The Dutchman was tense as a wire. Hawthorne felt his own briefly relaxing sinews grow taut again.

"Well, Wim?" he said.

"Certainly, certainly!" said Dykstra. He had grown pale. The cigaret fell unnoticed from his lips. "I am still not absolutely convinced, but that may be only my own disappointment. The chance of genocide is too great to take.''

"Good boy," smiled Jevons.

Dykstra smote a fist into his palm. "But my report," he said. "What shall I do with my report?''

So much pain was in his voice that Hawthorne felt shock, even though the ecologist had known this question must arise.

McClellan said, startled: "Well, it's still a nice piece of research, isn't it?''

Then Cheng-tung voiced the horror they all felt.

"I am afraid we must suppress the report, Dr. Dykstra," he said. "Regrettably, our species cannot be trusted with the information."

Jevons bit his lip. "I hate to believe that," he said. "We wouldn't deliberately and cold-bloodedly exterminate a billion or more sentient beings for our own . . . convenience."

"We have done similar things often enough in the past," said Dykstra woodenly.

I've read enough history myself, Wim, to give a very partial roll call, thought Hawthorne. And he began to tick off on his fingers. *Troy. Jericho. Carthage. Jerusalem. The Albigensians. Buchenwald.*

That's enough for now, he thought, feeling a wish to vomit.

"But surely—" began Jevons. "By now, at least—"

"It is barely possible that humane considerations may stay Earth's hand for a decade or two," said Dykstra. "The rate at which brutality is increasing gives me little hope even of that, but let us assume so. However, a century? A millennium? How long can we live in our growing poverty with such a temptation? I do not think forever."

"If it came to a choice between taking over Venus and watching our civilization go under," said McClellan, "frankly, I myself would say too bad for Venus. I've got a wife and kids."

"Be glad, then, that the choice will not be so clear-cut in your lifetime," said Cheng-tung.

Jevons nodded. He had suddenly become an old man,

whose work neared an end. "You have to destroy that report, Wim," he said. "Totally. None of us here can ever speak a word about it."

And now Hawthorne wanted to weep, but could not. There was a barrier in him, like fingers closing on his throat.

Dykstra drew a long breath. "Fortunately," he said, "I have been close-mouthed. No hint escaped me. I only trust the Company will not sack me for having been lazy and produced nothing all these months."

"I'll see to it that they don't, Wim," said Jevons. His tone was immensely gentle beneath the rain.

Dykstra's hands shook a little, but he tore the first sheet off his report and crumpled it in an ashtray and set fire to it.

Hawthorne flung out of the room.

VII

The air was cool outside, at least by contrast with daytime. The squall had passed and only a mild rain fell, sluicing over his bare skin. In the absence of the sun he could go about with no more than shorts and mask. That was a strangely light sensation, like being a boy again in a summer forest which men had since cut down. Rain washed on the decks and into the water, two distinct kinds of noise, marvelously clear.

The waves themselves still ran strong, swish and boom and a dark swirling. Through the air shone a very faint auroral trace, barely enough to tinge the sky with a haze of rose. But mostly, when Nat Hawthorne had left lighted windows behind him, the luminance came from the ocean, where combers glowed green along their backs and utter white when they foamed. Here and there a knife of blackness cut the water, as some quick animal surged.

Hawthorne went down past the machine gun to the trading pier. Heavy seas broke over it, reaching to his knees and spattering him with phosphor glow. He clung to the rail and peered into rain, hoping Oscar would come.

"The worst of it is," he said aloud, "they all mean so well."

A winged being passed overhead, only a shadow and whisper.

"The proverb is wrong," babbled Hawthorne. He gripped the rail, though he knew a certain hope that a wave would sweep him loose . . . and afterward the Venusians would retrieve his bones and take no payment.

"Who shall watch the watchmen? Simple. The watchmen themselves who are of no use anyway, if they aren't honorable. But what about the thing watched? It's on the enemy's side. Wim and Cap and Jimmy and Shorty—and I. We can keep a secret. But nature can't. How long before someone else repeats this work? We hope to expand the station. There'll be more than one geophysicist here, and—and—Oscar! Oscar, where the hell are you, Oscar?"

The ocean gave him reply, but in no language he knew.

He shivered, teeth clapping in his jaws. There was no reason to hang around here. It was perfectly obvious what had to be done. The sight of Oscar's ugly, friendly face wouldn't necessarily make the job easier. It might even make it harder. Impossible, perhaps.

Oscar might make me sane, thought Hawthorne. Ghosts of Sinaic thunder walked in his skull. *I can't have that. Not yet. Lord God of Hosts, why must I be this fanatical? Why not register my protest when the issue arises, like any normal decent crusader, organize pressure groups, struggle by all the legal proper means. Or, if the secret lasts out my lifetime, why should I care what may happen afterward? I won't be aware of it.*

No. That isn't enough. I require certainty, not that justice will be done, for that is impossible, but that injustice will not be done. For I am possessed.

No man, he thought in the wet blowing night, no man could foresee everything. But he could make estimates, and act on them. His brain was as clear as glass, and about as alive, when he contemplated purely empirical data.

If Venus Station stopped paying off, Venus would not be visited again. Not for a very long time, during which many things could happen . . . a Venusian race better able to defend itself, or even a human race that had learned self-control. Perhaps men would never return. Technological civilization might well crumble and not be rebuilt. Maybe that was best, each planet working out its own lonely destiny. But all this was speculation. There were immediate facts at hand.

Item: If Venus Station was maintained, not to speak of its possible expansion, Dykstra's discovery was sure to be repeated. If one man had found the secret, once in a few years of curiosity, another man or two or three would hardly need more than a decade to grope their way to the same knowledge.

Item: Venus Station was at present economically dependent on the cooperation of the cetoids.

Item: If Venus Station suffered ruin due to the reported

hostile action of the cetoids, the Company was unlikely to try rebuilding it.

Item: Even if the Company did make such an attempt, it would soon be abandoned again if the cetoids really did shun it.

Item: Venus would then be left alone.

Item: If you believed in God and sin and so forth which Hawthorne did not, you could argue that the real benefactor would be humankind, saved from the grisliest burden of deeds since a certain momentous day on Golgotha.

The worst of this for me, Hawthorne came to realize, *is that I don't care very much about humankind. It's Oscar I want to save. And how much hate for one race can hide under love for another?*

He felt dimly that there might be some way to flee nightmare. But the only path down which a man, flipperless and breathing oxygen, could escape, was back through the station.

He hurried along a quiet, brightly-lit corridor to a stairwell sloping down toward the bowels of the station and down. No one else was about. He might have been the last life in a universe turned ashen.

But when he entered the stockroom, it was a blow that another human figure stood there. Ghosts, ghosts . . . what right had the ghost of a man not yet dead to walk at this moment?

The man turned about. It was Chris Diehl, the biochemist. "Why, hi, Nat," he said. "What are you doing at this hour?"

Hawthorne wet his lips. The Earthlike air seemed to

wither him. "I need a tool," he said. "A drill, yes—a small electric drill."

"Help yourself," said Diehl.

Hawthorne lifted a drill off the rack. His hands began to shake so much that he dropped it. Diehl stared at him.

"What's wrong, Nat?" he asked softly. "You look like second-hand custard."

"I'm all right," whispered Hawthorne. "Quite all right."

Hawthorne picked up the drill and went out.

The locked arsenal was low in the station hull. Hawthorne could feel Venus' ocean surge below the deckplates. That gave him the strength to drill the lock open and enter, to break the cases of explosive and lay a fuse. But he never remembered having set a time cap on the fuse. He only knew he had done so.

His next recollection was of standing in a boathouse, loading oceanographic depth bombs into one of the little submarines. Again, no one stirred. No one was there to question him. What had the brothers of Venus Station to fear?

Hawthorne slipped into the submarine and guided it out the sea gate. Minutes later he felt the shock of an explosion. It was not large, but it made so much noise in him that he was stunned and did not see Venus Station go to the bottom. Only afterward did he observe that the place was gone. The waters swirled wildfire above it, a few scraps of wreckage bobbing in sheeting spindrift.

He took a compass bearing and submerged. Before long, the coralite city glowed before him. For a long moment he looked at its spires and grottos and lovelinesses, until fear warned him that he might make himself incapable of doing what was necessary. So he dropped his bombs, hastily, and felt his vessel shudder with their force, and saw the temple become a ruin.

And next he remembered surfacing. He went out on deck and his skin tasted rain. The cetoids were gathering. He could not see them, except in glimpses, a fluke or a back, phosphor streaming off into great waves, with once a face glimpsed just under the low rail, almost like a human baby's in that uncertain light.

He crouched by the machine gun, screaming, but they couldn't understand and anyway the wind made a rag of his voice. "I have to do this! I have no choice, don't you see? How else can I explain to you what my people are like when their greed dominates them? How else can I make you avoid them, which you've got to do if you want to live? Can you realize that? Can you? But no, you can't, you mustn't. You have to learn hate from us, since you've never learned it from each other—"

And he fired into the bewildered mass of them.

The machine gun raved for a long time, even after no more living Venusians were around. Hawthorne didn't stop shouting until he ran out of ammunition. Then he regained consciousness. His mind felt quiet and very clear, as if a fever had possessed him and departed. He remembered summer mornings when he was a boy, and early sunlight slanting in his bedroom window and across his eyes. He re-entered the turret and radioed the spaceship with total rationality.

"Yes, Captain, it was the cetoids, beyond any possibility of doubt. I don't know how they did it. Maybe they disarmed some of our probe bombs, brought them back and exploded them. But anyhow the station has been destroyed. I got away in a submarine. I glimpsed two other men in an open boat, but before I could reach them the cetoids had attacked. They stove in the boat, and killed the men as I watched . . . God, no, I can't imagine why! Never mind why! Let's just get away from here!''

He heard the promise of rescue by ferry, set an automatic location signal, and lay down on the bunk. It was over now, he thought in a huge grateful weariness. No human would ever learn the truth. Given time, he himself might forget it.

The space vessel descended at dawn, when the sky was turning to mother-of-pearl. Hawthorne came out on deck. Some dozen Venusian corpses rolled alongside the hull. He didn't want to see them, but there they were, and suddenly he recognized Oscar.

Oscar gaped blindly into the sky. Small pincered crustaceans were eating him. His blood was green.

Oh, God, thought Hawthorne, *please exist. Please make a hell for me.*

The Life of Your Time

The *Emissary* had been half a year under way before her people knew that something had gone awry within themselves. They could have noticed earlier—the human organism is that sensitive—but they were too occupied with their work and with getting used to the grotesquerie that gleamed and blazed and shivered and hummed around them. Also, the interior change was very slow . . . at first.

Isabel McAndrew broke through to the truth, but not till the end of the seventh month.

She stirred awake as a chime signaled the start of another watch period. Her husband Arch was moving likewise, beside her in the tiny cabin that was theirs. Gradually his red hair and angular features came from beneath the blanket, as if he were an animal grumbling out of hibernation. (They could have set room temperature higher and done without bed clothes. But they liked cool air for sleeping. Then, too, blankets were a homely remembrance of Earth, such as one needed here where the very stars crawled toward patterns of otherness.) He swung his feet around to the deck, yawned, and stretched.

But I didn't touch a drop last "night," he thought.

Isabel sat up and regarded him for a long while. Her heartshaped face was so grave, beneath the tangled dark locks, that he felt a stab of worry.

"What's the matter, sweetheart?" he asked. The words dropped out of his mouth one by one, like pellets of buckshot.

"You," she murmured. "Me." Drowsiness fled. Her eyes widened. "Every one of us!"

"Huh?"

"The way you feel. Have been feeling. More and more." Isabel took hold of his arm. She didn't move fast, though the gesture was almost frantic. "Suddenly, watching you, I know. And I know it's true of the others."

"You mean— Wait." The physicist curbed himself, wet his lips and said carefully, "All right. For some time I've felt, uh, a bit funny. It's progressive, I think, though too gradual for me to be sure. I didn't worry about it because, well, what I mainly noticed was that I seemed to be thinking faster than normal. I put it down to being stimulated by our situation. The first manned expedition beyond the Solar System!"

"But today," she said, "you were comparing it to a hangover."

"How do you know that?"

She didn't answer. Such questions had arisen between

138

them before. Unpredictably, but not unseldom, she had an eerily accurate intuition of what was going on in other people's heads. The psych team, probing every aspect of her mind before they O.K.'d her enlistment, had found indications of some telepathic talent. But that was as hard to pin down and study as most psi phenomena. So Isabel McAndrew was signed on just because she could rapidly assimilate training in advanced linguistics, and because she could cook, sing, organize games, soothe nerves: in general, be the morale officer of what was otherwise a crew of specialists.

I wonder, though, flashed across her husband's consciousness. When we get to Tau Ceti, when we're eye to eye with those beings whose radio we detected (if they have anything like our concept of eyes)—the psych men may well have hoped her gift would serve us better in getting to know them than any number of language courses.

Then he realized she had not spoken for what was apparently quite some time. He cleared his throat and said: "Don't get scared, sweetheart. I'm not sick. No headache. Only, well, when I do have a mild hangover, time drags for me. It takes forever to do something, even though the clock says I'm proceeding at my usual speed. I suppose it's because of being especially aware of my body. Or maybe, I don't know, maybe the aftermath of alcoholic irritation gears up the brain a little. But anyhow, yes, I do feel sort of like that, now."

"Me, too." Her fingers tightened on him. "It's been creeping up on me, too. I didn't mention it for the same reason you didn't. It looked like such a minor thing, something that'd cure itself. But if we *all*—!"

"How can you tell?" McAndrew grinned and patted her cheek. "Never mind. You've told me often enough that you don't know. Probably your subconscious puts different subtle clues together. Come to think of it, when we were last playing bridge with Jerry and Lisette, I did notice their manner was the least bit odd." Gently, he disengaged her grasp on him and hauled his lanky frame erect. "I'll check with Doc. Chances are that if this means anything whatsoever, it's due to environment. They warned us to expect psychological consequences. Doc will prescribe us a pill or a brain stimulation sequence or something, and we'll be O.K. again."

She smiled. He could read the tinge of forlornness underneath. They had more rapport than the other three couples. Theirs was the only love match aboard. The rest got along fine—they'd better!—but the marriages were of convenience. Even in ship's time, they would take a couple of years to reach Tau Ceti, and then they might spend as much as five years there before returning. So you had to have one woman for each man. And she must meet the same standards as he, of youth, health, skill, and dedication. McAndrew had found his girl for himself, before this expedition was organized, and the luck was fantastic that they both qualified.

He wanted much to comfort her. The eternal murmur of the vessel, ventilators, pumps, chemical converters, was as eternally underlaid by the bone-deep pulse of the drive. The deck thrust against him with an Earth gravity of acceleration, but metal, not the warm live soil he remembered. The overhead was no sky, the fluoropanel no sun, the ecological plant no forest. Outside this thin skin lay near-total vacuum, seething with hard radiations. Sol was shrunken to another star, ghastly far aft, and now that they had reached some sixty per cent of light speed, Doppler effect made it an ember. The same effect discolored the whole heavens, and aberration was drawing the constellations into distorted clumps. Not easy to ship on the Flying Dutchman!

But for that exact reason, you dared not confess to fear. You had to keep the tone light. He glanced at the indicator on the door to the bath cubicle, which the four residential cabins surrounded. "Well, whaddaya know," he exclaimed. "Unoccupied. The first time in recorded history. I better grab while I can." He popped in. Rather, he tried to, but somehow his body resisted speed.

Emerging and dressing, he was surprised to note how few minutes had passed. And, for that matter, how quick Isabel was in her turn; for she seemed to be dawdling. While he waited for her, he opened the panel which folded down to make a table and accepted what the autochef sent from the galley. Dinners were ceremonious affairs, cooked by Isabel and eaten in the saloon, but otherwise the couples clung to their privacy. They wanted to remain good friends.

Her normal breakfast chatter was absent, and he was too worried to jolly her. He swallowed his last coffee in haste and got onto the intercom. "Hullo, Jerry?"

"Hi," said Greenberg, who was his scientific assistant as well as the communications officer. The syllable was prolonged.

"I'll be late for work. Can you finish that spectroscope-computer linkage alone?'' They were gathering a glorious hoard of data, in this place and under these conditions which men had never known before. Hitherto it had kept them cheerful.

"I . . . I'm not sure."

"Something wrong?"

"No. Not exactly. But to tell the truth, I've been a little off my feed of late. Slow and awkward."

McAndrew exchanged a look with Isabel.

"O.K., then, wait for me," he said. "I do want to nail down those observations while we're still in this velocity range, but we're not accelerating that fast. And what the hell, if we don't make it, we'll get another chance coming back."

If we come back, said the forbidden part of him.

He called Vincent Norrington, arranged to see the biologist-physician, kissed Isabel—this time-stretching did have some compensations!—and left. The corridor reached blank and murmurous before him. On the way, he passed Denis Romano, the captain, and Sylvia Norrington, the engineer. Neither of them had any duties while the passage lasted. The *Emissary* was totally automatic en route: had to be, when such masses and speeds and energies were involved. But they kept busy, maintaining the ecosystem, tinkering improvements into the service equipment, assisting Clarice Romano with her biochemical experiments. Two years in space should not have proved a burden.

Nonetheless, McAndrew noticed that they looked haggard.

Norrington, a large and soft-spoken Negro, was already in his consulting room. The bulkheads were paneled in oak, hung with old-fashioned prints, dominated by a stereopic frame which showed moving, ever-changing scenes of Earth. A layout calculated to be restful, McAndrew knew. He wondered if Norrington's old briar pipe was part of the same act. No one else had wasted any personal baggage allowance on tobacco.

"Hullo, Arch. Sit yourself. What can I do for you?" Norrington blew a leisurely cloud and relaxed into his armchair.

"How have you been feeling lately?" McAndrew demanded.

"Hm-m-m?" Norrington raised his brows. "This is a new twist. I'm supposed to ask you that."

McAndrew tautened on the edge of his seat. "I mean it, Doc. I've got reason to believe something odd is happening to the bunch of us. Have you noticed anything in yourself?"

"I see." Norrington sat quiet a moment, before he opened the console on his desk. Switches, knobs, meters bristled forth. "Suppose you tape an account while I cover my ears," he said. "Then I'll do the same, and we'll play them back."

McAndrew nodded. "Good idea."

The reports were nearly identical. Even to the slowness of speech.

The men regarded each other while the walls seemed to grow close. Finally Norrington said, "Let's test this. Observe the sweep-second hand on my clock here. Count off time for yourself: one hippopotamus, two hippopotamus, and so on. Compare."

143

"I've always counted thousand-and one, thousand-and-two."

"If you prefer. I think hippopotamuses are more fun."

The results, for both of them, were oddly uneven. McAndrew noted down several series of correlations and averaged them. "The mean discrepancy," he said, "is about oh-point-two-five. That is, our personal time sense has accelerated by some twenty-five per cent. But why such a large probable error?"

"Because our biological clocks are out of whack." Norrington rose. "This apparatus here is only good for routine diagnosis. Come on into the med lab. I want to check you within a centimeter of your soul."

Even with the superb automated equipment available—it would later be used to study the unforeseeably alien life forms around Tau Ceti—the process took a couple of hours. They tried to joke meanwhile, but with scant success.

In the end, Norrington pondered the data printouts for minutes before he said in a flat voice, "Let's go back to the office." When they were there, he got out a bottle. "I know how small our liquor supply is," he said, "but I, at least, need a drink."

McAndrew's hand was not quite steady, taking his glass. "What's the verdict?" he heard himself ask.

"Clean."

"Huh?"

"As far as the tests can tell, you're in virtually perfect shape. A touch of neurological and physiochemical imbalance, but nothing to worry about, obviously a mere by-product of nervous strain due to this time phenomenon." Norrington sipped, put down his glass, stoked his pipe anew, and made an elaborate business of getting it lit. "I'll have to check everyone, including myself," he said, "but I'm quite sure the results will be the same."

"What can the cause be?"

Norrington shook his head. "I don't know."

"Our environment—"

"I doubt that. You remember that volunteer groups spent two years under identical conditions of confinement, noise, vibration, with no ill effects. And the plants and animals on the automatic probes came back in good shape."

"But people aren't animals," McAndrew protested.

"Oh, yes, they are," Norrington said. "I'll agree, though, the human mind is unique."

He scowled and puffed before continuing: "We have to take that into account, always and forever. Remember why a strictly American crew was selected? That made for a lot of grumbling and trouble throughout the Hegemony. Our troops even had to suppress riots, here and there around the world. But the reason was not imperial pride. No, it was only that the psych boys figured there would be enough mental stress without adding intercultural conflict."

"So maybe . . . you mean . . . the knowledge of how alone we are, that's causing us to break down?" McAndrew suppressed a shiver. The ultimate betrayal: one's own self.

"I do not," Norrington stated. "Each of us was hand-picked for stability. And nothing like this happened while the Solar System was being explored, nor on the Alpha Centauri expedition; and *its* ship could barely get up to a fourth of our ultimate velocity. No, men in the past have been just as isolated, and a lot less comfortable and safe.''

"So what is the trouble?"

"Some new kind of energy field? Maybe you'd better get busy looking."

"Nonsense!" McAndrew collected himself. "Sorry. But I can't see that either."

"We're edging toward the speed of light," Norrington reminded him. "Men have never gone this fast before. Couldn't there be some unsuspected effect?"

"We've pushed atoms within a cat's whisker of c, for centuries, and not found anything but—" McAndrew jarred to a halt.

"What?" Norrington took the pipe from between his lips and clenched the bowl close to breaking force.

"Wait a minute." McAndrew leaned across the desk and scribbled with a stylus on a reusable tablet. How well their loneliness was measured by the fact they couldn't afford scratch paper. "Damn," he muttered, "but I wish I'd brought my slide rule . . . Yeh. Got it."

Norrington waited. The bleakness grew and grew in the other man. Finally he spoke:

"I've inverted the time relationship we found. Are we really thinking twenty-five per cent faster? Or are we thinking at our ordinary rate, while everything else has slowed down to eighty per cent of normal?"

"Is that even a meaningful question?"

"It sure as hell is. Look, we've reached sixty per cent of c. That gives you a tau function of oh-point-eight. In other words, as you well know, if an observer on Earth could see us now, he'd see our clocks, chemical processes, radioactive decay, everything—our time rate—going at eighty per cent of his own. Same factor as we've observed in ourselves, you and me. I can't believe that's a coincidence.''

Norrington's face turned a peculiarly horrible grayish color. McAndrew saw him sit motionless, as if he were already locked in stasis. The physicist nodded and spat:

"Yeah. Exactly what you're thinking. The tau factor approaches zero, faster and faster, as we approach the speed of light. We'll be very close to that in less than five months. What happens to us then?''

It spoke well for them that they were not shattered by the announcement. They had been worried when Norrington put them through his tests without saying why and McAndrew searched so desperately for a trace of some hitherto unknown physical phenomenon and didn't find any. The knowledge had become common, after they realized that *something* must be wrong with everybody, that time had gone askew. But most had thought of . . . well, psycho-physiology, energy seeping past radiation screens . . . not this.

They sat around the saloon table, couple by couple, when Norrington finished and seated himself. Husbands and wives clasped hands, except for the Romanos. The captain doubled both fists together and leaned on them, as if to crumple the tabletop.

Silence waxed. Weaving beneath it, around it, through it went the relentless rhythm of the ship. And McAndrew imagined crazily that he could hear the unhearable noise beyond the hull, hydrogen atoms dying in the fusion generator or flung aft in one torrent or shuddering with the shock waves of the *Emissary*'s transit; cosmic rays sleeting through light-years, photons that were old before this galaxy came into being, the synchrotron fury of magnetically whirled electrons. Certainly he felt the pulsations in the metal that enclosed him, and to his awareness they had dropped in frequency, become a bass growl within his flesh. The slugging of his heart, the acrid smell of his fear, were by contrast things of home, human, almost as dear to him as the pressure of Isabel's fingers.

"No!" Romano smote the table so it rang. "Impossible!"

"The truth is never impossible, Skipper," Isabel said quietly. Because he could have no secrets from her, McAndrew had told her the facts already, and there had been time for her to find some measure of calm. Which had helped him more than he dared reckon up.

"But your explanation's absurd," Romano sputtered. "What you're saying is that we're moving at six-tenths *c* while our brains are sitting still!"

"Not our brains," Norrington corrected. "Those are physical organs, subject to the same laws of nature as anything else. Our minds."

"You mean the mind is not subject?"

"Different aspect of natural law," McAndrew said. "You don't expect stars to act like molecules, do you? Or men like stones?"

He took some of the brandy Norrington had ordered set out. "I agree, Denny," he went on, "it is absurd to suppose that our bodies are moving while our minds are not. There must be some other cause. The fact does appear to be, though, that the human mind is permanently in ordinary cosmic time, and the rate at which it functions is not affected by speed.''

"Hey, wait!" Jerry Greenberg protested. "Do you mean there is a distinction between subjective and objective time? Everybody knows that. I seem to remember Einstein himself pointed it out. Wasn't his example the way an hour spent with your best girl on the porch swing is ever so much shorter than an hour spent sitting on a hot stove? O.K., no argument. I can see how our organisms might in some way resent these unnatural conditions and—"

"No, that is not what I'm getting at," McAndrew said. "Doc's tests pretty well rule out physiology or psychology as a cause for this thing. What I mean is that our minds, not our bodies or brains but our minds, are somehow still operating at the same rate as they did on Earth.''

Greenberg shook his head. "You're implying that there is one inertial frame of reference which is unique. That was disproved back when the foundations of relativity were first laid.''

"Not exactly," McAndrew said. "I've given this matter some thought. What we might as well call the cosmic frame does have one peculiarity, namely that most of the accessible physical universe is in it. I mean to say, after all, leaving aside the galactic recession business . . . throughout an enormous volume of space, not many masses travel at any substantial fraction of light velocity. We had to accelerate to get moving this fast, and we'll have to decelerate at journey's end. That takes the problem out of special and into general relativity. The old twin paradox doesn't arise. When we return to Earth—if we do—no,

149

damn it, when we do!''—he tossed off his drink—''we will in fact be younger than the people who stayed behind.''

"So?"

"So there is, strictly speaking, one *set* of inertial frames, not very different from each other, which are indeed unique within any galactic family. The low-velocity set, that all stars and planets and interstellar atoms belong to. The cosmic set. Evidently the mind—as opposed to the brain—is somehow tied in to the cosmic set."

"Stow that, you two," Romano barked. "We've got a survival problem to lick. Doc, if this goes on, what'll happen to us?"

"I'll tell you straight," Norrington said. His words lacked tone, and how slowly they fell! "Matters will get worse and worse as the tau factor shrinks. We'll feel more and more inert, less and less able to coordinate will and action. Only a nuisance, at first. But eventually, for practical purposes, we'll be stiffened into motionlessness. As far as our perceptions are concerned, that is. We'll stare at the same object for days, weeks, before we can drag our eyes away, or close them, or anything. We won't even have any noticeable sensation of interior life, pulse beat, breath, all stopped. It'll be the most extreme sensory deprivation human beings have ever undergone." He filled his lungs. "Eleven years of that before we commence deceleration. Forty-eight hours is considered sufficient to induce radical psychosis."

"We'll go insane," said Lisette Greenberg into the thrumming. She gasped and buried her face against her husband's shoulder.

"Whoa, there." McAndrew spoke briskly, as much for his own sake as anyone else's. "Things are not quite that bad. We have to get pretty close to light speed before the effect becomes overwhelming. Four months from now, we'll be moving at ninety-five per cent of c, but the tau factor will be oh-point-three. A little more than three hours will pass in your consciousness while one hour passes outside. No fun, of course, but you can stand it."

"Beyond that, though—" Clarice Romano whispered.

"Uh-huh," McAndrew nodded. "The process accelerates. In a couple of weeks more, the ratio will be ten to one. Four days later, two thousand to one. And on and on. But we can count on four months, I'd say, in which to solve our problem."

"Solve it how?" Sylvia Norrington challenged. "If we could get in touch with Earth, and they turned the entire scientific force of the human race out to help us, what could they do in that time? We've stumbled on a whole new field of knowledge. We don't even know what data to look for, let alone how to look or how to theorize about them."

She appeared calmer than the rest, whose jaws were clamped together as if they held onto sanity by their teeth. Only Isabel matched her evenness in asking, "Don't you plan to try?"

"Certainly, dear," Sylvia answered. "I'll work like hell, if we can decide what to work at. But let's be honest. We won't succeed." She shrugged broad smooth shoulders. "We knew there were risks. We were trained to accept the fact we might die. When I've failed, and can't stand any more what's happening to me, I'll ask Doc for some pills and go quietly to sleep."

Norrington traded a glance with McAndrew. They'd talked about this. A mind, trapped in dreams for the days or weeks the brain took to die, would not go out easily.

But best not speak of that now.

McAndrew was jarred to note that Isabel's eyes had joined the silent exchange. Did she read this in them, too?

She smiled, released her clasp on him, and raised her glass. "The sooner we get organized, the better," she said. "But first, how about a toast to our victory?"

On and out the ship plunged, a web of force and a blaze of energy, within which the hull was little but a control center. As her speed mounted toward that of light, and mass with speed, she became herself a cosmic object; space was troubled by her passage, and perhaps—not impossible—a sun did or did not form, billions of years later, because she had crossed those particular kilometers.

Space is not empty. Look out a port and try to count the stars; and then there are planets, meteorites, dust clouds beyond imagination. True, the way is long from one to the next. But more than radiation pervades space. There is matter: the primordial hydrogen, and every other element born in the suns and spat forth in their death pangs, but all-dominatingly the interstellar medium is hydrogen. In our part of the galaxy, the atoms number one to a cubic centimeter.

The *Emissary* departed Sol on a standard reaction drive. Had that been her only means of travel, she could never have come near the ultimate speed. The mass ratio would have been too huge. But she had not accelerated very long when she could begin gathering the mass which every-where surrounded her, the hydrogen, and use it.

One atom per cubic centimeter? No, the thought is not ridiculous. At speeds close to light, every square centimeter of ship will encounter thirty billion atoms per second. And the energy of encounter is stupendous. Had the *Emissary* run directly into that interstellar atmosphere, her crew would have died: at one-half of c, they would have been blasted by thirty million Roentgens per hour.

Since the hydrogen must be warded off in any event, why not take advantage? Scoop it up and blow it backwards, a ram jet which becomes ever more efficient as velocity increases. Light speed is the limit, but you approach that limit asymptotically, you can accelerate the entire distance. One year roughly, to come very near it: in the course of which, you will travel half a light-year. Then—scarcely any time, weeks at most, just a few days if your route takes you through a denser-than-usual region—to cover the bulk of the trip; though the cosmos will measure your transit in years.

At midpoint, you make turnover and decelerate. A new configuration of forces is established, to interact with the gas like some titanic drogue. Even so, the engine must be operated, too. The atoms you collect must have their relative velocities reversed. No matter. You have power to spare, for the energies involved are enough to maintain a thermonuclear fire. In the end, half a light-year from journey's termination, you will begin to come down to something like a reasonable speed, and you will note the passage of a year while you brake to rendezvous with your goal.

Such was the theory. Practice was something else again. The airscoops, the jets, the very power plant could not be material: not when such orders of magnitude were involved, a trap whose diameter was four million kilometers at the mouth, an atmosphere cloven at three hundred thousand kilometers per second, a center of fusion reaction which was like a small sun, and which must be kept far away from the ship lest its own radiation pour too strongly through the hull shields. Nothing could have carried out the task, nothing could control that monstrousness, except the forces themselves. To balance those had been the work of three generations of engineers.

Nor could the ship maneuver. Once launched, she was less guidable than a hurled rock. The least attempt to change the pattern of action programmed into her would have upset the force equilibrium; she would have vanished in a novalike burst visible halfway across the galaxy.

She might yet. A single flaw, or an unnoticed pebble afloat in her path, would spell the end. Surely they were brave who launched her. Who had dreamed more majestically than those who rode her?

Arch McAndrew writhed in his bed. Horror mouthed at him. He had slipped into darkness, and now he fell, while an eyeless face that was his own receded before him, then came back, swelled until it filled the universe, until it was the universe, until nothing lived and nothing had ever been or would be except wrongness, they had put the sky on crooked so that he could see past the horizon into the nonexistence which lay infinite beyond, and for centuries he screamed.

Heavy as the world, arms enfolded him. He struggled through great waters that roared, up through a surface that resisted and clung, broke past and gasped for air. Light was hideous about him. Inchmeal, his wife's countenance moved into his view. He lay and drew life from the vision; now he could feel the breath that dragged in and out of him, the heart that wearily pumped a bloodstream gone viscous, the slow, slow cold trickle of each sweat drop down his ribs; Isabel, Isabel, you are become a statue, only an idol of what I have served, God has departed from the Ark of the Covenant and you are blank before me.

No. No. The same dear play of expression was there. He could see it creep across her lips and eyes, the words belled in him,

"Oh,

"darling,

"wake

"up.

"It's

"all

"right,

"the

"Face

"was

"only

"a

"nightmare,

"I

"am

"here

"and

155

"I

"love

"you."

He summoned what strength of will was left him. Not only had the past months of futile, frantic toil, scurrying from hypothesis to hypothesis and experiment to experiment like a rat in a bottle, worn him down. He could have taken that. But his body, his brain, no longer supplied what his mind needed at the rate he needed. And now they had come so far that he could feel the gap widen slowly—hourly.

Power, he thought. Rate of doing work. But rates are relative.

The dry physics concept was something to cling to in his exhausted confusion. He looked at the tears that slipped over Isabel's lashes and cheeks, and wondered: How did she know what I was dreaming?

Word by word—while goblin birds flapped wearily past, however much he tried to believe they were hallucinations spewed out by a mind starved for knowledge of any reality beyond itself—she answered, "You didn't yell. I just knew, in my own sleep."

Sleep, that knits up the ravel'd sleeve of care. Doc Norrington had gotten them onto that approach. They should be able, with a drug or a brain-wave playback, to knock themselves unconscious. They could have on Earth. They would rig automatic intravenous systems to maintain their bodies, and wait through the eleven years. Not too difficult; as far as those bodies were concerned, the question was of mere weeks, or even less.

It should be possible.

*   *   *

It wasn't. The mind does not cease to function during sleep. It only functions differently. Prolonged coma, through accident, experiment, or therapy, had not damaged the psyche before. But that was back on Earth, where the mind worked as the brain did, where thought or dream slowed down likewise. Here, the discrepancy had become too great. Even stunned, the self knew it was coffined in a darkness that would not lift for days, and went mad with terror and loneliness.

We're pretty near the edge, McAndrew rehearsed. Jerry's quit his own pet approach, finding some electronic means to slow down physiology, and sits and stares at his apparatus, the whole watch through. Lisette does nothing but giggle to herself. The Romanos have moved into separate quarters, after she tried to kill him. Doc's hogging the liquor supply, I suspect, unless he's raiding the drugs instead, to keep himself looped. Sylvia says never a word to anyone. And we two? Isabel's stopped cooking—not that the crew want to watch each other eat, any more. Mostly she sits and listens to her Beethoven collection on a speeded-up taper. Me, I get one idea after another, each crazier than the last; I can't concentrate; I can't sleep for the nightmares, and when I'm awake they go right on gibbering at me.

We'd better kill ourselves soon. I don't want to spend a year feeling the bullet crash through my head. As the brain disintegrated, day by mental day, I'd know I was becoming less than human, less than real.

—Are you so sure?

Of course I am. We dropped long ago the silly notion that this phenomenon proves we have immortal souls. If consciousness were not produced by the brain, how could we be destroyed as we are?

—Yet the mind isn't affected by speed.

Oh, it is, it is, as witness our destruction. I see what you mean, though. Well, Doc and Jerry and I developed a hypothesis that accounts for the facts. Obviously the mind is not a material object. Instead, we've decided it's a, well, a space-time pattern.

—Like music?

Hm-m-m, I never thought of that. A good analogy. (*That is NOT a real snake crawling down my throat!*) In one sense, music doesn't exist except when played: which requires material instruments and players. But in another sense, it does. I mean, the pattern of a symphony, the relationship between notes, is not identical with the sound waves. That pattern is as real on the printed page as in the air of the concert hall. It isn't affected by acoustics . . . or velocity, or anything. The mind must be something similar. Of course, it's a hitherto unsuspected law of nature that a pattern of this sort continues to operate within the inertial frame where it was first established.

—And maybe even when the brain is gone?

No! Can't be, or we wouldn't be going to pieces right now. The pattern is created and maintained by the physical organism; when that goes haywire, so does the output. When the brain dies, the process of maintaining the ego must end. Theoretically, you could recreate the ego in another matrix, just as you can play a symphony with different orchestras. But we've no means for doing that. We have to accept that we're under a death sentence, and make a decent end while we still can.

What the devil is going on?

*   *   *

He had been talking to himself, within his own head, as he did more and more. Only . . . this time it had felt different. There had been a warmth which had long left him, a resurgence of strength and courage that drove back the inward-crowding phantasms. Besides, why should he carry on such a mono-dialogue? He'd threshed this notion out with Jerry and Doc, *ad nauseam*. But not with anyone else. Denis Romano had been curtly uninterested, wanting only an engineering solution, until he sank into witless apathy. Clarice, Lisette, and Sylvia had become unapproachable even earlier. McAndrew had not mentioned the idea to Isabel, because speech had grown too hard, better that they simply smile at each other.

He looked into his wife's face and saw the same puzzlement there. Slowly her lips parted.

A scream came forth.

The sound dragged on, without end. He knew that they both surged from the bed and that she led him in a race through the door and around the hall enclosing the cabins; but he had multiple minutes to spend with his ghosts. He saw that a corridor fluoroplate had been installed half a degree out of true, and could not take his gaze away from that, but brooded on the fact, on the final ugly chaos which underlay creation, while his foot rose and came down; and the chill white light, the humming and seething, took him and he went under.

No! called through the dream. *Come to me, my only dearest!*

Like a fish on a hook, he was drawn back to the universe he did not want to be in. The door stood open to the Norringtons' cabin. Doc wasn't there. Probably in his office, drunk or doped. Sylvia lay stretched on the deck. The blood that surrounded her was impossibly red, a shout of scarlet that also went on and on. One of her husband's scalpels was in her hand.

I will turn her over, McAndrew knew, and stare at the gash which grins across her throat for a day that will become a month and a year. That will be the end of my own last sanity.

Isabel shrieked again. Not because of the sight. Through and through McAndrew burst the reason.

Blackness, nothingness, oh, help me, I am so alone. I cry and there is no voice. There is only myself, and I am nothing. I whirl away in a million fragments, horrible in shape, fading, dying, but why must I be so slow about ceasing to exist? I am dead, but it will not let me be dead, I did not know death was haunted, I thought there would be nothing except the blessed peace. There is no silence WAIL BUZZZZ MMMMM no darkness HELL'S BLUE FLAMES no end no end no end.

Isabel stumbled toward her man. But long before she touched him, they were one.

—Arch, she cried, Arch, she's gone and still I hear her!
—And I hear her through you, he answered.

Eyes were upon eyes, hands reaching toward hands, he had time in which to savor the beauty before him, until contact was made and he could know warmth and litheness as well. But meanwhile his mind leaped into the Real.

The whole of six fellow human beings was opened to him. He felt Isabel's self: no more should be said. He felt the anguish in Doc, the inward-aimed rage in Denis, the

160

ultimate surrender of Jerry; so strange and wonderful was it to sense, to be, the femaleness of Lisette and Clarice that he did not at once read their thoughts. Lunacy fled like mist before the sun. For beyond them and beyond them— the fire that was an atom, a mind old and wise in the body of a creature light-years removed, a planet which would be born fifty million years hence and bear a race which was to find one salvation.

But he had no chance, then, to explore. Poor Sylvia screamed so loudly. Before she became the nothing she had wished to be, she must be helped. Arch and Isabel meshed their minds. They were awkward as yet, but they spanned death and touched her.

—Sylvia, here-now we are!

The howling gave way to stillness, despair to joy. She clung to them, and they pulled her from the dark, world-drowning tide, made her one with them, shared what they sensed and gave reality back to her.

All the while, McAndrew's body had been in motion. He paused for the briefest of instants, not even many interior minutes, to hold Isabel. Then he stooped, picked up Sylvia's drained flesh, and ran toward the hospital bay.

His thought ran before him: Doc! Without words, he projected the entire pattern of what had happened.

—She's dead? wept Norrington.

—Clinically, yes, McAndrew flung in reply. But that simply means the body has stopped functioning. Not even in entirety. Most of the cells are still alive.

—Can you bring me back? swirled Sylvia.

—Sure. Why not? We've supplies and equipment. Brain

deterioration doesn't set in for five minutes or so, even at room temperature, and yonder clock says it's only been two minutes since we found you. Put your body in an ice bath, hook in a heart-lung machine, supply blood and oxygen, clamp off the slashed vessels till we can do surgical repair—of course, of course.

The wave of shame and grief that smote McAndrew was so monstrous that he lurched. Almost, he could materially hear Norrington's cry: "I can't! I'm too doped, too clumsy. My own wife has to die because I was a coward."

—No, laughed Isabel. Don't blame yourself. You did your best, and when that failed, you didn't surrender, you merely tried to numb yourself as much as necessary. Don't be afraid. You still know what to do. You can tell us. We have hours to learn the motions before we need start to work.

A chorus of selves shouted the length and breadth of the ship: What's happening? What woke us?

Together, McAndrew and Isabel told them, and healed them.

—The mind is a pattern, created and maintained by the nervous system as music is by an orchestra. But music is also a set of sound waves: physical. Even so must the set of experiences-thoughts-emotions-memories which is the mind have some physical embodiment. In the light of what we have just learned, we must think of the brain as a transducer, coverting the energy of the cells into that ever-changing energy-field we name the human psyche. Because of its pattern character, the self remains in the cosmic frame of reference where it was born. How that can be, we don't know; but we'll find out! (I/We think perhaps there is some kind of signal involved which is not bound by the speed of light; because we are now listening in across the whole space-time continuum. Perhaps that signal-energy is the simple existence of everything that is.)

—But what happened when I died? asked Sylvia, calm now, save as wonder filled her awareness.

Grimly: Much the same thing, dear, as was happening to us. The mind-pattern does persist, for a while, after the brain ceases to work—like a note of music continuing through the air. But there are no more senses. No more data come in. The final isolation. The mind belongs in the cosmos. Cut off, it disintegrates and goes back to nothing, to noise, to chaos. (Oh, our beloved dead whom we are too late to save!)

(Unless one day we can reach into the veritable past.)

—How did you save me? Sylvia sang.

—Isabel, said McAndrew, as much by himself as was possible. She had the greatest telepathic potentiality; though some must be latent in every human being. Under these conditions, with less and less distraction from outside, while her own inner strength was so complete that she could endure the aloneness, her power grew. It was spurred on by her wish to live and to keep me with her. It burst into bloom when she sensed death beyond the bulkhead. Now she is awakening it in all of us.

We will not go crazy. For eleven years, we will explore ourselves, each other, the universe: more data input than we'll know what to do with. We'll change—it hurts to put away childish things—but we'll grow. And . . . maybe we will never die. When our bodies are too old to live, as long as there are younger beings who will take us into their fellowship, our selves will continue.

This is the first word we must send back to Earth. By radio from Tau Ceti, if we can't trumpet it from the ship before then. No matter the expedition. We'll carry through with that, and have a glorious time doing so. But this is more important. This is what we came to find.

Time Heals

Hart followed the doctor down a long corridor where they were the only two in sight and their footsteps had a hollow echo. The fluorescent lights were almost pitilessly bright, and the hall was silent. Silent and empty as—death? No, as the Crypt at its end, as timelessness.

Hart's lips were dry, his throat felt tight, and his heart beat with a rapid violence that dinned faintly in his ears. He was frightened. Why not admit it? The feeling was utterly illogical, but he was scared silly.

He asked inanely, as if he and all the rest of the world didn't know, "There won't be any sensation at all?"

"None," replied the doctor with a patience suggesting he had led many down this hallway. "You'll stand on a plate between the field coils, I'll throw the main switch and—as far as you're concerned—you'll be in the future.

Time simply does not exist, as a 'flow' at any rate, in a level-entropy field.''

Hart licked his lips. "It's like dying," he said.

The doctor nodded. "In a way, it is death," he replied. "You'll be leaving everything behind you—family, friends, the whole world in which you have lived. You can't go back. When you're released from the field—ten, fifty, a hundred, a thousand years hence maybe—you'll be irrevocably in the future." He shrugged. "But, of course, you'll live, whereas your only choice in this era is death."

"Don't get me wrong," said Hart. "I'm nervous, sure, but I'm not scared. I have every confidence in your machine. It's just that I never did understand the principles of it, and of course one is naturally skittish in the face of the unknown."

"It's very simple," said the doctor. "The newspapers have, as usual, made a horrible mess of trying to explain it to the public, and all the legal and moral argument it's stirred up have further confused the issue. But the scientific basis is very simple indeed." He adopted a lecturing tone: "Time, of course, is a fourth dimension in a more or less rigid continuum—that's putting it very crudely, of course, but it shows that simple relativity gives no reason why time should flow, or if it flows, why it should do so in one direction only. That difficulty was resolved by suggesting that the increase of time was the general increase of entropy throughout the universe with respect to the 'rigid' time dimension. Again, that's a clumsy way of putting it, but you get my general idea. I don't pretend to understand the details of it myself.

"Anyway, just a couple of years ago, in 1950 I believe,

Seaton found an effect, a field, in which entropy was held level. An object in such a field could not experience any time flow—for it, time would not exist. The generation of such a field turned out to be fairly simple once the basic principles were discovered, so that before long we had—the Crypt.''

Hart nodded—although he didn't understand it even now. Science had bored him; he regarded himself as a natural-born aesthete and observer of man, a pursuit which a medium-sized independent income made possible. He wrote a little, painted a little, played the piano a little, went to all the exhibitions and concerts, chose his friends and occasional mistresses primarily on a basis of conversational ability, and in general had a pretty good time.

The fundamental idea of the Crypt was hardly new to him. He had read the old legends—the Seven Sleepers, the tales of Herla, Frederik Barbarossa, and Holger Danske—of men for whom time had stopped until the remote future date when they awoke. Only last night, his last night in this world, he had played the whole *Tannhäuser* in an orgy of sentimentality.

There was always a catch. But he had very little to lose. A cancer which had metastasized to the lymph glands meant a short and unpleasant life, perhaps prolonged by operations hopelessly carving away more and more of his flesh—better to take some poison and go out like a gentleman.

Or, better yet, go into the future when they would have worked out some sure and easy cure for his sickness. And perhaps, he thought, a cure for the political cancers which ate at his own society, a cure for war and poverty and misery. Utopia was not inherently unattainable, to a close approximation anyway. . . . For a moment he was almost looking forward to the adventure, but the tightness and the heavy pulse wouldn't leave him. He liked his present existence, and the future would have to be pretty good to make up for his present.

Though I'm lucky, he thought. *I have no really close ties, none who'll really miss me or whom I can't live without. And I have a high I.Q. and adaptability, I can get along with almost anybody. I won't suffer.*

He asked, "Are there any people besides those with diseases at present incurable going into the Crypt?"

"No," answered the doctor, "except, of course, husbands and wives who wish to accompany their sick spouses, and a few other special cases like that. We just don't have room for any more.

"Naturally," he went on, "we're swamped with applications from people who want to escape the tribulations of the present for a presumably happier future. But those we ignore. There's been talk of developing level-entropy units which can be used for everyday purposes like preserving food or other perishables, or even in the household. Imagine cooking a chicken dinner, putting it in the field, and taking it out piping hot whenever needed, maybe twenty years hence! But the manufacturers are very careful about releasing stasis generators, precisely because too many people would try to take a one-way ride into tomorrow. What would become of the present—and would the future want our neurotic escapists?

"Several state legislatures have already tried to regulate the use of the Seaton effect, and Congress is arguing about a Federal law. Meanwhile, the Crypt staff uses it simply to save lives which are lost to the present anyway.''

"If you can be sure they are saved—" murmured Hart.

"Of course, we can give no hundred-percent guarantee," said the doctor with elaborate patience, "but I think it's a very safe bet. The Crypt is in an underground vault well away from any area which might be presumable atomic-bomb targets. Not that even an atom bomb could penetrate a stasis field. Once the fields are set up, they're self-maintaining until neutralized from outside. Information about the Crypt is diffused throughout the world by now, even if something should happen to the permanent staff, which is unlikely. Whenever a cure for a specific disease is found, we will consult our records and release those suffering from it."

"Yes, yes, I know all that," said Hart. "But what kind of future—?"

"Who knows?" The doctor shrugged. "But I don't think it will be too hard to adjust. I rather imagine that a smart Roman or Elizabethan Englishman, say, could do very well for himself in the present. Besides, at the rate medical science is advancing, I don't think anyone will be in here longer than fifty or a hundred years."

"And making a living—"

"You invested all your money as safely as possible before coming here, didn't you? You'll still have it when you awake, then, or the equivalent of it if they change the fiscal system. The Crypt staff will see to that if it isn't taken care of automatically. You'll also have quite a bit of accumulated interest."

Hart nodded his sleek dark head. "It seems as sound a

proposition as human ingenuity can make it," he said. He added wryly, "Anyway, there's no point in quibbling, not when the old man with the scythe is so close."

"Quite so," said the doctor.

They came to the end of the passage, where a great vault door sealed off the Crypt itself. The doctor worked the multiple combination lock, remarking idly, "Even if this whole place should be destroyed, the sleepers would be safe. Literally nothing from outside except a neutralizing field can penetrate the stasis. You could be buried under ten tons of earth without its making any difference—till they dug you out and opened your field."

"There are things worse than death," muttered Hart, and then added quickly, "but hardly worse than death by cancer."

"Quite." The doctor started the little motor which opened the huge door. "In a way," he said, "I envy you. You'll wake up rich, in a society which is better than ours—it must be, it couldn't be much worse—and has all the great new adventures we're just beginning to glimpse—the planets, the stars. . . ." He shrugged. "I may see you again, of course. They're working hard on the cancer problem right now. But I'll be a pretty old man then."

Hart nodded. "Benjamin Franklin once said he wished that, after he was dead, somebody would wake him every hundred years and tell him what happened. I see his point."

They entered the Crypt. The room was a huge one, cold in steel and concrete and the white fluorescent lighting. There was little about to suggest the sensation it was arousing in the outerworld. It looked much like a burial vault—a sinister thought, that, and one which Hart did his best to abolish—with its long row on row of steel caskets sliding into the walls. Each box, Hart noticed, had a complete case history engraved on its end.

The doctor followed his eye. "Those supplement our other records, in case they get lost," he said. "The future physicians can read directly what is the matter with each patient. And just in case something should happen to the Crypt itself, everyone takes another case history into stasis with him, like the one you're carrying now. So if it should become necessary, if nothing else survived, you could always be 'wakened' for the sole purpose of reexamination. But all those precautions are more for the benefit of worriers than because we think they'll ever be needed."

"The patients are actually in those—coffins?"

"Yes. The Seaton generator throws an almost cubical field about the subject. You've seen pictures or movies of it—a totally reflecting region, six or seven feet on a side. This field is, as I said, inherently self-maintaining. I heard Seaton himself lecture once, and he said something like the field requiring finite time in which to break down— only there is no time in it. Anyway, we find it most convenient to store those, uh, blocks of frozen time in the vaults you see."

Hart licked his lips again. He had always had a touch of necrophobia, and his hands were damp and cold now. To be frozen in time like a fish in a chunk of ice, and stowed away in a steel box for no one knew how long . . . He had a morbid desire to see his own coffin, but did not indulge it. That would not have fitted the picture he had of himself, which was somewhere between Epicure and Stoic.

They came into a smaller room at the end of the Crypt. It was crowded with apparatus which was meaningless to Hart. A couple of technicians stood by, smoking and talking and most infernally casual about it all.

"Well," said the doctor, a little awkwardly, "I guess this is it. Are you sure you don't want to leave any farewell messages or—?"

"No," said Hart. "I hate good-byes. I've said mine, and don't want that railway-platform waiting at the end. Let's get it over with."

"Okay. Mount that plate over there, please, between those four big coils. And—good luck." The doctor extended his hand and Hart shook it, thinking to himself that it was a wholly unnecessary gesture. Maybe they'd have better taste in the future.

He climbed up onto the silvery disk and stood looking out between coils that were taller than he was. His knees were a little weak—almost, he was tempted to shout, to call a halt—but that would be silly, of course.

The technicians busied themselves about the generator with that casual competence he had always found irritating in their breed. He heard the list of instrument readings called out, someone else said, "Check," and he thought briefly and wildly, *Maybe it's also mate*. A switch slammed down and a blue glow hovered over the coils. He heard a low, rising hum.

It faded. "Alri, no," said the doctor. "Du can downstep no."

Hart had a moment where his mind wobbled, where he thought wildly that it hadn't worked after all. Great Heaven, he was still in the world, still at home—

172

What had happened to the doctor? Where were the technicians? These weren't the same men they had been an instant ago!

An instant—no, an age. There was no time flow in the stasis field—he was in the future.

He had thought himself mentally prepared. But it was too sudden. The shock was too blurringly great—shattering, devastating shock of suddenly alien men, alien speech, alien world. He staggered a little, and the doctor stepped up on the platform to support him.

Hart leaned on the man's arm—a big, solid fellow, which was somehow reassuring—and let the soft, lilting words slide over the surface of his mind. Almost, they were familiar. For a moment he couldn't follow the speech at all, then he caught words and recognized the changes in accent. Except for the foreign terms and the slang, he could follow the language. Certainly he could get the drift of it.

Only—how long would it take to modify the tongue so much?

He almost croaked the question. The doctor said slowly, "Dis are yaar 2837, du would say. But bay chronomizing nos, are yaar 2841."

"What on earth—?" The sheer incongruity of it jerked Hart from his daze. He might have accepted a wholly different chronology, but—four years' difference! "How the hell did that ever happen?"

"Hell?" For a moment, the doctor was puzzled, then his face cleared. "Oh, yes, medyaeval belief." He smiled. "Skood du raaly ask huw de Heaven. See du, in su-named Second Dark Ages Americas waar under rule of de Kyirk

173

of de Second Coming. Dey waar religio-fanatics whuw
held dat chronomizing skood be set up four yaars since dey
claimed Christ waar rally borned in 4 B.C. bay uwld
chronomizing. Bay time yoke of de Kyirk waar overthruwn,
everybody waar used to new style.''

Hart nodded, a little overwhelmed. ''I . . . see. . . .''

It didn't matter, though. It didn't matter. The . . . the
Church of the Second Coming was in the past now, the
dusty buried past which had still been in the future—ten
minutes ago!

Almost nine hundred years. Nine hundred years!

''Here.'' The doctor gave him a little flask. ''Drink du
dis.''

He gulped the liquid. It was tasteless, but it seemed to
lay a great calm hand on him; his mind steadied and the
trembling went out of his knees. He looked around him.

The chamber was different. The Crypt was not nearly so
full, and it bore signs of extensive repair work. Many must
have been released, many. . . . But lymphatic cancer was
really a tough disease, it would have taken time to work
out the cure and if ages of barbarism had intervened—

His eyes swung to the men. There were, as before, two
technicians and a doctor. (And the three men of *his* time
were dust these many centuries.) They were large, well-
shaped fellows, with dark hair and skin, eyes with a hint
of obliquity, high cheekbones—but, clearly, the Caucasoid
strain still predominated, however great an admixture there
had been. They looked curiously alike, as if they were
brothers, and were dressed almost identically—sandals,
kilt, and tunic of some faintly iridescent material, with a
curious involved pattern reminiscent of Scottish tartans on

the left breast. There must have been immense folk wanderings during the dark ages, thought Hart vaguely, fantastic interbreeding and a rise of composite types of man.

He said aloud, slowly, "You have a cure for my case?"

"Of cuwrse, Tov Hart. De uwld records did not survive, but de Crypt and traditions abuwt it did. Su alsuw did de case histories engraved on de metal. We are ready for du no. De meditechnics have bee-an perfected uwnly in de last fifty yaars, and of cuwrse we wanted to be shoor we waar right before waking any of de 'sleepers.' "

"I seem to be one of the last."

"Indeed, Tov Hart, du are. Case duurs proved more difficult dan had bee-an antsipated. But we have a quick and aisy treating no."

"Well . . ." It might only have been the stimulant, or maybe the words, but Hart felt immensely braced. He was going to live! And in a superscientific world of friendly people, he should be able to make his way. His money would hardly have survived all the changes of history, but—well, there must be some provision made for the "sleepers."

The world wasn't such a bad place. Even in the far future, it wasn't bad.

"I'm afraid you have the better of me," he said to the doctor. At his puzzled look, he added: "With regard to names, I mean."

"Oh. Pardon, Tov. We are all Rostoms here. I are Waldor Rostom Chang, here are Hallan Rostom Duwgal and Olwar Rostom Serwitch."

The three men bowed formally. Hart tried to return the gesture, but couldn't quite imitate the slight knee bend and the position of hands and head. "Philip Bronson Hart," he said. "But the middle name isn't the family name, the last is."

"As wit us," said the doctor, Waldor Chang. "Family name nos come last, group name in middle, gived name in front. But dey had not de groupings in time duurs, did dey?" He smiled. "Come du no, towarish, above ground. De clinic are quite nea-ar, and we will suwn have du well."

The landscape hadn't changed much, there were still the same hills and trees, the far shining thread of a river, and the wind cool and fresh on their faces. White clouds walked overhead through a sky of sunny blue, and a thrush was singing in a little thicket.

But there were few signs of man. The little village which had once been visible down beside the river had long since moldered into the earth, and the buildings of the Crypt center were gone, replaced with a single-roomed frame hut over the vault itself. Above the trees Hart could see a structure of stone and sun-flashing glass which must be the clinic, but otherwise there was no trace of civilization.

"This region must have become pretty well depopulated in the time since I went to 'sleep,' " he remarked.

"Why, nuw. It are raader heawily settled," replied Chang. "Dere must be-a, oh, all of a million people witin a radyus of a tousand kilometers."

"But—that's less than— How many people are there in the country?"

"About tirty million in Nort America. Or on all Eart, abuwt haaf a billion. Of cuwrse, dere must be-a a good ten million on de oder planets of de Solsystem, and perhaps

176

anoder haaf billion in Centaari and elsewhaar—but little are knuwed abuwt dat.''

''But—in my time, there were over two billion people on Earth!''

Chang gave Hart a quizzical look. ''Su I have heared,'' he said slowly. ''But times have cha-enged, Tov. It may taak du some while to reelayze huw much dey have cha-enged.''

They entered the clinic. A blond young woman who was apparently a nurse stood waiting for them. She wore a crisp white skirt, and nothing else, and she was gorgeous.

She and Chang gave their patient an examination which for thoroughness surpassed anything in his time. He didn't pretend to understand the machines that buzzed and clicked and glowed around him, the serological tests and the curious symbolic notation. But he hadn't expected to—naturally, medicine would be far advanced, and he hadn't troubled himself to learn the details even of the past techniques.

''Very good,'' said the doctor at last. ''Satisfactry reactions tuw virus Beta, good Delta cofficient—yes, we skood suwn have du well, Tov Hart.''

''What's the cure?'' he asked idly. ''In my time they were beginning to think there'd never be a specific for cancer.''

''Dere aren't, but dere are specifics for de difrent kinds. Artficial diseases have bee-an developed which attack uwnly de disorganized cancer cells. Frinstance, for cancer of de liver we inject a disease of de liver, but one which healthy tissue can resist. De sick cells are eaten away sluwly enough so dat normal tissue gruws back to replace dem as dey disappear. It are more complex dan dat, of cuwrse, but dat give du de genral idea-a.'' He smiled. ''A mont or su in hospital skood suffice for du, and we ran give du de oder tests in de mea-anwhile.''

''The . . . other—?'' It sounded faintly ominous.

''Classficating and su on. Worry du not abuwt it no.''

''Come du,'' said the nurse. ''I will taak du to ruwm duurs.''

Hart followed her to an elevator. It went up with a pleasingly low acceleration, but his pulse went a little fast just the same. She was exciting!

''What's your name, please?'' he asked. He put on the smile which had usually worked in the past. ''We'll be seeing a lot of each other, I hope.''

The girl frowned, then seemed to make an allowance for him. ''Mara Sorens Haalwor.''

''This is a pleasure . . . you're not married?'' Hart edged closer.

''Mayried? Oh, de uwld style. Nuw, but—'' She backed away. Her face bore an expression of distaste, barely covered by politeness. ''Please du, Tov Hart—''

''Oh. Sorry.'' Hart moved from her, a little chapfallen. Oh, well.

He had a room to himself—he found out later that all hospital patients did—which delighted him. It was large and sunny, more like a living room than anything else. The furniture was curious, rather hard and low-legged— Asiatic influence during the Dark Ages?—but he could get used to that. There was a set of buttons on the wall which he learned how to use when he wanted to read. Central ''libraries'' had all the books and music in existence, no one owned volumes or records privately anymore. To read anything in existence, one simply called the nearest "library" and asked for it; automatically, the books—actually, record tapes—were flashed onto a screen, the speed being regulated by the reader. Likewise, any music was played directly into the citizen's own room. There were enough copies of all record tapes to take care of any reasonable number of simultaneous requests, and if a local "library" didn't happen to have a certain item, it would be relayed from one which did.

Curiously, there were no movie records, and no regular radio or television programs. Hart was too busy catching up with history and language at first to wonder why.

His synthetic disease and the physiological strain of growing new tissue left him a little weak. He stayed close to his room and only went out in the hospital gardens on orders of the staff. Nor did he have any visitors except the medical workers. After a while, he began to be lonely.

He was put through a series of psychological tests more exhaustive than the physical checkups. Here, too, he was baffled by the intricacy of a science evolved immensely beyond the older one which itself had puzzled him. Some of it was recognizable—word-association, elaborate questionnaires much of which seemed to be completely irrelevant, long informal talks with a psychiatrist. And the huge machines which studied him seemed remote descendants of the electroencephalographs he had known. But he went through completely bewildering processes—hypnotism, drugging, physical exercises.

"What's the idea?" he demanded, a little indignantly. "You seem to want to know me better than I know myself. Why?"

"Psychoclassificating," said the tester. "All citizens undergo it, with periodic rechecks."

That sounded ominous. *What kind of totalitarian state have I landed in?* "What do you do with the results?"

"Counsel, advise, straighten uwt conflicts. And, of cuwrse, arra-enge introductions." The psychiatrist looked troubled. He kept looking at the elaborate data sheets in his hand, as if he couldn't quite believe what he saw. "Suwcial integrating of individual depend on what psychotype he are, Tov Hart. No, if du will excoose me, must study dese results—"

Hart went back to his reading. He was having trouble finding out what kind of world he lived in. There were plenty of histories, but they said little about the details of daily life, and they grew remarkably uneventful as they neared the present time. There were also plenty of sociological texts, but these were written in a technical language that left his head whirling—much of the material, indeed, was mathematical. He recognized the symbology as descended from the symbolic logic and calculus of statement of his own time, but since his acquaintance with those had been completely superficial, that didn't help much.

But manners, customs, family relations, all the million little details which make up life—rather than the abstractions of life, such as history and sociology—were nowhere explicitly described. After all, why should a people concern itself with its own mores? Such things are learned in childhood, are absorbed unconsciously as the individual grows through life. Had any twentieth century anthropologist ever described the habits and customs and beliefs of New York as carefully and objectively as he did those of the upper Congo? Hart found himself in the curious position of having learned more about the social organization of the natives of Procyon IV than those of Sol III.

He went back to history. That he could learn objectively, and with such a background feel his way around contemporary Earth until he learned the social ropes.

But it was not part of the matrix which had produced him. The Church of the Second Coming, the Asiatic invasion of America, the mechaniolatry of the Australian Reformers, the invasion of Luna by the weirdly changed descendants of Earth's old Martian colonists, the Scientific State, the Overthrow, the retirement of the Dissenters, the evolution of the family groups . . . Well, what was it? A story, a dream which had passed by while he slept, the thoughts and deeds and struggles of men unthought of in his own age.

Napoleon had been an almost living reality to Hart. He had read Emil Ludwig, he had listened to *Die Beiden Grenadiere,* he had heard all the tired old jokes about crazy men with hands in their coats, he had been subjected to the wistful reminiscences of old men who had grown up in that forever lost world which came between the Congress of Vienna and the murder at Sarajevo—he had, without being unusually interested in the Corsican, lived in a world where the little man had been a dominating influence even a century after his death. Napoleon was as much a part of his background, part of the complex of events which had, *inter alia,* produced Philip Hart, as the sun or the moon or the banging canyons of New York.

But could an imperial Roman transported to the twentieth century *feel* that a defeated dictator of a hundred years ago had existed? Would Napoleon be more than a dusty fiction? Would the Roman consider it logical that Frenchmen should be below the average European height, that the French law should be completely revised, that the Louisiana Territory should be American and Haiti independent, that the Nelson column should rise in London, that the whole existing world should *be,* all because of one little *condottiere?* The Roman might realize the fact, with the top of his mind, but it would not look reasonable to him. Because *he* would not be one of those inevitable results.

Hart gave up trying to make more than superficial sense out of all that had happened since the twentieth century, and simply learned the salient facts. He got a rough outline of the present political and economic status of man.

Earth—and the Lunar cave-cities—were under one rule. The colonists on Venus, Mars, and the outer planet satellites had evolved their own societies, often radically different from that of the mother world; man himself had had to become modified before he could settle the reaches of space, an evolution which had been carried out by the eugenics of the Scientific State with ruthless completeness. There was still regular interplanetary contact, but it was infrequent. The different branches of man had too little in common by now. Once in a great while there would be a ship from one of the colonies on the nearer stars, but distances were too great; even Alpha Centauri was fifty years away, and social evolution was diverging out there.

But could it be said that Earth was—ruled? Not in any traditional sense. The social organization was uniform, and a single council did what little administrative work the planet required. But there was nothing like a real government.

History—wars, social changes, migrations, important new discoveries and concepts, events of any great significance—had been slowing for the last three centuries, ever since the family-group society had gained the ascendancy. For the last hundred years or so, nothing had really happened to mankind as a whole. *Nothing!*

It might be called a philosophical anarchy. Superficially, there was perfect freedom. The general law had almost no regulations on individual behavior. There was, apparently, universal content.

Decadent? No, not in the usual sense. These people were too magnificently healthy, too full of life and laughter. But they were certainly not progressive.

Hart tried to make friends with the nurses, and failed completely. They were all frigidly polite. The male staff members were cordial enough, but there was an inward reserve which increased with the days. Hart wondered what was the matter. His unhappiness waxed with his returning strength.

Chang came in at last. "I think du can leave clinic no," he said cheerily. "Du have best undergo periodic checkups for a yaar or twuw, but all medics are shoor du are guwing to recover completely." He handed the patient a set of clothes like his own, but without the group insigne.

Hart got out of the hospital robe and climbed into the garments. "And now what?" he asked. "I've tried to plump everybody on what I'm supposed to do, but they're all so evasive I haven't really learned a thing."

Chang looked uncomfortable. "We have place for du," he said. "It have taak unusually long time to analyze

183

psychometric results duurs. Dey are su very different from ordinary.''

"Well . . .'' Hart waited impatiently. They'd been stalling him long enough.

Chang explained as well as he could. Psychometry and preventive psychiatry were really the basis of society. The fundamental personality of the individual was determined at an early age and he was "developed" throughout life in accordance with that—conditioned to society, but not in such a rigid fashion as to interfere with really basic urges. Vocations, recreations, social life were all planned in accordance with psychometric data.

"Planned?" exclaimed Hart. "How on earth can you plan everything?"

Well, not exactly planned either. Guided. An individual had such and such an I.Q., his main interests were so and so, his personality factors were as follows—it all went into a great electronic "file," in the powerful psychosymbology of the time. And any citizen had access to that file, with technicians to help him in its use. Thus you could find your likes, your associates, wherever they might happen to live, rather than leave it to chance encounters. It was scientifically predictable whether a friendship, a marriage, a business association, would be really of mutual profit. Naturally, everyone made use of the service, and adjusted his life accordingly.

"But—ye gods! You mean *anyone* can find out all about you at any time? What kind of privacy is that?"

Privacy? Chang was puzzled now. The word still remained in the language, but it had come to mean simply solitude. Why should you care whether or not anyone else knew just what you were? It didn't make you any better or worse, did it? You could find your kind in the world—those whose company was most pleasing to you. You could know yourself, and set your goals accordingly; you could change most really undesirable characteristics, with the help of psychiatry or even endocrinology and surgery.

The "groups," originally simply clans formed for mutual protection, were increasingly becoming endogamous associations of similar people. It was the group which was the real unit of society. Business, social life—all were integrated with the needs of the group, and of the world as a whole.

For instance, it was desirable that population be limited. Overpopulation was probably the most basic cause of misery in past history. Thus the group council regulated how many children there should be in a given family. It decided how long a marriage—family association was the term now—should last; a person might have children by three or four different people, if that seemed to be for the good of human evolution.

"But suppose your individual doesn't want to obey? I noticed nothing in the law compelling him to."

"Obedience are customary, and psychoconditioning in childhood delibraatly plants reflexes of conformity wit custom. No sane person *wants* to do oderwise."

"But—but—talk about tyrannies!"

"Why, nuw." Chang was taken aback at Hart's violent reaction. "All societies in past conditioned young. Waar du not telled to obey law and worship flag—dey still had flag-worship in time duurs, did dey not?—and how it are wrong to kill and steal? But such conditioning waar superficial, it did not always affect basic impulses, so dat dere waar tragic conflicts between individual needs and desires and de laws and customs. Frustrating, crime, insanity? No wonder de dark ages came. Today we simply condition so thoroughly—and de inculcated desires do not conflict wit basic instincts—dat no one wants to break rules which fit him su perfectly.''

"Everyone?"

"Well, dere are exceptions, ewen today. If dey cannot be adjusted, or will not be—since noting is legally compulsory—dey must eider be sent to space colonies or struggle though an unhappy life on Eart, witout friends or marriage, witout ewen a group. But numbers deys gruw less all de time.''

"Hm-m-m . . . well . . .''

"Ewerybody have his place in society. Ewerybody happy wit life, nobody have conflicts wit felluw man—dat are goal nos. And we are close to it.''

"It sounds nice,'' muttered Hart. He shrugged. "Not much I can do about it, anyway.'' His eyes swung back to the doctor's. "Now what about me?''

"Well . . .'' Chang was obviously steeling himself. He smiled with a false geniality. "Well, we have sewwral possibilities. Dere are a weader station in Greenland, or a small farm in Brazil, or—''

"Hold on!" Hart reached out and grabbed the doctor's tunic. His throat choked with a sudden rage and, under that, a gathering horrible dismay. "What do you think you're doing? Am I going to be stuck somewhere out of the sight of man and forgotten?''

"I—''

186

"Come on," snarled Hart. The fist he lifted was shaking. "Spit out the truth, or you'll be spitting out your teeth."

Chang disengaged himself and held the smaller man with an effortless strength. His face was twisted. "I—I are sorry, Tov Hart," he said, very quietly. "It waar raally a cruel kindness to wake du. But I are afraid dat—du are right."

Hart sagged, the anger draining from him and leaving only a vast hollow void. Dimly, he heard Chang's voice: "Du have nuw place in world. Du belong to nuw famly or group. Du have no traits wort perpetuating—indeed, we would not want children wit cancer tendency duurs. Psychotests show du as unstable, egocentric, unable to adjust to cityless world, to close familial relationship, to—anything. No one would want to associate wit completely unintegrated, hopelessly neurotic—foreigner.

"Best du find a quiet place where du can serve—out of sight."

Hart rebelled. Bitterly, desperately, he tried to escape. There must be something. He had been the admired leader of his little clique. Broad knowledge, sardonic humor, a way with women, ready money, all had combined to impress and delight. Surely the world had not changed so much!

No compulsion was put on him. He went where and when he chose; he spent a good three months prowling this new Earth, riding the free public transport and using an unlimited government credit card to buy necessities. And he found that the world had indeed changed.

The tall, healthy, serene folk were polite to him, and no more. But they had nothing in common with him. He belonged to no group and, for eugenic and other reasons, could not be adopted into one, and all social functions were within such alliances. He did not follow their jokes, his manners were gauche compared to the formality now accepted; his learning and background were from a period too remote to interest any but scholars. There was no underworld, no demimonde. Morality was somewhat changed, but it was never violated.

For his part, Hart began to be bored. It was not entirely a subjective attitude rising out of resentment at inferiority. These people were slow-speaking, formal, calm; they lacked the tension and the acrid mirth of the twentieth century. They were not weaklings in any sense, but they were—innocent.

There was no entertainment except what groups provided for themselves—singing, dancing, amateur showmanship, a great deal of hobbycraft. The reason for the absence of professional entertainment was basically the same as that for the lack of large-scale industry. The group society was deliberately throwing the individual and the family on their own resources. Now that there were no external challenges of war, poverty, famine, disease, now that history had slowed almost to a standstill, man must return to a degree of primitive self-sufficiency and independence if he was not to become the glorified termite inhabiting a purposeless machine city.

Hart saw the reasoning, but it seemed puritanical to him. And he could not sympathize with a people who deliberately submitted to it. A man who plowed his own fields when science had advanced to the point where everyone could eat out of cans was a fool. To be sure, the man was conditioned to like it, and certainly the food was better than the sterilized pap of twentieth century canneries, but even so . . .

Hart tried to leave Earth altogether. But he lacked the physique and the technical skill which would justify a spaceship in hauling him. And from what he read of the spatial colonies, he was likely to find a still more alien society out there.

In the end, desperately, he took the weather-station job.

For a while that was better. He was alone, away from the subtler and crueler isolation of strangers' company, and he was not entirely useless. The vast windswept snowfields, the far mysterious glimmer of northern lights wavering over enormous mountains, the snug hut which had access to the books and music of all history, were all somehow comforting. He barely spoke to the pilot of the occasional supply rocket, and refused to be relieved.

He couldn't go back to a world which had no use for him. He could stay here and dream of what had been, out here in the wind-whining loneliness, alone in the dark with the ghosts of his own time whispering to him. . . .

They muttered in the dark corners, they wavered in the auroras and the pale cold sunlight, ghosts of the past, calling to him over a gulf of time. Time began to be meaningless, and space. In this unreal landscape of ice and snow and dark, wind blowing up between the frosty stars, it was hard to say where the solid world left off and the dreams began.

Hart realized vaguely that he was slipping. But it didn't matter. Certainly he couldn't return to the politeness of the world, more cold and remote than the flying haggard moon, he couldn't leave his old friends here. . . . Why, his relief would sweep the dust out of the cabin, dust which had once been human, dust which had once lain in his arms or laughed at his humor. . . . Now the wind laughed, hooting around the house and rattling the shutters in appreciation of Hart's jokes.

Waldor Rostom Chang looked, with horror creeping behind his eyes, at the thing which mumbled on the floor of the airjet. Hart was almost completely catatonic now.

"If we had knuwed!" said the doctor. "If we had uwnly knuwed!"

"How skood we?" asked the pilot, a weather-service technician. "De job waar just 'made' work, to give de poor felluw someting to do. Reports his waar filed in de wastebasket. And he had bee-an su unsuwciable dat de supply pilots simply left stuff his witout ewen seeing him. It waar uwnly when he had quit reporting for seweral days dat we got alarmed."

"I newwer drea-amed he would go crazy, ewen when he had bee-an dere two yaars witout relief," said Chang. "After all, a modern man could stand it easily. And de twentyet century mind waar too strange to mind nos, completely unintegrated as it waar, for de psychotechnics to spot de instability in him."

"And nuw what will we do wit him?"

"We cannot help de poor jorp. Psychiatry nos are preventive, mental disease su long forgetted dat we have no real curative technique—teories, records of old cure metods, yes, but nuw experenced mental doctors." Chang shrugged. "All we can do is put Hart back in de Crypt till such day as psychiatry have evolved cure for su extreme a case as his. And dere are su little need for psychocuring today dat I fear it will be a long, long time befuwere Hart can be outtaken again.''

The pilot grinned mirthlessly. "By den," he said, "society may be su alien dat Hart, once cured, will relapse into insanity too deep for dem to handle—so dey will have to put him back in de Crypt. . . ." He spied his goal and sent the airjet slanting downward.

SOS

MOSCOW, 1 June 1966—Dr. Bruce C. Heezen . . .
at the second International Oceanographic Congress
. . . said studies of ocean bottom samples showed
that in the last 23 million years a number of magnetic
field reversals had occurred. Magnetic strength dropped
to zero and then returned with an opposite orienta-
tion . . . "The result of the increased cosmic radiation
reaching the earth apparently was the complete killing
of some species and the mutation of others" . . . Magnetic measurements made of the earth for the past
120 years show a decrease that, if continued steadily,
would lead to zero magnetism and a reversal in about
2,000 years. . . .
—Associated Press (Archives of the Awaiian Histori-
cal Museum)

AUSTRALAO COMMAND, 13 Heros 4127—General order . . . to . . . Space Force of the Autarchy of Great Asia. . . . With due regard to the requirements for achieving surprise, you will occupy the station and promptly deploy ground and ground-to-space defenses. They should not be needed except in case of failure. For success, it is absolutely essential that your presence remain unsuspected by the Kinhouse units until the moment of your missile strike . . . Immediately afterward, you will assume Earth orbits according to pattern . . . The importance of your mission cannot be overemphasized. On you may rest responsibility for the survival of civilization, quite possibly of the human race. You are reminded of the recent, unexpected acceleration of the decrease in field strength . . .

—Archives of the Astromilitary Institute

I

Ing Jans was the first to see them.

He had gone out after work to be alone. His need did not arise from any physical crowding. Chandrasekhar Research Station in its best days could spaciously and graciously house fifty scientists, their assistants, any family they cared to bring along and a large service staff. Of course, in the past two or three centuries, as things worsened on Earth, there had been too few personnel or resources to maintain everything. Meteoroids, moon-quakes, thermal stress had caused damage that was not repaired. But most of the big rooms, tunnels, domes and blockhouses were intact. The score of people who now inhabited them rattled around

Thus the pressure on Jans was not material—nothing he could name. Suspicion? Ostracism?

Suppose he went to the chief, Rani Danlandris, and exclaimed: *Yes, my mother was born in Great Asia—she was fifteen before she came to Normerica. My father's a native Kinsman, all right, but yes, he does sympathize with the Asians. He isn't disloyal to the Westrealm but he does think—and say—Autarchism's egalitarian and collectivist philosophy gives more hope for saving Earth than our own neofeudal timocracy, as he calls it. And I haven't disowned my parents. Can't you see, though, I've broken with most of their ideas? I support the Westrealm. I prefer its way of life and think it can cope better with the crisis than Autarchism. I've only said that the Asians may have something to teach us. Besides, we aren't at war with them. Incidents, diplomatic maneuverings, armies along the borders, true, but no war. Anyway, under what circumstances could I be a threat here on the far side of the Moon?*

Rani Danlandris would probably look down his long aristocratic nose, arch his brows and drawl, *Has anyone said otherwise? I fear you are a bit overwrought, my boy. You need a rest. The next supply car can take you back to Tycho and, scarce though spaceflights are these days, I daresay you shouldn't have to wait too long for passage to Earth.*

And maybe that was the best move, Jans thought bitterly. He wasn't accomplishing a great deal, after alienating his colleagues till they were barely polite to him and his subordinates till they had grown downright insolent.

Go home, young man. Get a position somewhere. No

195

problem about that. A planet on the brink of the abyss has use for every technologist. You can serve humanity well on Earth. Does anything except selfishness convince you that you can serve better here? Go; find yourself a wife, a good solid Kinswoman; forget all dreams about a Luna girl who can live and dream with you in this stark, starry land. For you will not return. Somebody else will have taken the laboratory you now hold and resources are too lean for lifting a man for whom there is no positive call. In Great Asia they allocate spaceship passages by official assignment, in the Westrealm they do it by letting the price of a ticket soar beyond reach of whoever had not the backing of a Kinhouse. For both, the effect is the same.

Go home, Ing Jans.

To Earth. To deserts spreading like cancers. To poverty, unrest, fear among the commoners, leading to manias whose suppression perforce makes their overlords ever more harsh. To spending your nights and as much of your days as possible underground—for, while atmosphere will always shield the planet from the full irradiation that Luna gets, exposure is cumulative. There are only so many genetic repair facilities to go around. You have seen the stillbirths and the weeping barren women (and men) and the mutants who are forbidden to have children and the figures on population decline. When you go outside, even if it never troubled you in space, somehow on Earth you cannot ignore what is sleeting through you—you are never at ease in guts or groin.

Man expected conditions elsewhere in the Solar System to be unnatural for him. Your forerunners provided the snug little caves of environment, the technological and medical buttresses that let life exist—that make it actually comfortable when it is not being adventurous and glorious. But that's for a few people in a few ships and bases. On Earth they are too many and the planet is too big.

In the long run, we realize, if the mother world goes, so does man everywhere. But the privileged handful scattered across the sister planets can repay what they have enjoyed—by finding the means to rescue those who supported them.

Given the chance, they will.

Jans climbed swiftly from the plateau edge toward the peak of Mount Einstein. After three years in low gravity his muscles continued to exult in the lightness, the bounding strides, gentle descents, the spacesuit exactly a sufficient burden to make him fill his lungs and to send a little shiver of boot impact up his legs. His nostrils drank a clean odor of machine and his own flesh. The air pump, the chemical bubbling of the oxygen renewer on his back came no louder than his bloodbeat; and beyond them reached a majestic stillness. It was hardly broken by the faint seethe of cosmic interference in his radio earplugs. Briefly he thought he heard a message. Like everyone who went beyond atmosphere, he was trained in dot-dash code. But no, a random fluctuation—the galaxies were not talking to him.

He stopped on the heights and looked down. Farside night lacked the glory of Earth in its sky. But more stars than he could count crowded the crystalline dark overhead, unwinking and jewel brilliant; his eyes traced the Milky Way's cataract and the nebulae. In their light he could clearly see the crags and steeps that fell away beneath him, a ghost-gray valley and the thrust of huge mountains over the horizon. He could see individual stones underfoot, for Jupiter and Saturn were both aloft, blazing so bright they cast shadows.

Here was peace. No work of man remained on Farside save the station, the road that slashed a ribbon down from its plateau toward the opposite hemisphere and the microwave relay towers that stood along that road. Stray radiation must not be allowed to hinder the quest that went on here.

Not that Jans didn't like the Nearside centers. They were busy and friendly and filled with visions of a future which, if the quest succeeded, might yet encompass new suns. They were fun. But his real life was in this station.

It sprawled below him, turrets and sheds and fortresslike housings. What he saw was a fraction: most lay underground. His gaze went to the masts and webwork of the radio telescope, the mirror gleam from an optical observatory.

His own deeds were done beneath a roof that fenced the plateau edge for five straight kilometers. At each end of it stood a house, one for the physicists and their controls, the other for certain types of target. The roof was a hemicylinder on concrete posts, shielding the particle beam from cosmic rays but otherwise open to the Moon's bountiful vacuum.

Sometimes, guiltily, Jans caught himself failing to regret such catastrophes of the past as the Population Wars or the collapse of the Syntechnion. Had they not been followed by hiatuses in astronautics, the last secrets of high-energy physics might have been unveiled centuries ago. Then he recalled how desperately those secrets were needed today, and he cringed.

Oh, Deity, he thought, how can my fellows suspect me?

And supposing I were an Autarchist, how would that matter? This isn't a military base, we hide nothing, our service is to all mankind . . .

Flame blossomed among the stars. His faceplate didn't darken fast enough. Light blinded him. He crouched down, crying out. The soil began to shiver beneath him, under the thrust of nuclear-driven jets. By the time his vision had cleared, it was over. He stared across a near distance at a dozen landed spacecraft. Upon their hulls fluoresced the Sun and Man emblem of Great Asia.

II

Hours later the view glittered with torpedo shapes: missiles. The ships loomed gaunt and tall over them.

Likewise did Pitar Cheng stand in the station's conference room, whither he had summoned its personnel. On his scarecrow form the green uniform failed of its usual neatness. But his tones fell crisp across the murmur of ventilators. And behind him, against the wall, stood a pair of his soldiers, stutter-guns in their arms.

Cheng's gaze swept down the table. The scientists, assistants and technicians made themselves look back at him. They were an unimpressive lot in their working clothes, though some had pinned on the badges of the Kinhouses to which they owed fealty, a forlorn defiance. Chief Danlandris alone had military garb to wear. It was peacock gorgeous and his bearing remained haughty. But he was no soldier either, simply commissioned by virtue of his birth, and Cheng knew it.

Cheng knew disconcertingly much. He had named each of them individually, without asking to be introduced. He obviously carried the layout of the station, the entire map of the surrounding country, in his head. Not that anything had ever been secret about it. Plainly, though, Asian Intelligence had gone to immense trouble to compile data. Cheng's operation had to be important, too important for the lives of a few researchers to be of any account.

Yet the fleet commander spoke to them with correctness, if not total courtesy.

"Chief Danlandris and gentlemen, I have summoned you in order that I may explain what is happening. It is unfortunate that our landing produced such confusion among you that a man was killed. We had no wish to inflict casualties."

Near the center of the table, Ing Jans bent his head and clutched the board till his fingers hurt. He had witnessed Edard Lierk's death. The invaders were swarming from their vessels and up onto the plateau as he got back. Big, merry Lierk had seen they were Asians—and his family had been for generations in Kinhouse Eyra and two of his brothers were in its armed service. He charged forth, a wrench in his hand, knocked loose the gun from an enemy's grasp and retreated, firing, toward the shelter of a blockhouse. But he hit no one and return fire cut through his spacesuit. The pieces of him lay frozen in outside storage, to be buried when a chance for mourning him should arrive.

"After all," Cheng said, "our ultimate objective is nothing except the victory of the people as a whole over their oppressors and the establishment of a rationalized world government which can cope with the magnetic emergency."

Danlandris' response was dry. "The majority of the

Westrealm's people, at least, do not seem to agree that they are oppressed, Admiral. Nor does the voluntary cooperation of the Kinhouses appear to be doing too badly at maintaining the biosphere.''

"I do not propose to argue politics," Cheng snapped. "You are under martial law. Conduct yourselves accordingly."

Danlandris stroked his beard. "I can guess how you managed to get here unobserved," he said. "You approached within the Moon's shadow cone. Orders from Australao went out on a tight, scrambled maser beam and were relayed by a communicator boat. I ask you, however, why?"

"Is it not obvious?" Cheng threw back.

Danlandris raised a hand. Somehow, through the horror, Jans envied that schooled, stoic coolness of a nobleman born. He himself was struggling not to weep or vomit.

"If you please," Danlandris said softly. "I quite understand that your government has decided to break the deadlock and force us to agree to its policies by an act of undeclared war. But are your leaders suicidal? Has the latest wave of hysteria, religious frenzy, whatever it may be, smitten them, too? The Westrealm has double the space navy you do. Granted, no one can afford many warcraft these days. That doesn't matter. Many are not needed. I know approximately what fighting strength you possess in space. And you have used practically the whole of it to seize one unarmed research station!'' He paused for effect, continued: "Were blackmail intended, the threat of destroying this place, a single vessel would have been ample. Instead, you cluster here where a single detonation can finish Great Asia as a spatial power. May I ask for an explanation? Or shall I assume we deal with insanity?''

Cheng drew breath. ''I will tell you, in general terms,'' he said grimly, ''because you must realize why we require your cooperation and will take any measures necessary to get it. Any.''

He leaned forward, resting his knuckles lightly on the table.

''Earth cannot be saved piecemeal.'' His speech stayed quiet, but with what an edge! ''If half of it dies, how can the other half live? The Kinhouses maintain that their loose combination within a framework of traditional social forms, their encouragement of diversity, gives mankind the best chance of finding solutions. They are wrong. The magnetic reversal is too huge a phenomenon. Nothing can deal with its consequences except world-wide mobilization, directed effort on the part of every last individual, according to the principles discovered by Autarchism.

''As you say, Chief Danlandris, the Westrealm has put its superior space navy in the way of thus organizing humanity. And since no one is mad enough to bar the Inspectorate there are no nuclear weapons on Earth and hence no defense against attack from above. At the same time, gentlemen, when it is a question of naked survival one eventually stops playing by pretty little rules.''

His voice lifted, rapping forth. Jans heard as through a fever's delirium: ''The space fleet of the Confederated Kinhouses of the Westrealm is currently on maneuvers. Our Intelligence has discovered that plans include a massed landing on Nearside, in Mare Nubium, two terrestrial days hence. At that moment, missiles will be launched from here—not on trajectory, which would mean detection and interception, but on the deck—specially developed missiles that dodge between mountains, craters, gorges, and emerge from concealment too late for counteraction.

"With nearly all of its navy gone, your High Council must change its blind, man-destroying attitude, accept an Autarch—or have its centers of government and military power destroyed by bombardment from orbit, after which occupation of the country will follow. I trust it will see reason and yield peacefully. If not, then the harm done, the radiation released, by us is infinitely less than the damage that must result from the present fatuousness of the Kinhouses."

His eyes smoldered at them. "That is why we are here," he said. "Had we landed elsewhere on Farside, your instruments would have noted signs of it and this could have brought investigation. You will recall that, while descending, we blanketed your communications with a magnetic pulse-field. Now they are restored. Our technicians have sent a standard machine-machine signal to Tycho: 'Temporary difficulties resulting in blackout have been satisfactorily resolved.'

"Should a real message get through—please disabuse yourselves. You will not be given the opportunity to send one. You will be under guard. Your guards will not be fools. Any rebelliousness will mean immediate execution. By contrast, cooperation will be rewarded generously.

"No supply car is scheduled to arrive here within the critical period. No spacecraft is expected to pass by. You will continue to send your regular reports and other messages. My Intelligence officers have studied the records of these and know what they are normally like. They will rehearse you in what you are to say.

"Perhaps one of you is thinking that when his turn comes he will shout, 'The enemy has landed!' and die a hero's death. Forget it. Before he makes his call every man will be given a bracelet to wear. The vidiphone pickup scans his head, not his wrists. The bracelet will be wired to a neuromonitor. The upsurge of nervous activity before any extraordinary action will be registered and the transmitter will instantly, automatically be cut off. The man will be shot. A few minutes later another of you will call back, explaining that you are having a little more trouble with your gear, nothing you cannot fix yourselves.

"Is this understood?"

Silence dropped, pressing inward. Cheng watched them for a whole sixty seconds before he continued, suddenly looking tired and speaking almost gently.

"I do not expect you to believe how we who have come—and those who have sent us—lament this necessity. The killing of gallant men, the loss of irreplaceable machines and materials, will always haunt us. But your overlords have left us no choice. We act on behalf of every child that will ever be born. Few among you are fanatics. Most of you have families, friends, lives that are dear to you. Some admit that we Autarchists are not monsters, that indeed there is something to be said for our position. Never fear but we will get help."

His glance ranged round the table, came to a slender form, and rested.

"For instance, from you, Ing Jans," he finished.

III

They walked down the tunnel toward the accelerator—Jans, a soldier and the security officer assigned to the physicist. This was a small, dark, earnest man named Lal Grama. He kept talking. The soldier cradled his gun and spoke never a word.

"Surely you, a scientist, do not exaggerate the ideological conflict," Grama maintained. "Oh, ideologies are involved, two opposed concepts of what society ought to be. But the essential, the vital dispute is about immediacies— how can we best meet the magnetic crisis?"

"That was being worked on here, among many other places," Jans answered, "until you came."

"How effective was your work? The rate of decline has increased alarmingly, you know. We have less than the fifty-odd years to zero magnetism, maximum irradiation, that we were counting on. Perhaps much less." Evidently, Grama had a technical education himself, since he added: "A number of specialists are wondering now if there may not be a threshold value of field strength, below which self-inductance no longer operates to resist change."

"Well, Earth has a thick atmosphere," Jans argued. "It's been through episodes like this before and wasn't sterilized. The average background count at sea level won't become anything that can't be lived with. Even the peak dosages, on mountaintops during solar storms, will fall within the permissible range as long as antirad medicines are available.''

''Ah.'' Grama lifted a finger. ''No doubt. You ignore the weakening of the body's resistance to disease, the shortening of lifespan, the increase of mutation and sterility—with what that means in terms of social inefficiency as well as private tragedy. Can we maintain civilization under those conditions? And remember, massive extinctions did take place at every past reversal. Might they include man in the present case? Consider microecology, for a single example. Imagine the disappearance of a key type: say, nitrogen-fixing bacteria on land or phytoplankton in the seas. What then, Scientist Jans? Is it better for men to starve or to strangle?''

''I don't believe that can happen,'' Jans said. ''Nothing so drastic happened before. You're stretching the probabilities entirely out of shape. You talk of making ready for the troubles before they get worse than they are. Well, the Kinhouses are making ready, stockpiling, doing research and development, training professional cadres. You've created a bogeyman for an excuse to regiment our part of the planet. I'd rather go through a little extra hardship and danger than become a slave to the almighty state.''

But he had to force his words out and they had no ring to them. Too long had he wondered—sometimes in open argument, which was what had made him unpopular—if the Kinhouses were in fact doing enough. Suppose their programs did prove inadequate, whether to the Westrealm alone or to the whole globe. No political theory, no ideal of a commonwealth organized in small blood-related units

206

which let the individual be more than a cog—nothing was worth risking failure.

" 'Slave' is a meaningless noise," Grama declared. "Put your prejudices aside and consider—"

Jans forced his attention away from the seductive, reasonable-sounding voice. He was glad when the ramp led up into his laboratory.

Grama stared at the array of meters and controls that filled every wall. A low power throb dwelt in the air, which was slightly chilly and held a tinge of ozone. Viewscreens showed the outside. He focused on the display of the beam path. Concrete floor and roof defined a cavernous stretch to the target house, dwarfed by its distance of five kilometers. Supports, instruments, massive control rings and magnets, cryotrons, booster generators lined that covered road; between them peered the stars.

A single assistant was on hand, Ridje Tommin, a burly man in coveralls. He stood aside, glowering.

"Impressive," Grama remarked. "The engineering by itself—Am I right that the builders actually had to extend the original plateau?"

Jans blinked in surprise at the Asian's honest interest.

"Why—yes, a ways. Mainly they chose Mount Einstein because the plateau was here, easy to recontour for a flat surface. Can't normally travel five kilometers in a straight line on the Moon. It curves too fast."

"I know. Superb accomplishment." Grama paused. "But is it, today, relevant?"

"More relevant than you imagine," Jans told him. "Have you forgotten, has propaganda made you forget, we aren't doing research for its own solitary sake? Our stations, our laboratories throughout the Solar System, are after knowledge. Pure knowledge, the kind of facts that can't be foreseen, that upset old theories and open the way to new realities.'' His utterance gathered force and speed as it heartened him. ''Perhaps a discovery in quantum exchange physics, giving us a basis for finding a way to screen large areas with strong magnetic fields—if not to recreate Earth's. Perhaps something in biology, suggesting how to make the organism more resistant to radiation. Perhaps—I don't know what. You don't know either. Nobody ever will unless we search. Deity, Grama, you can't really mean to attack our ships and close down our projects! You've got to see what they mean.''

''I do,'' the officer answered frostily. ''I see resources and labor spent on a reckless gamble—effort that could be devoted to methods less spectacular than those you rave about, but proven methods, methods that won't save everything but will save a minimum.'' He pinched lips together and obviously decided to cleave to his task. ''This station maintains close contact with another on Nearside,'' he said. ''I want the details concerning that.''

''I suppose you're thinking of Kapitza,'' Jans mumbled. ''It's precisely antipodal, to help in conducting various types of experiments jointly with us.''

''You must have a direct line to it, then,'' Grama pounced. ''Show me.''

Vague ideas had churned in Jans . . . a secret call . . .

His eyes flickered to the man with a green uniform and a gun. The barrel shifted a little toward him. Jans swallowed, went to the vidiphone line and explained his use of it.

Grama fired questions so fast and shrewdly that he had no chance to invent lies.

At the end, the Asian nodded.

"It accords with what information I had. At the moment Kapitza Station is engaged in measurements of the Virgo supernova and has no particular reason to keep in touch with you. Rather, both will report directly to Tycho." He rubbed his chin. "Still, if they came upon something exciting they might call to share the news. Eh? If no one were present at this end the 'phone would notify you over the intercom. Therefore I think best that no one be here except a guard."

Jans shrugged. The spirit within him had utterly slumped.

"I am not unaware that your work has importance," Grama said in an effort at politeness. "I regret the interruption to it almost as deeply as I do the need to assault your fleet."

Jans might have answered: *If your side wins my work could be interrupted forever. You'll pull everyone, everything back to Earth for your hysterical "preparation."*

He felt too tired.

Still trying to be friendly, Grama asked, "What have you yourself been doing?"

"Isotope bombardment," Jans replied listlessly.

"Your staff is rather limited, no?"

"The equipment doesn't need more." Some life came back to Jans when he gestured at the magnificence around. "Totally automated, computer-controlled, versatile. We can shoot any kind of particle with any energy in any direction we choose. You see, we don't always want our target in the house yonder. Sometimes we want it closer,

209

for intensification. Or we may place several targets in different positions—even outside the roof, on the bare ground, if the cosmic flux is low—and sweep the beam across them in succession. That way we obtain—"

He stopped dead. A shudder went through his body, a shout through his brain.

"Yes?" Grama tensed and took a step toward him. The soldier hefted the gun. Ridje Tommin knotted his fists.

"I— I—" Sweat prickled cold on Jans' skin. His heart banged. He swallowed dryness.

Grama seized him by the shoulder. Amiability had vanished; the officer's face was like iron.

"What have you thought of?"

Jans crumpled into a chair. He stared at the floor and said with the awkwardness of fear, "Just remembered. Lately I've been reporting every Earth day to scientific headquarters in Tycho. If I stop they'll wonder why."

Grama glanced from him to Tommin.

"Is that true?"

Tommin spat.

"Answer me," Grama said, not loudly.

"Wouldn't know," Tommin got out. "I stay away as much as I can—from this Auty lover."

Grama turned back to Jans.

"Well," he said, "you needn't report actual results. You can, ah, fake your data."

Jans looked at Tommin.

"I have to tell Commander Grama something in confidence," he said. "The reason is strictly scientific."

Tommin's mouth twisted.

Grama bent close and Jans whispered, "I'm afraid fakery would make them wonder, too. What I'm doing at the moment isn't original. I give out that it is to avoid any conscious or unconscious bias among my helpers. If they knew we're supposed to get certain results they might try too hard to get them. Or, in my case, not get them, to spite me."

Grama scolded. "I should have expected that kind of snobbery in a Kinsman. Well, go on. What is your real purpose?"

"To check the calibration of some newly developed instruments. We're repeating experiments that were done when the station was first built. My data are processed in Tycho as they arrive. Now I haven't the mathematics to calculate to the last decimal what the results should be. That involves distribution curves for several simultaneous variables and—a computer, analyzing what I sent, would spot an anomaly at once. And that would have such big implications—"

"Your colleagues would swarm to check in person," Grama concluded. "Or, if you claimed you were having trouble with your apparatus, they would send a repair crew. Yes. Best you do proceed with genuine tests." He stood stooped for a while longer in the pervasive generator pulse before he said, "The appearance of a crew like that—any small group of men—would inconvenience us. However, we have provision for minor emergencies. The newcomers can be arrested and— But you would be shot. Suspicion of treachery suffices."

Jans raised his head.

"Why do you think I'm warning you? I want to live."

211

"Indeed. Indeed." Grama nodded again. "Reorganize. Get started. I will give you what help I can."

"Not I!" Tommin yelled. His countenance burned red. "Be damned if I'll work for a traitor—"

The soldier pointed his gun.

"No," Jans pleaded. "Let him be. I don't need help. Not for something routine like this. Especially when I might be—uh—sabotaged."

"Good logic," Grama approved. "We'll confine him and his partner to quarters." He studied Jans. "I am hoping to win you over. The new government of the Westrealm will need every capable person. Nevertheless, understand this: I shall be with you each instant of the next day and a half."

"I understand," Jans said heavily.

The computer keyboard danced under his touch. Behind a mask of meters, electrons swirled through vacuum and solid-state cells. The machine hummed, then clicked forth a printout.

Grama moved catfooted in Lunar weight. His shadow fell suddenly across Jans. The physicist started. He turned his head and saw the dark face, hollow-eyed with weariness, aimed at the papers and references before him.

"I'm ready to start the first run now." His pulse drummed.

"Explain to me precisely what you intend doing," Grama ordered. His hand darted to an open manual on the desk. "What have selenological tables to do with nucleonics?"

"Why, everything." Mental rehearsals paid off and

Jans spoke more steadily. "We aren't on Earth—we're on the Moon. Completely different environment."

"Go on."

"I mentioned the curvature of the surface several hours ago, remember? No Lunar magnetic field to bother us, which is why we don't need walls around the beam path. But there are quanta from both sky and ground, induction effects of certain minerals—we even have to allow for gravitation, yes, for mascons, in the case of low energies and long path. Our instruments are that sensitive. I was making the necessary calculations." He gestured at the viewscreen. "I'm about to send a series of pulses of different durations and intensities," he went on. "Different compositions, too. Protons, neutrons, alkali metal ions . . .

"You can see how I've positioned the target blocks outside on the ground as well as in the target house proper. What will actually be measured are parameters like scattering, excitation, capture cross sections, re-emission—"

"Never mind. I have the general idea." Grama rubbed his eyes. "Oh, Deity, but I'm tired! Do you never sleep?"

"You didn't have to stay awake just because I did."

"I did have to. Our force is too busy to spare me a relief." Grama smiled. "Please, as one human being to another, won't you bunk down soon?"

Jans thought, *What about the human beings you intend to slaughter?*

He said shortly, "In an hour, maybe," grinned a little and jerked a thumb at the soldier who dozed in a chair, gun on lap. He himself was strung taut beyond any sense of weariness. "Why not send him for coffee?"

"Why? Well—" Grama hesitated, touched his own sidearm, made a quick decision and issued the order.

"That's better," Jans said. "Sit. Relax. I'm only going to program the system. You needn't fear any melodramatic leap at your throat."

"I don't." Grama followed his second suggestion also. His gaze never left the younger man. "I do worry somewhat about your mind. You proclaimed your loyalty to the Kinhouses very strongly when we first talked. Now you are more than cooperative. Why?"

"I can simply try to tell you. Who knows what really drives him—down underneath?" Jans clipped the result of his computations, a string of zeroes and ones, to the main console. A scanner read it and, with his guidance, instructed the accelerator. A light flashed Ready. Jans leaned back in the control chair. The hum around him deepened to a drone. "As I told you before, I'm not interested in dying," he said. "If I refused to help you—and got shot for it—a team might arrive from Tycho to ask what went wrong with my latest experiment and why I didn't report the trouble. You've explained to me that you can handle that sort of contingency. My death would be for nothing." His tone grew harsh. "And it would be for a cause that, well, has faults of its own. And my fellows are already convinced I've scuttled to your side. I may as well have the game as the name."

"Suppose we do, despite everything, lose?"

"Then I'll move to Great Asia, I suppose. Nothing worse. The Kinhouses aren't totalitarian. They'll set reconciliation above revenge."

"Whereas we are the contrary? My friend, you have entirely the wrong impression. Let me explain—"

"Later. I have to begin."

Jans closed the master switch. The drone became a triumphant song. Needles quivered across gauges. The outside view showed no change visible to human eyes, simply the beam tunnel, the cliff edge, the distant peaks, the timeless stars. But pulse after pulse was leaping forth.

It ended. Jans let go a breath. "Run number one," he said. "Next we do it with thermal neutrons."

"Eh? Will that not confuse the results of what you have already done?"

Grama was intelligent, Jans realized not for the first time. "Those results are being recorded, on the spot, at this instant," he replied. "It just takes a few minutes; half-lives are short. We want to know what happens during a sequential bombardment—to our new instruments, I mean."

The soldier came back with coffee cups on a tray. His face was flushed.

"What kept you?" Grama asked.

"Damned Kinhouse-lover in the cookshack, sir. I had to rough him up some before he'd do what he was told."

Grama's smile was thin.

"You should be happy you are under armed guard, Scientist Jans," he said.

Jans made no answer. He was busy.

Run two. Three. Four.

"That's all for today."

"We can rest?" Grama asked eagerly.

"I'd better 'phone in my data first," Jans said. "I'm already several hours behind schedule."

"With your permission, then." Grama didn't seem to notice any humor in his words. He locked the neuro-monitor/bracelet onto Jans' wrist and considered the readings. "You're overtired and nervous," he decided, "but not gathering energy for a sacrificial effort."

"Of course not. Where would I find energy? Let me finish, will you?"

Grama connected the monitor to an amplifier and this in turn to the vidiphone's circuit breaker. Jans punched a number.

A face appeared in the screen and said, "Physical Laboratories Headquarters—why, good watch, Scientist Jans. Whom do you want?"

"Lord Scientist Bradny. Who else?"

"Well—" the technician grinned—"Astry Coner's been wondering aloud when you'd be back here. She—"

"Lord Scientist Bradny," Jans barked. "Now."

Offended, the man shrugged and touched the appropriate button. A robot lacked the discrimination to protect the higher-ups from idiot calls. But Jans prayed the research director would not be in his office, so that he need merely record a message.

His prayer was denied.

Bradny's white-bearded image said, "Good watch— What's wrong, Ing? You look like fury."

Jans spoke as fast as he dared. "A collywobble in the machine. We got it fixed. That's why the delay. I'm worn to a bone. Do you mind waiting for a full report? Here are my latest readings." He laid the figures, printed off from the outside instruments, onto the faxer. Bradny registered surprise. Jans trampled any possible remark under in his rush. "Sir, I'd like to sleep for about twenty hours, so please don't call me back. I'll call you when I can for discussion. Thanks. Good watch to you." He blanked the screen.

"Well done," Grama said and relief turned Jans boneless.

"I ought to go out and dismantle things," the physicist said faintly, "but let that wait. I want my doss as much as you two want yours."

He went through the tunnels with them, in the silent hatred of those teammates he passed. When he reached his quarters, he hardly stopped to remove his clothes before he tumbled into bed. Grama and the soldier took cots, the latter disposing his across the doorway.

Jans had some trouble getting to sleep. He kept waking with a gasp. Finally exhaustion claimed him.

Until, several hours later, thunder woke the whole station.

He sat bolt erect. Noise rolled around him, the bass toning of ground-borne explosion, the shouts of frightened men. Floor and walls shivered.

He looked down the mouths of Grama's pistol and the soldier's stuttergun and said, "Yes, they're here. You can kill me but that'll put you before a firing squad. You've lost."

Curiously, for he was no hero, his main worry then was about his instruments. He should have taken them inside where they would be safe.

The conference room was crowded with pride. Here were gathered the space navy captains of the Confederated

Kinhouses of the Westrealm. Uniforms glowed, medals glittered beneath the faces of men who commanded men. At the head of the table, between Rani Danlandris and Admiral Anwarel, Jans did not notice his own drabness. It was wholly exterior. Glory blazed from him.

Anwarel was saying: ". . . decisive battle indeed. Not that I'd call it a battle. Absolute surprise. One megaton shot wrecked every last ship of theirs. We took out their missiles with lasers. I doubt Great Asia has three warcraft worth mentioning left in the whole Solar System."

"What do we do next?" Danlandris wondered.

Anwarel shrugged his gold-encrusted shoulders.

"That's a political decision. If I were the High Council I'd order us into bombardment orbits and deliver an ultimatum. The Asians would surrender as fast as Cheng's gang did here after we landed."

"M-m-m—I'm not certain they would, Admiral. And supposing you're right, do we want their surrender? Dare we tie down men and equipment in military occupation, political reconstruction, when— Well, as you say, it's for the Council."

Anwarel's sternness relaxed. He addressed Jans.

"They'll have an even knottier problem finding a suitable reward for you, young man," he rumbled. "I haven't yet been told how you did it. Why not tell me yourself? We're waiting for word from Federal City anyway."

"Uh—well—" Thus called on, Jans became shy again. He stared at the table. "Not hard, sir. Except for inventing a reason why I had to use the accelerator and keeping the people at Tycho from letting out that there was no reason. Otherwise, uh, besides that, I mean, I knew the particle detectors at Kapitza Station were running wide open. They'd register anything that came in. So, uh, what if a beam—better still, three or four different kinds of beam in a row—what if they arrived? Pulse-coded. Telling what the situation was at Chandrasekhar. Asking the men to alert you, sir. Your fleet had to be near the Moon if it was due shortly to land on it. Of course, I didn't know for sure you'd get authority to strike without warning but, uh, since the enemy did have GTS missiles in place—'' He took a deep breath, went on: ''My main worry, once I saw Grama had swallowed my play-acting in front of Lord Scientist Bradny, my main fear was that someone would call me back and ask what I was up to. I did my best to make sure nobody would but— Well, it wasn't just that my pretext was a lie and my section doesn't report to Tycho that often. It was that my data were weird. Because, naturally, they weren't from any particular experiment. I'd only swept the beams briefly across the targets to make the instruments show something. Anything at all. And the rest of the time the beams were going straight across the valley, above the mountains, into the sky.''

''Why weren't they lost in space?'' Anwarel demanded.

''Because they didn't have escape velocity, sir. They had Lunar orbital velocity, more or less. About one-point-seven kilometers per second. I, obviously, I couldn't fire them in a circular path. They'd have hit something on the way. I had to calculate an elliptical orbit for them. But I was helped by the fact that, uh—well, it was shown ages ago, before the Population Wars. A spherically symmetrical inverse-square field, like the gravity of a planet, will partially focus particles traveling great circle paths, after a hundred and eighty degrees. And Kapitza is antipodal to Chandrasekhar.

"I didn't have to be too exact. I only had to get enough stuff there to produce flutters in the detectors. Which are quite sensitive, you know—and my beams were strong." Jans was warming up to his subject. "Even in the case of neutrons, whose decay reduces beam intensity by a factor of about twenty during an orbital flight of approximately thirty-two hundred seconds, the initial impulse could be such that—"

"Never mind." Danlandris smiled. "We get the general idea. And the Kinhouses do know how to show gratitude."

"They won't be too hard on Cheng's people, will they?" Jans asked. "Lal Grama, especially. He was pretty decent. He might be—well—useful in negotiations."

"Might be," Anwarel said skeptically.

Jans fell back to dreaming about a Luna girl who could live and dream with him.

Anwarel broke a lengthening silence with: "Why not interview Cheng? Get a notion what sort of chap he is. If nothing else—it'll keep us occupied till we hear from somebody."

He issued an order to a rating, who went off toward the room where the enemy commander was held. That was no vindictive detention. While Edard Lierk lay dead, any number of Asian boys did, too. Cheng had been left alone with his grief. Probably the telescreen had taken some edge off it. He had doubtless hunched over the relayed newscasts from Earth, though equally doubtless, word of this clash was being suppressed on both sides until . . .

* * *

The tall, spare figure entered, stumbling. They thought at first his loss had affected his mind. He looked on them with glaze-eyed horror and the breath was harsh in his lungs.

Jans rose.

Danlandris, "Do you feel well?"

"No." Cheng shook his head violently. "No. None of us. Ever again."

"What do you mean?" Anwarel replied. To the rating: "Here, get the man a chair. Can't you see he's about to crumple?"

Cheng stared from his captors to the wall and beyond.

"I heard the broadcast," he said. It was as if someone else, whom they did not recognize, were using his throat. "You have not? You will. Oh, you will."

Anwarel surged to his feet.

"What do you mean?" he roared.

"Public announcement. The truth cannot be hidden. It must be revealed, in full. Measurements . . . the newest studies . . . extrapolations . . . Earth's field is taking another nosedive. We now have a year. At most. A year." Cheng's gaze returned and became aware of them. "Meanwhile we fought!" he screamed. "Meanwhile we fought!"

Conversation in Arcady

So that's what a spaceship looks like, Bill thought.

It rested in the valley beneath him, near the river, with an arm of the woods for background. Mist flowed like white smoke around the lancehead shape. Where sunrays struck across the eastward trees, the metal shimmered. High overhead a fish hawk went circling.

Linda caught his arm. "Did that really go to the stars?" she asked. "It seems awfully small." Her voice fell low in the quietness, which nothing but the birds broke otherwise.

"Well, not under its own power," he admitted. "The mother vessel's too big to come down. Has to stay in orbit. That's one of the shuttle boats. But, yes, it was there." He squinted into the light, trying to make out details, as if he could see the scars of cosmic dust and strange landings. The distance was too great, though.

223

"C'mon," he said.

Charlotte made a face. "Nothing doing. My feet ache."

They had come only a few miles from the chalet, but she wasn't used to walking. And, of course, they'd had quite a night. Bill knew that before long he'd start feeling the effects himself, and curl up for a ten- or twelve-hour sleep. But the stim pills hadn't worn off yet. He'd taken an extra dose yesterday evening—Charlotte and Linda were plenty healthy girls—and still felt fine. It had been his idea that they stroll around and say hello to the spacemen, seeing how near they happened to be to one of the announced landing places.

"Don't you want to meet the boys?" he asked. "They should be quite a novelty. Not just that they've been so far away they couldn't see the sun without a telescope, but they were born more than three hundred years ago. Some of them may have known Thane himself. It's a safe bet they've lived in cities—"

"Why, they'll be *ancient!*" Charlotte said with a shiver. She wasn't stupid, but she had no more information about technical matters than the average person.

"Nonsense, dear," said Linda. "When you move almost at the speed of light, time slows down for you. I never could understand why, but it does. I don't guess they've aged more than twenty or thirty years in their traveling. If you take your Anti-Eld—they did have Anti-Eld back then, didn't they, Billy, darling?—that's not too big a percentage of a lifetime. I'm sure they're fascinating."

"Well they can fascinate me some other day," Charlotte grumbled. She yawned, shook the yellow hair off her shoulders, and drew her cloak tight around her. "I'm cold and sleepy and I'm going to call me a flitter and go to bed.''

"As you like,'' purred Linda, and held Bill's arm close.

Charlotte touched the cab summons button on her talkie bracelet, with a defiant little look at him. He grinned, chucked her under the chin, and started downhill. The grass was cold and wet where it brushed her bare legs and sandaled feet. Linda paced him. A breeze fluttered her dark locks and her cloak, which she hadn't fastened.

Bill gave her a sidelong glance. "So you do figure to latch onto a spaceman, sweetheart?'' he murmured.

"Why not? He'll be something different.'' She patted his head. "Not that I've got any complaints, Billy. Let's make a private date sometime, hm-m-m?''

"With pleasure. Uh, do me a favor, though, will you? If I get talking to one of the crew, don't wiggle yourself at him. Pick somebody else. You can take your pick, I guarantee.''

"Sure. But what, if I may ask, do you want with your man?''

"Gab. A lot of gab. I've often wondered what it's like out there among the stars.''

"You're a funny one,'' she said with amused affection. He allowed himself an inward smirk. Though his intellectual curiosity was genuine enough, his flaunting of it was calculated. You needed some point of uniqueness these days.

A flitter must have been hovering quite near, for it landed by Charlotte at that moment. Linda and Bill turned to wave good-by. The shimmer of the drive force distorted his view of her figure, which would ordinarily have been a pity. But he wasn't feeling frustrated about her, or anyone, this morning. She waved back, drowsily spoke an order to the robot, and took off. The egg shape was soon lost in that big empty sky.

A rustle of underbrush yanked his attention downward. Having no enemies that he knew of, he didn't draw the blastgun on his hip, but he kept a hand near it as he turned around. People didn't often sneak up on you unless they were looking for trouble.

Or were spacemen, he realized. The tall, black-clad form that stepped out of a stand of beeches could only be from the ship. Clothes like that hadn't been seen on Earth since the Dispersal. And the man had short hair, and a beard, and unhappy eyes. He was weaponless, too. Must simply have been out for a walk, Bill decided, had seen the flitter descend and headed in its direction.

"Oh!" Linda exclaimed. Remembering what they were here for, she gave the newcomer a slow smile and let her cloak fall so it showed exactly as much as she wanted him to see for a beginning.

A flush went up his long cheeks. He shifted his gaze to Bill, who considered that foolish. *Though come to think of it, didn't I read, or hear on a sensecast, or something, that the expedition had women along?*

No. He was wire tense.

Bill made a formal bow, gave his own name and Linda's, and said, "Peace to you" with hands held open.

The spaceman took a jerky step toward him, and another, before stopping. "Lieutenant Owen Garst," he said thickly. "At your service."

"Three names?" Linda raised her brows.

"Two names and a title," Bill told her. "The ancient style. He'd be Owen." To him: "Pleasure meeting you. We came to visit, if you're willing."

Owen's mouth twitched. "Willing? Oh, yes. Very much so. After all, you're the first. We landed three days ago, and you're the first who've come to see us." His accent was harsh and Bill couldn't follow some idioms; but on the whole, language hadn't changed too greatly since the starship left.

"He's terribly hurt about that," Linda whispered to her companion. She approached Owen, holding out her hand. "How strange," she said aloud, "but I guess not many people have heard you were here. And then, this is a wilderness area, sort of."

His eyes locked with hers, his arms remained at his sides, and he answered grimly: "That makes no difference when you have flycars. Does it? Besides, we spotted our boats evenly around the planet, to give everyone an equal chance. We've kept in radio contact with each other, so I know what's happened—or not happened. No boat has had more than a dozen visitors."

"What'd you expect?" Bill asked in surprise.

"Five million people came to see us off," Owen said, still watching Linda as if he accused her of something. "They estimated that three billion more watched on television."

"Three billion?" Bill whistled. "Were there really that many then?"

"More. What's the population now?"

"Gosh, I dunno," Linda said. She noticed that her hand

227

was still ignored and withdrew it. "Ask Billy. He reads books."

As Owen's gaze smoldered toward him, Bill shrugged. "How should I know? Nobody's counted. If I had to make a guess . . . uh, let me see. I never thought about it much. A hundred million? Maybe something like that."

"On all Earth?" Owen's bony head shook, back and forth, like a stunned animal's. "We saw from space that the cities were abandoned and falling to ruin," he sighed. "But we heard some radio talk. The one we contacted invited us right on down—and then we couldn't find him. What's happened?"

Suddenly he sprang. His fingers clamped onto Bill's shoulders with bruising force. *"What's happened?"* he screamed, and shook the other man till teeth rattled.

Bill jerked free, crouched back, and drew his gun "Hold on there!" he rapped.

"Billy!" Linda seized his wrist.

Owen stood gasping. The young sunlight glittered off sweat on his face. "Don't hurt him," Linda begged.

"Then let him behave himself," Bill said through his anger.

"Can't you see, he doesn't know any better?"

As if her words had opened a valve, the emotion drained from him. He even laughed a little as he holstered his gun. "All right," he said. "You're excused, friend. But watch your manners. Not everybody's got an easy temper or an understanding girl like me."

Owen blinked rapidly. For a moment he stood slumped. Then he turned blindly away, stumbled a few steps downhill, jackknifed his long black form onto a boulder. He sat there with hands hanging between his knees.

"Maybe you better run along, honey," Bill muttered to Linda. "Nothing here for you, I'm afraid."

"I'll say! But I'm sort of interested anyhow. I do think of something besides men, you know, once in a while."

She had, in fact, done a few water colors. It was one thing that had attracted Bill to her. He liked women with brains. He spread his cloak on the grass near the rock and sat down. She joined him.

A shudder went through Owen. He lifted his face, looked squarely at them, and said in a flat voice, "I'm sorry if I've violated any code of behavior. Obviously things have changed in three hundred years."

After a pause, he went on, almost too low to hear: "We expected that. We knew we, our wives and children, we'd come back as strangers. It's so horribly far to the nearest star with a planet men can live on. We had so long a hunt—cold red dwarf suns, worlds with poison in the air and things walking the land such as you don't see even in dreams . . ." His words trailed off.

"What's a wife?" Linda asked in Bill's ear.

"A permanent sex partner," he told her. "They used to have them."

She frowned in puzzlement. "Whatever for?"

"But we found it!" Owen shouted. "A planet like Paradise, waiting for us these five billion years. And we came back. And what's happened?"

Bill began to see what a shock it must have been. He had read some of the history books lying around in the old

229

libraries, which helped him remember the smattering of the subject he had gotten in autocation. He drew a breath and picked his words carefully. "Well, the Bio War must have broken out a . . . uh . . . about a century after you left."

Owen's fists lifted, and fell again till they rested on his knees. "We didn't believe Earth could go on the way it had been going," he said. "Overcrowded, overcivilized . . . One reason why the expedition went. To find another planet, an outlet. Did the war destroy civilization, then?"

"Oh, no," Bill said, amused in spite of himself. "The buildings and machinery and such weren't hurt at all. But the germs got nearly everybody. After that, the others had it good. Each man could use what thousands, maybe millions had been using before. Robots to do the work, even skilled work like doctoring."

"And bringing up children?" he flung at them.

"Why, of course," Linda said. "Not that there are a lot. Most girls would rather not be bothered. But when they come along, we're fond of them, really we are. My half-sister has her Tommy living right with her."

"And maybe you didn't have autocation in your time," Bill suggested. "Machines to put what you need to know right into your brain."

"You don't seem to have much use for knowledge," Owen said furiously.

Linda laughed. "Whatever for?" she said again.

The spaceman looked away, across the valley and the hills toward the snowpeaks that seemed to float in the western sky. "To know. To have a foundation for new knowledge, discoveries, things never done before."

"Shucks, there're too many new things for one lifetime already," Bill said. "Like me, I've never yet been in Carlsbad Caverns, or smoked sho-nuff opium, or made love to Linda's half-sister—"

"From what I hear, you haven't missed much," she said.

"But don't you care about the future?" Owen's voice cracked. "What'll become of your grandchildren?"

"That's their problem," Bill shrugged. "Though I don't expect the world'll be any different for them."

The conversation was beginning to bore him. He had wanted to hear about romantic adventures on foreign worlds, not argue psychologics or whatever it was called. So he noticed how tiredness had crept into his muscles and decided that a large breakfast and a long nap weren't such a bad idea.

"No directing purpose," Owen mumbled. "Don't you even have a government?"

"What's that?" Linda asked.

"People used to tell other people what to do," Bill explained, hiding a yawn.

"Huh? Sounds crazy. How'd they make them do it?"

"Ask him." Bill jerked a thumb at Owen. But the spaceman looked so woebegone, sitting there shivering in the dew, that Bill had to continue in a kindlier tone:

"Look, friend, when there's plenty of elbow room, and the machines give you everything you need, what more does anybody want? I suggest you fellows catch flitters to the nearest supply depot and outfit yourselves. Then settle down, take rooms in a hostel or find a house, some area you like, and wait. You'll get lots of invitations, as the

231

word spreads. Novelties are always welcome. You've done a long, hard job. Now relax and have fun.''

Owen stared at him. The landscape grew so still that you could hear the air whistle in the pinions of the hawk. Bill's eyes wandered drowsily away from the spaceman's. The fog was vanishing down in the valley; a hundred different shades of green showed through.

After a very long while, Owen's mouth gashed open and he said unsteadily, ''Is that all it means to you, what we did? A job?''

Sleepier by the minute, Bill couldn't think of any reply.

''It was a mission,'' Owen said. ''We went to plant the seed of man among the stars. A whole universe is waiting for us out yonder. We found one planet to colonize; but there must be millions. And men can learn, and strive, and . . . No, you can't just stay here. You mustn't!''

His yell jarred Bill awake. Linda felt how her companion bristled. She squeezed his shoulder as if to say once more, He doesn't know any better. Her words were quick and polite. ''Well, I hope you can get somebody interested. It must be real thrilling. Very glad to have met you.'' She rose. ''Let's go, Billy, shall we? I'm dead on my feet.''

''Me, too.'' Bill got up. Owen remained seated. The muscles jerked in his face, and Bill wondered if the man was about to cry. ''Good day, friend,'' he said.

He walked back uphill with Linda, to get out of sight before calling a flitter. Otherwise he might have had to continue that embarrassing session while they waited. At the edge of the woods, they paused to glance back. Owen was still sitting on the boulder, an angular black blot under the sky.

232

Bill chuckled. "Want to try another spaceman?"

Linda wrinkled her snub nose. "Not if they're all such crawlies."

"Oh, well," he said, to maintain his reputation as a thinker, "times change."

They flitted to Pike's Peak Chateau, where the robots were taped for a champagne breakfast, and afterward went off to rest. When they woke, he called Bertie in New Zealand, who said there'd be a party at Marie's, so they went on over. Linda got considerable conversational mileage out of the morning's encounter. Bill avoided the subject. It made him feel a little uncomfortable, somehow.

Not long afterward, he heard that the spaceboats had lifted. Since they never came down, it appeared that the starship had departed Earth. He often wondered why.

Dialogue

Forget not yet the tried intent
Of such a truth as I have meant;
My great travail so gladly spent
    Forget not yet!
        —Sir Thomas Wyatt

(The story has come to light even later than the teller
intended—almost five centuries later. He left it in a goods-
deposit box at a financial institution in Bienvenida, which
was then the only town on Arcadia, Epsilon Eridani II.
He likewise left instructions that the box be opened after
the last survivor of a certain trio died, and funds to cover
its rental meanwhile. Unfortunately, an earthquake later
wrecked the building. In the confusion everybody seems
to have forgotten these orders. A new structure incorpo-

235

rated rubble from the old, the box therewith, in its foundations. Well-built, it lasted to the present day, when a remodeling project forced demolition and the container was discovered. If nothing else, the voice tape it held is interesting for the confirmation it lends to a suspicion which some historians have long nursed.

(The text here derives from a translation. For the sake of intelligibility, certain passages have been condensed or eliminated, others expanded or added. It was a very different universe in those days. Many modern readers may not be familiar with the details. Therefore, a brief summary:

(Men had established scientific bases on several planets of the nearest stars. However vital to the advance of knowledge, this was a desperately marginal operation. Each voyage was a huge undertaking, over-costly to an Earth impoverished in natural resources. Each light-year traversed meant a decade in cold-sleep for the passengers and, once they had arrived, a year of time for beaming back what information they could gather. Arcadia, hospitable to our species and possessing no intelligent aborigines, was permanently settled, and had been so for about a century. But it was at the feasible limit of travel, since any longer time would have wrought irreversible changes in the live cargo, and only a few thousand individuals had been shipped there. The messages which they and their descendants returned, or received, were a ghostly contact indeed, and their culture was inevitably drifting from those upon Earth.

(Then Verizelos found how to produce tachyons at will, with any desired superlight velocity. Developmental teams solved the problem of modulating beams of these particles.

After a laser message had crawled for eleven years to bring Arcadia the plans for a transceiver, near-instantaneous audiovisual communication soon went between all men. Rejoicing was general—but not universal. Here is the story that Igor Simberloff has to tell.)

I wanted a talk with somebody who understood cities. Of course we're bound and determined we won't repeat the old mistakes. Arcadia won't be gutted, poisoned, scarred as the mother world was. But what *were* the mistakes? Thus far, a fistful of people in a planet-wide wilderness have been more concerned with nature than themselves. By and large, we seem to be doing pretty well there, reaching ecological understanding, introducing terrestrial life which thrives but doesn't overrun. However, our population grows fast. Already 10,000 live in Bienvenida, and hamlets elsewhere are becoming villages. What awful urban experiences have they had on the old globe, and how can we avoid the same? Our records don't say much.

My secretary reported, "I'm sorry, Igor. The starcom's engaged: Has been for over an hour." We still had just a single unit on Arcadia, capable of handling just a single channel. Tachyon streams, necessarily pulse-coded, can't have the bandwidth of electromagnetic radiation. The engineers had said we could carry several conversations simultaneously if we settled for voice only; but I opted for full eidophonic capacity. One hologram was worth any number of words, to convey data and make us less alone.

I frowned. Transmission took a monstrous lot of energy, which could otherwise have gone into capacitors for vehicles, 'dozers, power tools, all the machines which would always be short of power till we got more fusion generators built. I had nearly a full-time job discouraging an open-ended increase in the burning of coal, petroleum, even wood. Everybody authorized to use the starcom was supposed to keep that use to a businesslike minimum. "Who's on the line?" I asked.

"Becky Jourdain," my secretary answered.

My heart stumbled, picked itself up, and ran, singing. "I . . . didn't know she was back." *Why didn't she call me? Doesn't she think I'd care?*

"Yes, she's at home," the technie said. "Shall I have a runner tell her to cut it short?"

"No," I mumbled. "Never mind. I . . . I think I'll go over there in person. Maybe I'll learn something interesting." Was he looking at me in sympathy? I wasn't that transparent, was I? Commanding forth a smile, I added, "Science, thy name is serendipity." Rising, I promised to return in time for an appointment with our superintendent of mines, and limped out of the presidential office.

There was no reason not to. "President" is a big name for the chief public administrator of 30,000 mostly wide-scattered, mostly self-reliant people. They must think I do a good job, since they keep re-electing me, but I don't delude myself it's a very demanding job. It's about right for my frail, crookbacked organism.

And the day was perfect for a walk. The sun's big ruddy disc stood near the middle of a violet sky where wings and a few clouds went gleaming. When I cut through the park, sweet warm odors of growth flooded me. Chime blossoms rang tinny, scattered around in a soft terrestrial lawn. Roses bloomed, python trees swayed and waved their branches, water danced in silver and rainbows at the fountain. Everybody I met gave me a friendly hail.

I'm afraid my replies were absent-minded. I'd no room in me for much except Becky. She'd been weeks gone in the field, fifteen hundred kilometers distant, Lake Moonfish area, botanizing. Both she and the biolab staff here in Bienvenida were excited about it. She'd told me she was finding clues to a whole new concept of certain food chains. Then why had she come back this early in the season? (Not that I objected, oh, God, no.) I decided—correctly, I soon learned—she had reached a point where she needed to confer with a place where they kept bigger data banks and more kinds of specialists than we were able to. A portable radio can't link to the starcom like a home phone.

Her battered old flitter was parked in the street outside her cottage. She'd planted the grounds entirely in native species, choosing and arranging them so they wouldn't need care in her absences. That kind of ingenuity left me helplessly awed; and the effect was beautiful, blue-green leaves and golden blossoms where peacock moths loved to hover. As I climbed the porch steps, a pain began in my left leg which I tried to ignore. This was Becky Jourdain's door I was knocking on again.

She let me in after a minute. Her cynopard padded at her back, claws a little extended on all six feet, fangs showing bright against forest-colored fur, beneath a scarlet stare. Originally I'd scolded her for bringing the animal into town. It was an excellent companion and guardian in the wilds—most members of the Faun Corps keep a cynopard—but too big and dangerous around here. "Poof," she'd said. "William isn't the least bit dangerous. He doesn't need to be." At last I'd agreed, as far as that beast was concerned, though I still didn't believe anybody else could raise a pup so well . . . so lovingly.

"Igor!" she exclaimed. "Hi!" And she grabbed both my hands.

She's taller than me, slim, supple, sun-tinged. Her hair falls amber past a wide brow and blue eyes, straight nose and full mouth, down to her shoulders. This day she wore a blouse and shorts. I stood mute in the shining of her.

"Look, I'm connected to Earth and better get straight back at it," she went on. "But come and meet the fellow."

Barefoot, she led me through the comfortable clutter of a living room which was half workshop, to her study. It took me seconds to focus on the hologram.

Seated, the man rose when I entered the scanner field. A wry smile suggested he knew how odd that courtesy really was. He was young: about 60, I guessed, which would be perhaps 28 revolutions around his own star. Plain gray tunic and slacks covered a big frame. His hair was dark, his face sharp and crag-nosed.

"This is Igor Simberloff, Ken," Becky said, a touch breathlessly. "Or, oh, should I have made the introduction the other way around? Anyhow, he's our president, but he's not one for ceremony. You may call him simply Glorious Leader." She turned to me. "Igor, meet Kenneth Mackin, of the Life Studies Institute in, m-m, Edinburgh, Scotland. His field is bioenergetics, and we're both learning a bundle." Laughing: "You needn't either of you try to shake hands." The starcom was that new to us.

"A custom Earth has abandoned," Mackin told her. He

bowed to me. "My pleasure, sir." I must make an effort to understand his dialect of English, common tongue of Arcadia though it was, but his voice had a rough music. "Dr. Jourdain's discoveries suggest rather dazzling possibilities. Already I think I see practical applications—pelagiculture, for instance—which could more than repay the cost of all space exploration since Armstrong."

"Ken, I've told you, I'm not a 'doctor,'" Becky interrupted. "We don't have time here to fool around with degrees. Either you can cut it in your job or you can't."

"I envy you that," he said. To me: "I know, Lord President, this conversation bears a large energy cost. But I do hope you can let us carry on."

"Often," Becky added. She wrinkled her nose at me. "Don't fear for our morals. Two batches of photons can't carry on very much." But did I see her flush the least bit? "Have a chair and listen. Butt in whenever you want."

No, whenever you want, I thought at her.

Talk flamed up afresh between them. It was mostly in technicalities which passed me by; but they did tell something of themselves. Quite a lot of themselves, I realized later when thinking back. Sparks of reality. He spent a good deal of his life at sea, as she in her woodlands, not only on the job but in free-time search of uncluttered horizons. Little of those remained on Earth, and he sighed at what she had to relate. She for her part envied the intellectual stimulation he got, and even the harsh political challenge of making the post-Imperial Union work. He smoked tobacco in a pipe, voted Independent, fenced with a prospect of becoming regional champion; she had to trick that last information out of a certain shyness. They both liked

241

working with their hands, playing chess, listening to Beethoven and Nakamura, having a personal go at melodies less meaningful but more lively. Both had living parents and other kinfolk, but both dwelt alone.

Once when I chaired a heated discussion of policy objectives, a committeeman declared in his excitement: "I tell you, the inevitable can happen!" That's become almost a watchword of mine.

As the next weeks passed by, Becky did not return to the field, though the season wanes fast in our short Arcadian year. She hogged the starcom—her phrase—for at least an hour a day, sometimes twice and at peculiar times, Mackin in his position being closer bound to a 24-hour rotation period than she to 35. This got in the way of others who wanted access to Earth, partly because of that same scheduling but mainly because the power we could spare for tachyon transmission was limited.

Juan Pascual was the one who finally protested to me. He's a decent man, but peppery, and was anxious to discuss his planetary physics data. "I come to you, Igor, because she won't get off the line," he said in my office. "You have authority to allocate time. Well, do it fairly!"

I expected this. That was a gray thought to have. "I think what she's doing is important," I told him.

His small body bounced in the chair. "In the word of my ancestors, *¡mierde!* She flaps her eyelashes at you and—" He caught himself. "I'm sorry. A wrong thing to say. But she can't have collected enough data to need this long to send. She ought to be out after more."

"M-m-m, I hadn't mentioned this. She asked me not to,

242

figured it'd be too controversial till it was finished." And what could I refuse her? "But I suppose you do rate an early explanation. True, her professional talks ended for now, a while back. But since, she's been gathering facts we need. Facts about Earth, what it's like, what people believe and do and hope—"

He bristled. "Do you mean a holographic Grand Tour, all for herself?"

"Well, that saves time, doesn't it? I mean, a single person needn't be reintroduced to the guide or have basic information restated. And Juan, this is essential. We've become a new breed of society here. Earth has too, as far as that goes. How can we understand, sympathize with citizens of a polyglot megalopolis, for instance, or they with us? I think Becky's right, the ignorance gap could grow too wide to bridge. Which might be downright dangerous when faster-than-light spacecraft are developed."

"They won't be for centuries, if ever," he snorted.

"She records," I pointed out. "The stuff needs editing, she says, but in due course it'll go in the data banks for anybody to play back anytime."

"Have you studied those tapes?"

I flinched. "N-no. Been busy."

He cocked a brow, then scowled. "Do it, Igor," he said. "I warn you, I'm appearing before the next Council session, and I won't be alone. You'd better make ready to prove that what she's getting is worth the price."

We shook hands, friends regardless, and he departed. I sat long by myself, stared out the window at a rainy day and never really saw it. At last I instructed my secretary to get Becky's newest recording projected.

My office had a cabinet for the purpose, occupying a corner of the room. It was often quicker and energy-cheaper to show me the colored shadow of some place or person that I must make a decision about, than to fly me there—the more so when this carcass couldn't get around very much on the scene. I was used to it. I had supposed I was even used to contacts with Earth, infrequent though mine were.

This time, when the sight and sound sprang forth, they hit. Seated in darkness, for a moment I couldn't see what glowed at me. Shapes, movements, all things were too alien. I'd talked glibly enough about the mother world having changed. But this—? Offices and the people in them were what I'd met through the starcom. Maybe they are much the same throughout human space and time. And maybe this is because they are not in the forefront of life after all, but only foam and bubbles on top of its chaos.

The scanner was looking—had looked—from a window of a flitter. In the background, growing larger with approach, was a complex of frameworks where humans and machines swarmed tiny. Sections of wall had begun to cover the metal. I heard Mackin's voice: "Restoration project in Old Peking, what was once called the Forbidden City. I thought we might inspect that. Example of an attitude of piety toward the past which we're seeing quite a lot of nowadays. Three urban clans have organized to support this particular undertaking."

Meanwhile my gaze was locked onto what passed directly beneath. Like a sea from which there lifted the occasional island of a conurb—an island that I now saw, from the outside, was time-worn, scars and gaps not altogether repaired—shimmered what could not really be frozen iridescent fountains beneath the pale-blue sky of Earth. No, it had to be a kind of architecture. I remembered hearing a little about the use of light, cheap, interchangeable parts by individuals, to build homes and shops which were not solid for generations like our works on Arcadia, but ever-variable parts of an uncontrollably fluid megalopolis. . . .

Becky's troubled tone called me back. "Ken, don't you think— Well, I'll speak plain. Isn't this just another tourist sight? I do have a duty, some return to give my people for so much use of the starcom. What's a restoration to them? They need to know about things like, oh, those clans you've mentioned, or the Australian Mysteries, or—" Her words trailed off.

"I know," he answered. "Believe me, I'd do a proper sociological study for them if I could. But not only am I not a sociologist, I doubt if any would perform much better. Too many matters would take a lifetime to explain; and meanwhile the world, both our worlds keep on changing."

"Can't you at least land and, well, walk around a bit with your scanner, talk to a few individuals, the way you did in places like Merville?"

"I'm afraid that wouldn't be safe. They're staid engineer and worker types in Merville, in spite of their webs and gills. Here and now, it's Fire Revel. Outsiders aren't wanted. . . . Wait, yonder comes a troop. See for yourself."

The view steadied as the flitter halted in midair, then swung about as the pickup did. I glimpsed Becky and almost cried out, *But you aren't on Earth, you're here!*

—before I realized she'd been projecting her image to a receiver aboard the vehicle, cost be damned. The scene lost her. My heart stammered. When it steadied, I could observe at optical close-in those hundreds who leaped and whirled among the bright frail eccentric buildings. They were naked except for dragon masks and body paint; torches flared and streamed in their hands; they shouted and whistled, in curious harmony with the groaning of gongs.

Vaguely I heard Mackin: "I could land elsewhere and search for anti-believers, but—"

"Oh, no!" Had he deliberately evoked her terror on his account? "Go ahead the way you planned. Do."

The rest was merely a visit to the worksite. My anger at Mackin faded as he went about peering and interviewing. His effort was amateurish, useless to us, but I sensed it was real, if only for Becky's sake.

When the data ended, I hobbled to the nearest window and raised the shade. My watch said half an hour had passed. But the log showed she'd been on the line a good 90 minutes that day.

I left the office. Rain turned the world silver. It beat on my cowl and ran down my poncho to the pavement, swirled and gurgled and carried along bright leaves fallen off elms responding to an autumn that was not Earth's. It tasted warm on my face. Native trees still flaunted their foliage, of course. A wyvern passed above them, bound for the countryside to hunt.

When Becky admitted me, I saw she'd kindled a hearthfire. Otherwise her living room was in dusk. Wordless, she took my garment and drew a chair alongside hers. The cynopard lay on the rug before us, flamelight asheen off his pelt.

"I can guess why you're here," she said, very low.

I nodded. "Did you imagine you could steal private use of the beam forever?" My own voice was quieter yet, and I stared into the dancing, crackling colors.

"No. Why didn't you check before?"

"I did play your first couple of tapes. Then . . . well, I assumed there was no immediate need" to watch her and Mackin in the dawn of their happiness. "Now Juan Pascual and the rest are on the warpath. As is, I'll have a bitch of a time explaining away those hours already missing."

"You will, though? Oh, Igor!" She reached out and seized my hand.

I nodded and dared look at her. "Hm, if Mackin can supply canned stuff of the right length, we can probably work it in to replace what you wiped."

"Not wiped. Kept for myself, for always." She blinked hard and rubbed her free wrist across her eyes. "I will *not* bawl. Igor, you—I love you for this. If it weren't for Ken—"

"And a mutation which I ought to keep out of the gene pool," I cut in. My tone sounded overly harsh to me. I swallowed and tried again: "You . . . chromosomes like yours should be passed on. How're you going to do that with a shadow?"

Her grip on me grew hurtfully tight. "Don't blame him. My fault, the whole way through. When we recognized what was happening, he wanted to break off; and I wouldn't let him."

I never thought I might ask for a look at those stolen hours. But ashamed of myself, I have imagined:

He sees her in the room that, like all this house, is so wholly her own, though he does not see the room itself—that part of it which blurs off at the edges to nothing—for there is only her in the middle of it. She reaches for him. "Ken," she says. Her hand touches the scanner. His comes in answer. They stand with eleven light-years between their fingertips.

We can measure, but cannot imagine how far. If Sol let go of Earth and the planet whipped off into space like a stone from a sling, it would get here in a thousand centuries. Twenty times the length of our history since first in Sumer they scratched on clay what they knew about the movements of the stars, twenty processions of pharaohs and prophets, empires and hordes, discoveries, dreams, and deaths, would meanwhile pass by among the constellations. We traveled faster than that on our way outward, we humans, because we are mortal and could not wait so many cycles. Nonetheless our ships, the building of which dwarfed Pyramids and Chinese Wall and conquest of the Solar System, crept as motes through endless emptiness. Only the pulses of particles, which, being phantom, are not bound by space and time as we are (who are phantoms to them), bore news between our ten lost tribes.

"Becky," he gets forth in his awkward way. "How, how're you doing, lass?"

"Lonely," she says. Then, defiant, she tosses her head; the bright locks fly. "But oh, I'm glad to see you again!"

"And I you." The silence of space rises between them while they look. Finally his eyes break free. He smites fist in palm and says, "Can this Heloise and Abelard business go on much longer?"

"What?" she asks, bemused.

He has told her a great deal about Earth, as she has told him about Arcadia—and everything else they could share—but now he only jangles a laugh and replies, "Never mind. Not the same case. We've neither of us taken vows, and I'm not in his condition, and we can see and talk to each other—" His control snaps across. "We're crazy! Or I am, at least, my darling. Give me the courage to tell you goodbye."

"I can't," she whispers. "I don't have it myself."

Rain filled the windowpanes.

"Becky," I forced out, "I've known you for our whole lives. And, okay, if you tell me to go to hell I'll board the next bus. However, my job does make me a professional busybody, as well as arranger, fixer, shoulder to cry on—May I try to help out?"

She nodded quickly and repeatedly. Her lips had grown quite unsteady.

"The news that tachyon communication existed got me thinking," I said. "I've kept at it, off and on, ever since. Not that any unique, guaranteed inspirations have come my way. Maybe a vague idea or two, broached on Earth 20 or 30 years ago. I must know better what the situation is there. When can you call Mackin?"

"In a, a couple of hours. He'll be off work, at home, and he's got a standby connection." If she knew offhand what the time was on a planet eleven light-years away, more than a pulse-beam tied her to it. And if he could promote such special privilege, he must be an able bastard, even though Earth has several starcoms and abundant power for them. He must be the kind of man who could keep her kind of woman happy and give her strong children.

"Meanwhile—" Becky rose, drew me after her, down to the floor in front of the fire beside her great pet beast of prey. "Meanwhile, Igor, w-would you lend me that shoulder for crying?"

Which shoulder, the high or the low? They're about equally knobbly. "Sure, kid. Be my guest."

The hologram included part of the room around Mackin. Books lined its walls, actual printed books, many old and leatherbound. Among them I saw a sailing ship model and a Hokusai print I'd had reproed for myself from our data banks. He'd lost weight, puffed ferociously on his pipe till he sat in a blue haze I could almost smell, and sipped from a glass of whisky. We two had sweet bronzeberry wine for our comfort.

"I've looked into the transport question," he told me after a difficult opening of talk. Becky had come near begging him to let me sit in. Not till she raised pride and temper did he smile a stiff trifle and agree. I suppose an Earthling who wants to remain an individual has to be fanatical about his privacy. "The *Shakespeare*, the *Virgil*, the *Tu Fu* are all in Solar System orbit, committed to nothing. But that's the exact problem. Given the starcoms, who wants to spend resources we can ill afford on ships? The Assembly has ordered the whole fleet retired as vessels return from their current trips. I do have influential connections, and maybe I could get a last Epsilon Eridani expedition dispatched on some excuse. Maybe. The politicking would take a decade or worse, and then probably fail."

"Becky'd be in her grave long before you got here anyway," I said, and enjoyed my brutality till I saw that she winced, not he.

"Can't you build a coldsleep facility on Arcadia?" Mackin demanded.

I shook my head. "Uh-uh. It was discussed in the past, for the benefit of rare disease cases that could wait for special medical gear to be produced. But the price was out of sight. We may not be short on resources here, but we are on labor; and a lot of items have a lot higher priority for our people as a whole."

"Price?" He was briefly puzzled. "Oh, yes. You let a free market govern your efforts, don't you?" Having read a fair amount of history, I expected him to get self-righteously indignant; but he earned my respect by taking the social difference in stride. "Well," he said, "let's drop talk about that kind of spacecraft. I've investigated the prospects of faster-than-light too." His face bleakened. "They aren't good."

"Why not?" I asked. "Look, since we can detect tachyons, we can modulate them; since we can modulate them, we can make them carry information; and if we can send information, theoretically we can do anything."

"I've heard that oftener than you, sir," he said rather grimly. "But electromagnetic waves have been available a great deal longer, and're a great deal easier to give bandwidth too; yet nobody's ever transmitted a material object by them."

251

"Nobody had any need to," I answered. "Think, though. There you are in your billions, trapped on Earth. FTL would open your way to the stars . . . all the stars in the universe."

"Besides," Becky interrupted with an eagerness that twisted in me, "EM waves *have* toted matter. The photon drives on those same spaceships."

Mackin sighed. "Oh, yes, I've seen the arguments, lass, over and over. It should be possible to use tachyons, or a tachyon effect, or God knows what, to travel FTL. But nobody can think how. Research goes on, of course. But when will it succeed? 'Tis like atomic energy before uranium fission was known, a theory waiting for a fundamental breakthrough discovery. And—I've studied this— between that discovery and the first crude nonmilitary industrial applications, well-nigh a generation passed; another till reactors were everyday; two more till fusion came under control— D'you see? Let them make the breakthrough tomorrow, which they won't, and let them make an all-out development effort, which they can't, and still at the very best we'd be old when I came to you, Becky."

Expensive silence filled the room, except for rain stammering on the windows.

Until—"Mackin," I asked, choosing each word, "what kind of program have you got for contacting galactic civilization?"

"What?" He blinked at me. I saw understanding flare in Becky's glance, and heard the breath burst into her.

"You know," I said, impatient. "Even here in the boonies we know. Already we've found enough planets with intelligent beings on them—Atlantis, Lemuria, Cockaigne, the whole bunch—technologically behind us, yes, but they make it a statistical certainty that intelligence is common in the cosmos. And that makes it sure our kind of technology is reasonably common. A single species which mastered FTL would explode outward like a dropped watermelon. They'd have bases, colonies, disciple races . . . communicating by tachyons. That's why we never got radio signals from them; they don't bother with radio. But they exist!"

He flushed, and I saw that I'd half purposely insulted him. "Aye, sir, I am likewise aware of this," he said. "Humankind is. We've beamed to selected stars. We've listened in different directions. Ley Observatory on Luna has an automated detector operating full-time. But the problems—simply recognizing a code as such, not background noise, to name a single example—the problems are steep, Simberloff."

"Touché," I muttered. He'd responded to me in kind. Louder: "What I'm asking you for is not the general principles but the specific details. Our two planets have had so much news to swap in the short while since we built this gadget here— How big an attempt is actually being made? How much bigger might it be jockeyed into becoming? What kind of signal do your best minds think would be most effective in drawing the attention of the Others? Assuming they do then respond, even drop in for a personal visit, what procedures are wise? You two people don't have to be star-crossed lovers. You've got a practical problem, and God damn it, I'm trying to help you find a practical solution!"

Becky sprang from her chair and reached for his image.

253

Her hands disappeared in it. She wasn't ashamed to weep before us both, not anymore. "Don't you see, darling? We could call us a lifeboat!"

Maybe. Nothing is guaranteed. Nothing is simple, either.

If we Arcadians built a second, higher-powered starcom devoted entirely to the search, continuously sending as well as listening, we could triple or quadruple Earth's half-hearted effort. I told the Council that the preliminary talks about this had had to be confidential, which accounted for the censoring of Becky's tapes, and they swallowed my story.

They did because they knew Earth's project lagged for more reasons than a shortage of materials. Too many thinkers had raised too many questions about it.

I was pleased to learn that nobody worth mentioning took seriously the notion that, when they realized we were here, the Galactics might come a-conquering. What could they possibly gain? What possible menace to them could we be? Nevertheless, ghosts from our past did linger in the cellars of my mind, heretic hunters, racists, displaced tribes looking for new real estate . . . that kind of thing was thinkable, unlikely but thinkable, and had helped make responsible men hesitate. (Might the fact that we could think it condemn us?)

More logical were the ideas that either they were hopelessly distant—we do live away off in a spiral arm, where the stars are thinning fast toward emptiness—or that, if they detected a signal from us, they wouldn't bother responding to such an obvious gaggle of primitives, except maybe for a quick secret surveillance. Or had we already been visited and dismissed as uninteresting?

"I doubt that," Ken Mackin remarked when we conferred. We did for about an hour per week, which satisfied Pascual and his colleagues. I didn't tell them that I spent the larger part of most such hours in Becky's living room, reading a book or whatever. "We find the nonindustrial, nonhuman cultures we know quite fascinating, don't we? For that matter, European man got plenty of practical value from the American aborigines, domestic plants especially but also tools, utensils, techniques, arts, enrichment of his whole tradition. No, if they have the curiosity to develop scientific method, they'll want to know us better than casually."

"I'd settle for being casually transported to Earth," Becky whispered.

"No, lass, I'd rather come to you—"

I left them.

More subtle objections had been imagined. A germ, to which one species was terribly vulnerable? Thus far men hadn't met anything extraterrestrial they couldn't cope with. However, all it takes is that first time. Besides, decades of travel between stars imposed a natural quarantine; passengers were in cold-sleep, but not the robots programmed to experiment on specimens and tissue cultures. Maybe when humans and Galactics met in person, they should do so as a few individuals prepared to spend years together in strict isolation from their races. Becky and Mackin said that wouldn't be too high a price. I said probably the Galactics knew enough biochemistry that there wouldn't be any real hazard.

Subtle to the point of unanswerability was the matter of psychic shock. On Earth, had not entire peoples died from a sense of being utterly and forever outclassed, after civilization found them? Mackin shook his head. "I've studied for myself," he declared. "Gone to the original anthropological material. The fact is, for the most part the civilized shoved the savage into territories where he could only starve, or exterminated him outright. Or took away the basis of the old culture—for instance, forbade hunters to hunt—giving naught in return but a beggarly handout. I think odds are high the Galactics are beyond that kind of thing; and anyhow, I believe we are, we're too sophisticated now to become pathetic victims. Whenever the savages got a decent chance, which did happen a few times, they adapted rather well. Or . . . we humans could keep our identity within a larger society, while contributing to it, as the Jews did within Christendom and Islam. Why not? I've faith in us."

You hound, I thought, *you keep making me like you.*

There's no point in listing every argument. I had to meet them all, first before the Council, next before the citizens of Arcadia.

"Yes, of course a big new starcom would cost a fortune. But strictly capital cost, if we relax the conservation rules a bit. For instance, Thundersmoke Falls could furnish it plenty of hydroelectric power. Maintenance would be slight. And remember, we'd be developing technology as we built, equipment and knowledge which'd be damned useful elsewhere. In operation, the outfit would advance our entire science. If we never catch a message, the information we collect about natural tachyons may revolutionize our ideas. This in turn should bring the day of the FTL ship much closer.

"Why did Earth send our forefathers here, at enormous expense and trouble, if not to get knowledge? We who enjoy this wide and beautiful planet owe them a great debt back there. Can we really pay it off in scraps of biology and physics?

"If Earth is afraid of risks, need we be? Let's draw the Galactics to us first. The risk is negligible. And from a purely selfish viewpoint, the benefits of being those who start negotiations are incalculable. Not that we'd cheat our fellowmen, or withhold anything from them. But we would be in on the ground floor. We'd no longer be a few backwoods dwellers on the edge of nowhere, brought into the game whenever a busy Earth got around to us. We'd be the leaders ourselves.

"And afterward mankind would remember us the way they remember Athens."

A prospect of glory is helpful, but only butter for the parsnips. In two years of talk, my partisans and I created an emotional climate which made the undertaking possible. What made it real was a whopping endowment from Jacob Finch, when I'd logrolled through the Council his damned franchise to stripmine coal and burn it in electric generators. His stockholders having made such an investment, the system will delay adequate fusion energy for a generation. Meanwhile a lot of land will be spoiled and a lot of air will stink; and a terrible precedent has been set. I didn't tell Becky the inside story of these maneuvers. She's still appalled at what she considers my failure.

* * *

That was the first two years—or the first single year of Earth's. I must now think in terrestrial time, when we of mankind search for every piece of common heritage we have left. Therefore let me remember in the old calendar.

Year two.

My office windows were shaded against a summer day. Ken's stood clear to a dusk through which tumbled snow. It was as if a breath of cold reached me across the light-years. I hunched my scrawny frame in the chair while he grinned.

"Congratulate me, sir," he said. "I've made Stage One. Wirepulled my way into what should be the exact strategic position, research administrator and advisor to the Secretariat."

"Well, good," was all I could reply. "I, uh, I suppose this will let you guide the project through at your end?"

"Not by myself. I'll need your advice from time to time, about how to politic for what we want, just as it was your idea I try for an appointment like this."

"Wasn't that obvious to you?" I asked, somewhat surprised; so much of our discussions had been with Becky present and thus with me paying him only mechanical attention. "We have to have assistance from your specialists and supercomputers. If the government denies it, we're choked off. And you told me yourself how many think we here on Arcadia are trying to make a reckless unilateral move."

"Yes, yes, of course. But please, you have talent for working with people, even foreigners like us. If I call you occasionally and ask what to do, will you mind?"

"No," I snapped. "I'm committed too, am I not?"

His gaze sought her picture, blurred on the very rim of the scene I saw. "You are that, sir," he said. "I can't help but speculate whether you're seizing a chance to do something for the human race—or simply for your friend. You know my own motive's selfish."

"Don't you imagine I'll have fun in the attempt?" I retorted, and wasn't entirely a liar.

His glance came back to me. He laughed. "Good, sir. Between the two of us, I confess the same."

Blast, but I liked him!

Year three.

For technical reasons, closeness to the power source and remoteness from radiant interference, they built the great transceiver on the peak of Mount Unicorn. When it was ready, I went there to get a tour a day in advance of the dedication ceremonies the staff and I must endure. We didn't finish till after sunset.

Leaving the control center, my guide Peter Barstow and I paused for a little before we walked down the trail to the cottages. Suddenly night overwhelmed me.

The air was thin-edged as a knife; its cold struck into our bones, and breath smoked from us like escaping ghosts. Ground lay hoar beneath our feet and rang to our footsteps. Above, the projector drew a spiderweb across heaven. Yet it had not caught a one of the stars which glittered beyond, and I didn't think it ever could.

They were too many. Their brilliances well-nigh crowded out the dark, though deepening it somehow, and seemed to crackle—the Milky Way seemed to rush in a froth of suns, thunderous off the brink of creation—through the frozen silence around. All at once I felt what we are, dust-flecks astir for a wingbeat on a single whirling pebble, and I nearly grabbed at the wall behind me to keep from being spun off to fall forever between the stars.

Barstow may have heard my gasp. His voice came slow from the shadow face: "This hits me also, now and then."

"More than size," I mumbled. "Strangeness, exploding galaxies, black holes, neutron stars with mountains on their crusts a centimeter high, matter and energy as singularities in a mathematical field, time and space bent back on themselves—why do I call them strange? *We* are the rare freaks."

"I've wondered how I dare work." Barstow's half-seen hand waved around the horizon beneath us. "Suppose we succeed. What might we let into our cozy little cosmos? I wonder if I haven't been taken to a high place and shown the universe."

"If you refuse, somebody else will accept," I said. "We're that kind of animal."

"True. I have not refused. But—I try to be honest with myself—not because of imagined benefits to mankind. I'm helping us take this huge risk because I'm more curious than is right."

"And I— Well, never mind. I'm no altruist either."

He shivered. "Come on, let's get down where it's warm."

Year four.

Becky had her work, which kept her often in the field, while mine was doubled. I actually saw more of Ken than of her.

She had returned from a long expedition, and I invited her to dinner. The Terra House had expanded its facilities, and we enjoyed an excellent meal at our half-secluded corner table. Light in the big room was romantically soft; we could barely see the mural of the ancient Acropolis and—because of fluorescent vividness opposite us—Apollo Eleven's liftoff. A small orchestra played for couples who danced.

She lifted her glass. The glow lingered on her hair and eyes. "Here's to victory," she murmured.

Unsureness touched her smile. Though I clinked rims and drank, I could not quite speak any response.

She regarded me for a mute while. The melody in my ears came as remote as the tang on my palate. (At the back of my mind I tried to guess what a violin sounded like that was made of terrestrial wood, what champagne tasted like whose grapes had grown in terrestrial soil.) The trouble in her would no longer stay down. "Not a sign of anything, is there?" she asked.

I shook my head. "You've read and heard the reports."

"But you might know—an announcement they don't feel ready to make—"

"Nothing more than interesting scientific data. I'm sorry." I gathered what courage I could. "We knew from the start we might well never get the reply you hope for."

She nodded. "We'll keep trying. Won't you, Igor?"

"Certainly. But"—I leaned toward her—"how long are you prepared to wait?"

She squared her bare shoulders. "As long as need be."

Again I shook my head. "Becky, I may be talking out of turn, but you and, and Ken have made me a sort of father confessor. You're healthy. So is he. Are you willing to keep *him* on the hook for the rest of his life?"

261

She winced. I barely heard: "No. Any time he wants—"

"And you?"

"I know, I know! Give us more of a chance, though!"

Did she sense what was in me? I dared not utter it. She wouldn't have recoiled. However, pretending my purpose was merely public, we could laugh together.

If, or when, she decided our whole effort was for zero, and she'd best salvage what life had left to offer . . . she was fond of me, grateful to me. No, I'd never wish any get of mine on her; but I'd have been glad for her to accept a donation. And, sure, she could keep in touch with Ken Mackin. The ghost you loved, the cripple who loved you, the faceless who fathered your children—Becky Jourdain, here are your men!

She straightened anew. Her head lifted. "We aren't licked yet, Igor. In fact, we've not begun to fight."

"I'll drink to that," I volunteered, and did.

The rest of the evening was quite merry. When she glanced toward the pairs on the floor, I knew she'd have liked to dance. But that would be ridiculous with me, and she wouldn't humiliate me by letting another man take her out.

Year five.

Each byte of the moment comes to my summons. There are the yielding hardness and leather smell of my chair, routine documents on my desk and one a-rustle between my fingers, the shabby rug beyond, a crack in the wall behind a faded photograph of my parents. Windows stand open to a mild springtime breeze, a hundred fragrances—I can count them—and sounds of children at play outside. A little girl sings, high and sweet, *"Here we go 'round the bowberry bush, the bowberry bush, the bowberry bush—"*

My phone chimed. I swore, being tired, and lifted a slightly aching arm to press accept. Peter Barstow's lean features leaped into the screen.

"Igor—they've come!"

"They've, they've what?" For an instant nothing was real.

"Not a message," he chattered. "A ship. Bound in from north of the ecliptic—unholy acceleration, no sign of jets, but the Skywatch satellite's caught an unmistakable image and we've made radar contact—and the tachyon screens have gone wild!"

"No possibility of its being human?" asked a far-off machine. As for myself, the one thing I cannot remember is just how, just what I felt. Maybe nothing, yet.

"From that direction, with the characteristics it's got?"

"They. Came. Themselves."

My machinery began to move. "Who've you notified besides me?" I snapped.

"N-nobody. Except us here on duty—"

"Hold the news for the time being. We don't want to be mobbed by the curious and the hysterical till we've done a bare minimum. Can you tell me more than you have? No? Well, transmit the visual data, and anything else you obtain, for this phone to record. If something radical happens, you'll find me here, and my override code will be, uh, ADVENT. Right now I've work of my own."

Thus undramatically did I switch him off. But it was crucial to get in immediate touch with others. Rescue forces must be alerted, against the slight chance of an attack on us—or whatever the stranger might bring. As per the contingency plan which had been a strong talking point for Ken, Earth and the colonies must be notified; every starcom but ours must be shut down.

We realized how silly this probably was. Galactics who wanted to find the rest of mankind, could. But it was a crude statement to them and to ourselves. *We put a few outliers at stake, no more, until we have learned what the galaxy is.*

Year six.

A heat wave had set in. Our sun hung monstrous in a sky which seemed likewise incandescent. Parched turf was harsh beneath the feet; leaves rattled when I brushed them. A smell of scorch lay everywhere. Seeking to ease our tempers, Juan Pascual and I went for a beer on the terrace of the Big Dipper. An umbrella above our table gave shade, and the brew was cool and tingly; but around us, streets, buildings, trees stood in a silent shimmer.

It was hard to imagine, let alone believe, that a shipful of three-eyed green-plumed fantasies still orbited such a world.

"Please understand, Igor," Pascual said, "I don't accuse you of wrongdoing. I do feel we—not only the rest of the communications committee but the whole population of Arcadia—we have a right to know more than you're telling."

I raised my brows above my goblet. "What can I hide, Juan, and how? I don't do more than preside over the committee. The scientists and technies do the real work, hammering out a mutual language and— And none of our operations are secret, even from the public. I couldn't sneak off to hold a confidential radio conversation with them if I wanted to. And supposing I did, what could I convey in the pidgin we've developed so far?"

"You *are* composing our main transmissions in their final form," he said roughly. "When I and others ask why you design a message this way rather than that, you grow evasive."

"Vague, Juan. Vague, not evasive—because I have nothing except my politician's hunches to go on. If we wrangled over each precise paragraph, we'd never get around to conveying a meaningful word. Somebody has to make quick decisions as to what we say to them and how. I'm always open to suggestions, and I do nothing without prior discussion, but ex officio I have the job."

"That's how you interpret your mandate. And you spend a lot of time pondering the replies, without ever explaining what conclusions you've drawn."

"You're free to do likewise, aren't you? I'm simply not about to make myself look silly by a premature guess at what such-and-such a jumble of symbols may mean . . . in connotation as well as denotation." I clanked my glass down. "I've told you before, I do have a notion that these particular Galactics are not here out of pure altruism. I believe they mean us well, but also hope to turn a profit, be it only in the form of their equivalent of thesis material. If that notion is right, then, yes, I do have a better basis for empathizing with them than an idealist like you. That's all." I drew breath. "If you think I'm mistaken, or unduly arbitrary, you can move a vote of no confidence."

For a second he stared, before he sat back. "You know none would ever carry," he sighed. "And I don't want to, anyway. I simply—simply—damnation, when the issues are as vast as this, I'd like to know more fully what you have in mind."

"I'd tell you if I knew for sure myself," I answered, and went on to soothe him with lies.

For his intuition was sound. If you've thought ahead, you can slant the key reports, overemphasize the key proposals, slip in personal preferences disguised as official policy, unbeknownst—the development of a common language when there is no common world being so intricate a task, so much of an engulfment in subtleties. What I was accomplishing was that certain eventual recommendations would get more weight than they properly deserved from the viewpoint of society or God.

But it hardly ever left me free to call on Becky, whose first jubilation had turned to loneliness.

Year seven.

When at last we had bargained and I knew, she was in the field again. I flitted there and we walked from camp, just us two except for the cynopard pacing at our heels. This was in North Julia near the end of summer, on a ridge above a wide valley. Wind soughed in forest leaves; they tossed blue-green under violet heaven and westering ruddy sun, and the slim white boles quivered. The open ground ran down and down, golden-turfed, long-shadowed, to where a river gleamed. High overhead cruised a wyvern. The air was pungent and cold; I drew my poncho tight around me.

"I suppose they're obliging what they regard as our overcaution," I said to the tall woman. "They call the cell samples we rocketed to them 'typical.' And they may well be politely faking ignorance of where our core civilization, our mother planet, is. But . . . whatever they think, in exchange for those coordinates, they have agreed they'll pick a man out of Earth orbit—Ken, of course—and bring him here, to live among us till everybody's sure he didn't catch something dreadful from them. Or they from him. Afterward they'll land freely everywhere, and cultural exchange will start in earnest.''

She gripped my elbow. I saw fine crow's-feet radiate from her eyes and a breath of gray here and there dimming the blonde mane. "Is there a chance—a danger—?''

"Oh, Lord, no. Why, already they've analyzed our DNA and— Becky, they believe, given a few years of study—what they learn from it will repay them for their trouble—in a few more years, they can rebuild carcasses like mine. They can set right what nature bungled.''

I stopped, there in the woods, caught both her hands, looked up and said through a grin while my pulse racketed, "Can you imagine me big and strong and handsome?''

"Did you ever need to be?'' she cried. "Igor, if anything could've made me happier than you've done yourself, this has!''

She kissed me. Many times. For a minute I was hoping.

The Communicators

After the thrust and hiss of orbital assumption, there was a great silence. The ship freefell around the Moon. She would complete a circuit while her crew verified that all was in order and got a lock-on to Ground Control, before starting descent.

Marbled blue and white, scars hidden by remoteness, altogether beautiful, Earth's lighted half-circle dropped beneath the Lunar horizon. That land became a jagged darkness; and because the Communicators had turned off their cabin illumination, fainter stars appeared to them until their viewport was one wintry blaze.

Brother Roban thought he had grown used to the sight during transit. But suddenly it was as if the knowledge entered him, not as before into his brain or his excited heart, but into his entirety—that the Order was indeed

269

bound home again; today, in his own young person; back to that web of whispers across space and the centuries which was its reason for being and perhaps the reason for life. Weightless in the chair harness, his burly body turned insubstantial as a dream and his awareness whirled forth among the constellations.

A hand fell upon his. A voice murmured, "Steady, son."

The tenderness in gesture and tone was astonishment enough to recall him. For a moment he gulped. One does not easily leave the fringes of eternity. Flesh enclosed him in pulse, breath, moist skin, the scratchiness of coarse fabric, a gust of faintly acrid-smelling air from a ventilator. Walls of metal enclosed him in narrowness and bleakness. Knowledge enclosed him in mortality, his own and mankind's.

Once a trip from Earth to Moon was nothing. Well-nigh flying themselves, the argosies plied in days from Mercury to Pluto. Treasure was aboard them, and humanity and human hopes. But the last such voyage ended more than three centuries ago. The means no longer exist to build that kind of vessel. We are lucky we can again lift off even this clumsily, from the wreckage of our latest dark age.

"You aren't ready for an ecstatic experience," Primary Luizo said, still with a gentleness Roban had never met from him before, "Later, yes. I am glad to see you are among those who can have them. But best with preliminary training, and the first few times under guidance. Otherwise it can overwhelm you. I don't think you would really be happiest as an ascetic."

"M-m-maybe not . . . sir," Roban mumbled.

The lean features of his superior stiffened into their usual mask. The accented Inglis harshened anew. Luizo came of the Ali de Marokh family, barons who held their Near Eastern marshlands against raiders from desert and sea when civilization had crashed to its nadir, and afterward were in the vanguard of its return. Though he himself had early joined the Order, the soldierly style had remained with him through the years of his life. Under his directorship, Australia Station operated as much like an army base as a conservatory of learning.

"Besides," he said, "we have practical problems. Two of us, to get the whole enterprise started over."

In Roban, anger shouldered wistfulness aside and filled the space where awe had been. "Among a pack of Dominists!" he exclaimed. "How much damage have those barbarians done?"

"Control your emotions," the Primary said. "Nobody would be sent here who was not a technological competent: not when ships and facilities are as crude as now. He wouldn't survive. It is a bare ten years since spaceflight resumed."

"That makes ten years they've sat on our property."

"I told you to curb yourself, Brother."

Roban looked into Luizo's eyes, glacial green in the dark, aquiline face. "Yes, Primary. I'm sorry."

He bowed his head, as befitted a mere techno reprimanded by an administrator who had, moreover, spent a working lifetime among the records of messages from the stars. His floating hands sought each other and twined fingers till the knuckles stood white. It was bitter for Brother Roban of the Order, who had been plain Roban

Stacket of Seattle in Norrestland, to be meek toward those who had conquered his country.

He often wondered why Luizo chose him to come when the Domination of Baikal announced it would ferry a pair of Communicators to Farside. He could readily understand that the Board of Directors would vote the honor of heading and organizing that mission to Luizo himself. The Primary had done more than turn half-ruined Australia Station into a secure and prosperous center for scholars and their families. He had also, alone in mystery, found new interpretations that answered old riddles about what the Others meant in certain of their transmissions. If anyone could bring humankind back into the transgalactic web—could even, maybe, regain the Order's ancient control of the transceivers—Luizo was the man.

But why, out of every possible assistant, did he choose me? I'm just a fisherman's son. I only joined a few years back, after I couldn't stand any longer seeing foreign troops on my soil that had been free.

Could that be his reason? Roban thought abruptly. *The Order of Communicators is supposed to stand outside all politics, all nationality; it speaks to the stars on behalf of our whole species. And by and large, our membership's really held that attitude. Otherwise I don't suppose we'd have lasted through the ups and downs and ins and outs of two thousand years. Myself, though—well, I've seen the vision too, when studying the archives or standing out in the night and looking upward—but I haven't forgotten bombs and fire when I was small, Mother crying when Dad never came back, slant-eyed men barracking to this day in* (whisper it) *Liberation House.*

With a tingle: *If a chance comes . . . to do something . . . I'm strong and ready.*

Swift in her low orbit, the ship raised the terminator. Day burned, first a thin line ahead, then a pockmarked stone waste beneath; and the constellations paled before human eyes while they reeled across heaven. Roban strained forward in his harness. "Can you spot the Station, sir?" he asked out of a tightening throat.

"No." The Primary stroked the pointed beard allowed his rank. "But I did not expect to. We are doubtless being guided from the new navigational posts . . . ah." He broke off. Expressionless, he crossed his arms in proper greeting. "Salutation, Colonel," he said to the man who had appeared in the companionway.

"Salutation to you bot'." Iwan Duna's accent was thicker than Luizo's; but the fact that he spoke Inglis, which had remained the common language of the Order since American times, helped qualify him as the expedition's liaison with its passengers. "May I join you?"

Roban clamped teeth together. The living tongue of Norrestland was not much different from this archaic version; and he had heard it spoken in just that way, by armed men in just that baggy uniform, along the shores of Puget Sound. *How can we stop you?* he wanted to say.

"Assuredly, Colonel," Luizo replied.

"You see," Duna explained, "you have de best view here, except in de pilot section w'ere dey are busy." His native speech governed his throat, imposing its own rhythms, softening and shortening vowels while forbidding such consonantal sounds as *th* and *wh*. But his fluency was such

that even Roban had almost stopped noticing the pro-
nunciation.

He pushed foot against foot against bulkhead, soared,
checked himself with a hand on the headrest of Roban's
chair. *I must not tell you to get away from me*, the techno
thought. Sweat welled in his fists. Some broke loose,
glittering, dancing droplets.

"We wanted your trip should be enjoyable as possible,"
Duna went on. "I am sorry you must be strapped in. Dat
iss for your safety in case a sudden maneuver is needed."

"You have made this voyage several times before, have
you not?" Luizo asked.

"Yass. I never tire of watching. Es-specially w'en we
pass Mare Tranquillitatis."

"Why that?"

"You do not know? W'ere de very first men landed."
Duna moved around to the side, so that both Communicators could see him. His gaze fell on Roban. "Your people,"
he said. "W'at iss your country wass part of deirs."

And now part of yours, seared in Roban. *Oh, a puppet
native government; a shadow Assembly; a pretense at a
mutual defense pact; but we are under your empire, paying
your tribute, quartering your troops, lately fighting in your
frontier skirmishes . . . oh, God, your huntsmen in our
clean mountains and forests, your Protector's yacht on our
clean waters, and the girl I'd hoped for giggling on the
arm of one of you!*

Still Duna regarded the big blond man. He himself fitted
Norrestland's popular concept of a Baikalan (though that
meant little, when his nation was such a kaleidoscope of
races and cultures)—short and stocky, broad in features,

high in cheekbones, slightly oblique gray eyes, head shaven except for a reddish scalp lock, face marked with clan tattoos. His coverall was similar to the Communicator's, but green where theirs were blue, sloppy where theirs were neat. At his waist he bore pistol and knife, surely no use here except to remind him that he was supposed to be a warrior-herdsman.

It had been no great surprise to find him affable. Baikalans were, as a rule, if you didn't cross them. His attempts to converse of scholarly matters had been less expected; but receiving no encouragement, he soon gave them up.

"Do you really not remember?" he persisted in the same mild tone.

Roban grimaced. "No chance for much education," he said. "We start work in childhood where I come from, and work hard." *In rain, fog, storm, hauling on lines and capstan bars till our hands grow too thick to hold a pen; but also on chuckling waves where sunlight dances and seals frolic, and woods stand green ashore, and Rainier's Peak floats holy in heaven. Our country, no one else's.* "We must . . . to pay the taxes that pay the tribute."

Luizo scowled, and Roban wished it hadn't blurted out of him like that. However, Duna was unruffled. "I know," he said. "I visited your home grounds once. It isn't de tribute, friend, it is de fact you cannot afford—you have not de resources—to build or buy enough machines. So you plow wit' animals and fish wit' sailing craft. W'at you call tribute is cheaper payment for your defense dan you could manage alone, es-specially if you count cost of dose raids de Eastmen used to make on you. Derefore you will shed de burden of toil quicker."

275

Luizo intervened, obviously anxious to find a different subject: "Most of the Order's recruits are commoners like Brother Roban. They have everything to learn—not simply our organization, rituals, traditions; no, astronomy, mathematics, the whole range of sciences; if they have the talent for it, interstellar linguistics and semantics. Brother Roban is as far along as he is, at his present age, because he started with the advantage of knowing Inglis. But he has not had time to study economics, politics, or the history of Earth."

Duna glanced ahead, where the blue half disc was rising. "He should. We happen to live dere. Have you explored de past, Primary?"

"To a degree. No more. Besides administration, my work in decipherment has kept me occupied. I need not remind you, in spite of a three-hundred-year hiatus, we are far from a complete understanding of the messages we already have."

"And yet you want more."

"Of course." Luizo gestured at what stars were visible, cold sparks beyond Earth. "What have they been saying to each other, and trying to tell us, while we were away?"

The ship passed over a crater. It resembled neither the volcanic nor the meteoritic sort, but shimmered like black glass under the harsh spatial sunlight; and from its shallow ringwall jutted metal snags. Roban could not forebear to ask, "What's that?"

"Site of a base," Duna said. "Struck by a fusion weapon."

Chill touched Roban. He had seen terrestrial ruins, beginning with those which surrounded Seattle's city wall.

But they were not so stark. Men had quarried them, weather had worn them, the kindly soil had crumbled and buried them with green life. "No wonder spaceflight came to an end," he said low.

Duna raised his brows. "Oh, dis is not from de last great war. Dis is from de t'ird. More dan a t'ousand years ago. Dat one brought its own collapse."

The wreckage slid out of sight. Raw mountaintops grabbed after the ship. Then they were likewise gone and a great dark plain lay beneath, curving away over the near horizon. The grimness left Duna's countenance. He stared downward and outward and whispered something to himself—curiously, in Inglis—that Roban overheard, something about an eagle having landed. The young man wondered what it meant.

Farside Station was near the middle of a natural crater; but Ley being big and the Moon being small, the ramparts could not be seen from it. The land reached ashen, boulder-strewn, pitted, footprinted. Shadows of early morning stretched west from every irregularity, making it stand out more sharply than any canyon crag on Earth. Silence and emptiness magnified other things as well for Roban, sounds of breath and blood, odors of sweat and air purifier. When he overstayed himself in a fixed position, he felt heat gnaw at his sunward side, warmth drain out of the opposite. Mostly, though, he moved, getting the hang of one-sixth gee in a spacesuit, long marvelous bounds through lightness.

Reflection from the ground made his pupils contract. No more stars appeared over the western edge of the world than he had seen where wavelets chuckled and rigging creaked. But a sickle Moon had stood in that sky; and Earth would never stand in this. *I am here*, he thought with wonder. *I am actually here*.

A jog at his elbow, a voice in his earplugs: "You start work, huh?"

His joy broke. He turned to confront the squat shape, masked by a self-darkening faceplate, a Baikalan who had acquired some Inglis while stationed in Alaska. "I'm about to," he snapped.

"You learn Moonwalking fast," Sergeant Aigunov said.

Roban ignored the attempt at friendliness. He admitted the need for guidance before he could safely travel on the surface; and, in fact, the rule that no one went topside alone was sensible. Nevertheless—

"I'll check the radio telescope first," he said.

"W'y? No good. Not fix yet."

"Exactly," Roban said. "But it, and the optical instruments for that matter—the X-ray receivers, the particle counters, the gravity wave meters, everything here—is the property and responsibility of the Order. You don't think we simply kept star talk alive for two thousand years, do you? We were always astronomers too. Each time civilization cut its own throat, or just wallowed back in swinish 'practicality,' we had to carry science on alone."

His gaze went to the huge spidery skeleton which overhung the area. Most of the Station was underground. Most of the exterior installations were in buildings sufficiently sturdy to survive three centuries of abandonment. The scattered blockhouse shapes, like the grounded spaceship, were dwarfed in this landscape but hardly touched by its meteoritic sleet. However, the radio dish and its field of antennae had suffered cruelly.

Repairs would cost wealth as well as time and skilled labor. Roban wasn't sure the Order could do the job unassisted. It had considerable holdings and revenues, but were they that great? Probably not. Earth was still crawling back from impoverishment. Had the Communicators been able to construct spaceships, they would not have waited a decade for the Domination of Baikal to offer two of them a ride.

Not that the Domination had regained all that was lost when mankind last went crazy. Technical knowledge didn't go up with cities in radioactive smoke. It was too widely diffused in too many books and microreels. The Order preserved most information; but between them, secular libraries doubtless retained as much of what had been generally known. No, the problem was scarcity of resources, including trained personnel. Theoretically, the first post-collapse spaceship could have been a System-spanning photon-drive giant, totally automated, able to take herself anywhere. In practice, she had to be simple enough for today's industry to produce.

"If you'd taken us here from the beginning," Roban said bitterly, "that observatory would be in action right now." *But no. You had to see if you couldn't read the messages that had come in, with the help of renegades from our ranks, and keep what you discovered to yourselves.*

He started toward the 'scope. Baikalan reports on it were available, but he ought to investigate personally. Motion eased his mood a trifle, until a grin twitched one corner of his mouth. In the end, as always before, the Order was prevailing over mere armed strength.

Its Board of Directors had protested when the Dominator denied repeated requests to send its people Moonside. Roban, then a boy, had asked with tearful indignation why it didn't call down the ban on Baikal. His arithmetic teacher, a female member of Seattle Station, which cooperated closely with what public schools there were, had explained quite frankly.

"Roban, dear, the Communicators haven't survived the rise and fall of civilizations by being impulsive. We serve the whole human race: eventually, we hope, the whole of intelligent life everywhere in this universe. We do more than gather and safeguard knowledge. We try to keep it working. That's why anyone who joins us has to renounce his nationality: so he can travel freely, judge and advise impartially. Oh, yes, we charge what seems right for our services, because we must keep our treasury alive. But the important thing is the services themselves, halting a plague, establishing a factory, educating a generation."

(An ideal, as the boy already vaguely knew. The truth was as complicated and disorderly as human affairs always are—episodes of corruption, crankery, schism, abasement, abuse of trust, over-weening arrogance; but also reforms, scholarship, reunity, martyrdom, honesty, humble helpfulness. The Order endured, in its quest for understanding, because ultimately that quest was religious. Whatever name a Communicator might give to God, including Void, his search across the cosmos was a search into the spirit.)

Sister Marja's eyes crinkled. "As for the practical politics, Roban, well, we can only invoke the ban—withdraw ourselves from a country—in the gravest cases. If we did it often, governments might decide they could manage without us! Worse, the mass of the people might lose their reverence for us. No, I think here we need merely bide our time.''

She was right. Key information lay hidden—somewhere—in the secret files of the Order. Renegades or no, the Dominator's agents could not interpret those sendings from the stars. There had been immense laughter in Australia Station's auditorium when Luizo read aloud the announcement by Yuri Khan himself: ''Thanks to the skill and devotion of our space project personnel, technical difficulties have been overcome to the point where it is possible to carry a limited number of foreign guests—''

Bouncing along beside Roban, Aigunov said: ''We not fix becausse got odder t'ings first.'' His hand chopped across the Milky Way. ''We got to reach Mars. Radio say colony did not die. Got to reach asteroids, mine again, use dose minerals to build up Eart' again. Stars, dey wait.''

Well, Roban thought, *the Baikalans are scarcely a sentimental folk.*

You couldn't even say that their adherence to dark-age tradition—bonds of kinship, old rites, hunting and herding, the warrior ethic—had such a basis. Rather, it was necessary. Their diversity of peoples, most still more than half barbarian, could never have formed a viable state on the melting pot theory. Nothing would have melted except the pot. Instead, ethnic identity, pride, vying for glory, must be turned into the engine of empire.

And—Roban admitted reluctantly—the imperialism was itself pragmatic. From the beginning, the Dominators had

Poul Anderson

made their objective clear. Several major nations were emerging. Rivalries were sharpening. Baikal would not attempt world conquest; that had always led to disaster. But it would try for military and economic hegemony.

The attempt was succeeding. Through fair means or foul—persuasion, diplomacy, purchase, conquest, alliance—in fact if not everywhere in name, the horse-tailed banner of the Lightning Bolt was flying halfway around the North Pole. And it stood on the Moon. And it was bound for Mars, the Belt, the verges of the Solar System.

But not for the stars, Roban told himself. *Those are ours.*

Stopping at the clifflike base of the radioscope, standing in its immense shadow, he became able to see better aloft. Sun after sun trod forth, unwinking, winter-keen, blue Sirius, red Betelgeuse, the galaxy's frosty rush across blackness, the Orion nebula where new suns were coming to birth as he watched, Andromeda's vortex whose light was two million years old, host upon radiant host, and those among them where planets circled unseen and minds yearned outward like his own and the signals winged away, Are you there, are you there, my brother?

He swallowed. His head whirled. He wanted to cast himself on his knees. Now he understood how, once that first faint cry sounded in its receivers, the Foundation for Extraterrestrial Communications was bound to endure, evolve into the Order, outlive wars, famines, pestilences, upheavals, ages of chaos and ages of indifference, kings and peoples and gods. A man asked a question knowing that he would be dust before the answer could come; was this not what made him a man?

"E-yi. Ya inyah," resounded through Roban's hearing. He turned. Aigunov was making gestures at the sky, mumbling some formula. *"Om mani padme hum. Om, om, om."* He might be a well-drilled spacehand, but down underneath he was a herdsman who shivered when demons galloped overhead on the night wind. *We'll be a long time about shedding the animal in us,* Roban thought.

Anger flared afresh: *Animals like him—walking my homeland with my girl!*

Returning hours later to report—dry-mouthed, sore-eyed, itchy and smelly with perspiration, shaky with fatigue, but borne on a tide of eagerness—he found Luizo talking with Iwan Duna. Roban waited by the door. He could not interrupt a Primary.

The office was cramped and austere. One wall was covered with bookshelves whose volumes had not yet been dusted. Opposite, beneath an air grille, hung a chart of known interstellar links; three centuries of underground darkness and vacuum had left it wonderfully clear, as if for a token of the Order's timelessness. Luizo sat behind a desk, Duna in front. Though he had thrown the embroidered cope of his rank over his coverall, the references and papers lay spread before him, the Communicator seemed to be the soldier, erect and correct. The colonel sprawled back in his chair, collar open, malodorous cigar between fingers, tattooed countenance loosely smiling.

"—you succeeded in beaming a message at Kappa Ceti," Luizo said.

"Yass," Duna answered. "Five . . . no, seven years

ago. Of course, wit' t'irty-two light-years to cross . . ." He shrugged.

"Have you tried no other star?"

"Not dat I know of. Kappa Ceti iss de closest dat transmits, no?" Lazily: "Unless you know of some closer dat you have not told de world about."

"None," Luizo rapped. "A priori absurd. First a star has to have a life-breathing planet, then intelligence has to evolve, then a civilization has to develop that is willing and able to exchange information with others. Our fore-bears were surprised to find that, judging from what they learned directly and indirectly, as many as one percent of the main sequence suns qualify—in this galactic neighbor-hood, at least."

"None of dem have told you how far de network reaches?"

"I doubt any are certain. A message from the center of the galaxy would take thirty thousand years to get here. Longer, actually, since it would have to zigzag between civilizations which could relay it. Under those conditions, one doesn't beam blindly into the wilderness. One holds regular discourse with his nearest available neighbors. Each party passes on what comes in to him from elsewhere. But that takes time itself; first one must *understand* what the newcomers are trying to convey, next put it into terms that one hopes the neighbors will comprehend. Our predeces-sors have recorded their belief that it is unfeasible to relay past the third or fourth stage of translation. The garbling would become hopeless."

Luizo tugged his beard. "To be sure," he continued, "man is a baby in this respect. We know the Kappa

Cetians have been in the network for some fifty thousand years. To them, it is only yesterday that they finally got a response from us. And others have been sending on the maser beams much longer than them. So our guesses about the system and how it works are apt to be wrong more often than right, I suppose.''

"You really have dat much trouble understanding?'' Duna blew a smoke ring. "I should t'ink, wit' deir experience, dey would know how to convey information fast to anybody.''

"How fast is fast?'' Luizo countered. "In two millennia, how many direct exchanges have we had with Kappa Ceti? The largest possible number is thirty-one; and the hiatuses in space, during our mad-dog history, have cost us ten of those chances.''

He cocked his head. "Colonel, why are you asking me about things that a school child ought to know?''

Duna laughed. "Because I am not a school child.'' He lifted a hand. "No, really. I have studied dis part of man's past as closely as odder parts. I have read, and seen in ancient films, how de world jubilated w'en first contact wass made. W'at strikes me as strange is dat it has had so little effect on us. Astronomy, physics, chemistry, plane-tology, biology . . . science, certain technologies, yas, we learned w'at we did not know, got ideas we might never have t'ought of by ourselves, like de tricky way to make a spaceship dat can really do her own sensing and computing, or de photon drive. But art, religion, politics, matters dat touch de common man w'ere he really lives—no, none, in all dis time. W'y?''

Luizo drew breath. Roban wondered if the Primary

really thought the Dominist was ignorant, or was quietly insulting him.

"If nothing else, transmission lag. Oh, yes, one does not proceed on a simple dialogue basis, one sends a long continuous program, even in the initial exploratory signal. But consider what happens when such a signal is acknowledged.

"The acknowledgers have to work out the code. Men had devised theoretical schemes, even before space travel. For instance, a set of on-off pulses could be arranged in a rectangle, each side a prime number of units, and form a crude picture. But in practice—as might have been guessed—the Kappa Cetians did not think that way. It took *them* a human generation to realize that we did not realize they were trying to send us a group of circuit diagrams. Then they had to regress to an elementary level and instruct us in their symbolism—and several times we went astray, which they could not know for thirty-two years—and we, in turn, eventually found out that they did not know we cared about the ecology of their planet . . . Well no matter. You can read the chronicles."

"I have," Duna said. "Not easy for alien minds to mesh. Like you and me, ha?"

Luizo's eyes clashed with his. "Yes, probably."

They noticed Roban. "Come in, Brother," Luizo said. "Be seated. What did you find?"

The Norrestlander placed himself nervously on a chair's edge. "As reported, sir," he answered. "Damage repairable, but will take time and be expensive." He hesitated. "Uh . . . I can't help wondering, sir, if we shouldn't let it go. Now that we're back in the network, or will be, the Others can surely answer our astrophysics questions for us, like they've done in the past.''

"When we knew what questions to ask," Luizo reminded him. He shook his grizzled head. "No, we will always have to do most of our own work. And we don't want to be parasites, either. We have something to tell the universe." He glanced back at Duna. "Concerning the point you raised, there have in fact been transmissions of literally vital importance. I might mention our learning about the variations and analogues of DNA on a number of different planets. You must be aware of the impact that a biological science thus broadened has had on fields like agriculture and medicine, in eras when we have the means to apply the techniques.''

In Roban's mind lifted the pictures (heartbreakingly blurred and few) that had finally been sent when the request was finally, perhaps, comprehended. "Intelligent life form'' . . . in every case, an equivalent of eyes and hands, or so men assumed, though the shapes were too strange and the accompanying text too meager for identification . . . but were those half-dozen species typical? More pictures should have arrived, after Earth's desire had passed along the network. Unless the theory was right that difference piled upon difference, from race to race, soon choked off the flow. Luizo himself, in spite of having mentioned it, was skeptical of that theory. Eventually proof or disproof ought to be forthcoming.

Patience. Patience. They've been talking out of Kappa Ceti for fifty thousand years. Elsewhere, we're told, for more than a million. Give us time—but I have no time!

Duna was scowling. "Dat is not w'at I meant." He

leaned forward. "You know, I t'ink maybe de reason we got trobble getting humanistic—" his earnestness shattered in a canine laugh—"or nonhumanistic information is, de Odders send too much t'rough robots—cybernets—you know, dey turn de job over to computers."

"That is no new speculation, Colonel," Luizo told him. "I consider it plausible. Wasn't the original search for extra-Solar intelligence—the beaming and listening—automated by us? It's obvious that the least of the alien civilizations is technologically ahead of us, and far older than any culture of ours has ever lived to become. With that kind of progress behind it, that kind of stability within it, would you not expect affairs to be rationalized, well-ordered, to the point where machines handle all routines?" He smiled. "I rather imagine that the early stages of communication with a race as primitive as ours count as routine."

Duna's good humor vanished. He chewed his cigar. "I don't like it, if dey really are no more interested in us dan dat. We may be less intellectual dan dem, but we are alive, and derefore we must have uniquenesses dey ought to ask about. Intellect should be de servant of life, not de odder way around."

"Your opinion." Contempt barely edged Luizo's voice.

Duna shook his cigar at the Primary. "And w'at about dis? We humans, soon as we could, we would make ships for going dere to see for ourselves. If dey are furder along dan us, w'y have dey not come here?"

"Maybe they did, in Earth's prehistoric past," Luizo answered. "Frankly, though, I doubt it. Have you not read the records of our inquiries about astronautics?"

"Yas, but—"

"Why should the Kappans lie to us? They explained that a spacecraft could be build to travel as fast as one-sixth light speed, but the radiation encountered—from the engine and interstellar gas—would pose difficulties." Luizo smiled with scant mirth. "Difficulties! Our own calculations showed that any living organism, behind any feasible shielding, would last less than one hour.

"As for automated probes: in the early days, to the nearest stars, perhaps. But no longer, at least not to stars within the network. Not when so much more information, from so much wider a range, can travel so much faster along the maser beams. I keep telling you, Colonel, those are rational beings out there."

"Maybe you have right." Duna puffed ferociously. "Me, I would not want to be dat rational." He swung to face Roban. "You! You are young. Would you not like to go?"

"Uh—well—" the Norrestlander stammered, "if it's impossible—"

"W'y do you say impossible? W'y not try to find a way around de radiation barrier? Or go off in a slow boat, take a t'ousand years for Alpha Centauri but wait dem out in biostasis along wit' friends and pretty girls. Or at minimum—send dat probe! If not'ing else, live to see television pictures, like people did who watched de first Moon landing and cried for glory. W'y not, Brudder Roban? I would!"

Luizo said bleakly: "The problem is that whenever man has gotten to the point where such an effort could be mounted, some lunatic or some barbarian comes along and smashes him back. We won't be able to reach the stars till we have the stable, rational civilization you affect to despise,

Colonel; and then we will be past the need for such children's outings."

Duna flushed. "Or maybe we could," he growled, "maybe we could have already, before I was born—except your precious Order sat on information from de stars dat made it possible, because you felt sure common men could not be trusted wit' dose powers—only you wise Communicators! Yass?"

A clenched fist on the desktop was Luizo's single sign of fury. "That is an old accusation," he said. "I neither admit nor deny it. I do state that no sane person gives a hand grenade to a homicidal maniac. In the present instance—by retaining the key to the language, we have assured that the Order gets back what rightfully belongs to it."

"And to us," Duna replied. "We—we howling, drum-beating, stinking savages—we got men into space again. Not you." He surged to his feet. "Dere are two hundred years' wort' of messages waiting to be translated. You will translate dem for us too. Good day!"

He stormed from the office. Luizo and Roban sat a long while unspeaking.

"Well," said the elder at last, "you need a shower and change of clothes before dinner. And I suggest you go to bed immediately afterward. I want you ready for work come mornwatch, and you look exhausted."

"I'm not really, sir, and anyway I'm too keyed up to sleep right off." Roban shifted in his chair. "Uh, that message the Baikalans sent to Kappa Ceti. Have you seen the record of it? Was it really no more than an invitation to resume transmissions?"

"Yes." Teeth gleamed wolf-white in Luizo's beard. "I wonder if the Kappans will be puzzled, or merely amused, when it reaches them. After that gap of three centuries, to start afresh in a completely obsolete symbolism!"

Roban must needs chuckle. Because the Order had trained him in machinery and circuitry rather than in semantics, he found himself briefly reviewing the linguistic problem.

A signal comes in, unmistakably modulated by an artifice of intelligence. But what is the code? What meaning is intended? You have your own ideas about how to establish a common language—beginning with mathematics, say, and progressing to physics and chemistry—but is that an obvious approach to the mind at the other end of the maser beam? In point of fact, as Luizo had told Duna, it was not. The Kappa Cetians assumed that humans naturally thought in digital and quantum-physical terms. For instance, the original Foundation was slow to realize that in a certain pattern they were not sending a geometrical theorem but a statement of Planck's law.

In their turn, the Kappans appeared confused at first by man's binary patterns which specified pictures. When they did get the idea, they returned drawings full of physical-science information, such as the layout of their planetary system and the detailed structure of its members. Biology was for centuries confined to the molecular level; they had trouble grasping that men could be interested in natural history or the very looks of another thinking race; and at the date of the last collapse of human civilization they had not yet, apparently, deduced that they were being asked for an account of their own past, their culture, art, religion, any matter transcending the material universe.

Either word spread that Sol had joined the network, or independent attempts at contact finally began to be received. At any rate, there were exchanges with other stars. They being still further off than Kappa Ceti, still less progress had been made. But the difficulties looked curiously similar—as if the human mentality differed radically from some galactic norm.

"Quite likely true," Luizo had once remarked to Roban. "Machine civilization—which one must have for interstellar communication—presupposes order, rationality, a logic which must be the same throughout the cosmos. We are infants. Give us a few thousand years of peace and sanity, and we will doubtless be thinking like the Others."

"I'm not sure I'd want that, sir," the novice, as he was then, had answered. "Not caring about . . . oh, outings in the woods, good food, beer, girls, games, books, music . . . only science and efficiency; it doesn't seem right."

Luizo had shrugged. "You will be dead well before it's happened, son." Gravely: "It won't be like that anyhow. A static society, with everything automated that we would call work, sounds like living death to you. But you have been conditioned by war, poverty, toil, misery, the whole cruel, pointless rise-and-fall we know as history. Once that has ended, we will be free to live for the things that really matter."

"If that's right, sir, then why aren't the Others telling us about those things?"

"Probably because they feel the mutual symbolism is

292

inadequate thus far. Be patient; that is what the Order deals in, patience.''

And in the course of lifetimes, information exchange did evolve toward precision and completeness. With Kappa Ceti alone was the code approaching a true language; but given it for a guide, the development with other contacts ought to be faster. Furthermore, the sheer amount of accumulated material was becoming sufficiently great to permit considerable analysis; for example, several binary-chart ''sketches'' could be combined to form one fairly clear picture.

But meanwhile tension mounted between Great Asia and the Empire of the Americas; Midafrica was torn by civil strife; a militant new religion was preached on Mars and found converts on Earth; again demagogues assured starveling masses that their wretchedness was due to somebody else's greed; the scope and weaponry of border wars increased; ever more carriers of nuclear explosive crouched underground, prowled sea and sky and space. This would not be the first dark age the Order had seen, nor the first time that its Directors considered unpropitious for the release of technical data possibly transmitted.

Accordingly, the newest developments in interstellar linguistics were not published. Secular authorities who monitored the messages from Outside were as puzzled as the Communicators claimed to be. And when the upheaval came, Earth was not burned sterile.

For three hundred years, a succession of a few trusted masters of the Order kept secret that a key existed to those last dispatches to arrive before the catastrophe, and those

which had come in while no one was there to read the
recordings of them.

Roban was told, after Luizo selected him to come. Now
he leaned forward and whispered in the Primary's ear,
"Should you mention you know what the renegade brothers didn't? This room may be bugged."

"No doubt it is," Luizo answered aloud. "You forget,
though, the Domination government *has* been advised that
I possess information that was never made public. They
don't know what it is, of course; if they did, you and I
would not be here."

Beneath his facade, he likewise stiffened. "I cannot just
project the taped messages on a screen and read them like
a book, you understand. We are not that far along. No, it
remains a question of interpretation, of finding sets of
possible meanings that look mutually consistent. You wi'¹
have work, Roban, never fear. Dog work such as frequency analyses on particular symbol clusters. Let me
illustrate."

He took pencil and paper and scribbled. Roban waited.
He wondered why Luizo should repeat what he had spent
the past year studying. The room felt very silent.

The Primary handed him the sheet. His heart jumped.

*I dared not tell you this before. You are no actor,
and your manner might have given hints to the Baikalan
secret agents who surely checked on you after I selected you. But there are no such specialists on the
Moon, and in any event you can be expected to show
excitement under present circumstances.*

I may indeed find something in those tapes that

should not be revealed. What we have on Earth is harmless, but we cannot predict what is here. Yet I am required to turn in a full translation, with an account of the system I used, and this will be carefully scrutinized by Dominist experts.

With the help of certain colleagues, I have prepared and memorized a false system. It is close enough to the real one that most interpretations will be plausible and even correct. However, to give you an example: toward the end, the Kappans stopped sending numbers in binary and saved time by switching to a duodecimal base. In the false system, the new base is said to be ten. That would make it impossible to build any machine that might be described for us. It is unlikely the deception will be suspected, when the most honest and competent readings always contain so many ambiguities. The Order can "explain" the difficulty as doubtless due to a misunderstanding, promise to send a request for clarification, and thus delay matters for at least 64 years, during which many things can happen.

Therefore, do not express surprise if you see me proceed in a way that your own knowledge of the data makes you think must be erroneous. And, while I trust no crisis will arise, be prepared to act in an emergency with the strength and courage for which I chose you.

Luizo's gaze gripped Roban's. "Do you see what I mean?" he asked.

The techno nodded. His neck was stiff, his palms wet. "Y-yes, sir. Absolutely."

"Good." Luizo laid the paper in an ashtray, touched a lighter to it, and watched it burn. "We will commence right after breakfast," he said. The flame went out. He stirred the blackened remnants, breaking them up, mingling them with the ash from Duna's cigar. "You really must go make yourself presentable, Brother. Never forget, we represent the Order."

The sun rose slowly to blazing Lunar noon. A week later, night was falling on Farside.

Roban was scarcely conscious of time. Luizo worked him too hard. As translation progressed, he must continually reprogram the computers. (They, and the associated scanners, projectors, cross-comparison playbacks, memory banks, every piece of paraphernalia, were the reason for working on the Moon. In former days, the information could simply have been transmitted to Earth, where a parallel team used the facilities of Alpine Station. But the dark-age Mechanoclasts had dynamited it.) And he was put to uncreative but necessary tasks like tracking down previous appearances of a given configuration or drawing up probability matrices. He grew red-eyed and insomniac.

He didn't resent it. The Primary was laboring more heavily . . . and growing more taut and taciturn for every watch that went by. Clearly the translation, as it developed, was revealing something of major import. But Luizo uttered no hint of what it might be, and kept his notes in a private cipher.

Neither man saw much of the Baikalans. A few soldiers

were posted with them. Besides keeping guard, they kept house. The Primary, who spoke their language, could have gotten their help, for whatever that was worth, if he asked. But the longest sentence he gave them was a conveyance of Roban's desire for a bit of variety in the Asian food. The cook tried to oblige, with no great success.

Duna was gone. His assignment was only concerned in part with star talk. Mainly he was on the project of expanding his country's military bases on Nearside. In one of his rare conversational moods, Luizo remarked what a prostitution of engineering that was. Roban nodded, though his own wish was that those could have been Norrestlander installations.

The colonel returned about sunset and inquired what had been accomplished. Luizo snapped, "Messages, long ones loaded with information, came in at intervals for two centuries before the Kappans gave up. Each included a further evolution of the code itself. Did you think I would have them read in two weeks?"

"You got any idea w'en you finish?" Duna asked mildly. "Our stores are limited, you know."

"Perhaps another fortnight. Mind you, I won't have a proper text then. I will simply have done everything I can with the apparatus here, so that I may as well take the material back to Earth for continued study. If you are in a hurry, Colonel, I suggest you stop delaying me yourself."

Duna guffawed and left the laboratory.

Several hours afterward, he found Roban alone. Luizo had finally needed a little sleep. The assistant did too, but his nerves were overly stretched—*What is turning the old man so . . . grim? intense? exalted*—and he wandered into the observation lounge hoping the view would relax him.

The sun disc had gone behind a supply bunker. A plume of zodiacal light rose pearly over that black outline. Occasional ridges on the crater floor still caught the glow, and the spaceship was a burning spear, but otherwise shadows had engulfed the land. It was, naturally, a simulacrum on a hemispherical screen that Roban saw; a dome would soon have been etched useless by micrometeorites. But the realism was absolute. You rarely got a presentation that fine on Earth these days, and nowhere an omnisensory program.

I wonder what life was getting to be like . . . would have become like, if the collapse hadn't happened, he thought. *No need to go anyplace, when any experience you might want is brought to you, nor to do anything when you need only issue an order to a machine that might be at the antipodes.*

He felt the weariness that slumped his shoulders and wished briefly for that lost ease. Then looked at his big fisherman's hands and wondered what he could use them for in such a world.

Hobbies, I suppose. My brain would do my real work. . . . Or would it? Self-programming computers could direct the machines better. In fact, at last the system would get so complicated that you wouldn't dare let flesh and blood meddle with it.

Arts, philosophies, the spiritual explorations Luizo talks about?

Well, maybe for him, but I'm afraid I'd be no good at them, especially if every piece of information I had was provided for me by the system. That's the trouble with organized perfection. No surprises.

His gaze went to the stars where they stood in darkness. *Is that why their people communicate? For newness? But why haven't they*—The sense of their isolation, and his own, stabbed him with cold.

Anticlimax, a whiff of cigar smoke called his attention back. Duna had entered the lounge. The Baikalan smiled. "Salutation, techno," he said.

"Brother, if you please," Roban corrected him annoyedly. "My title is Brother of the Order. 'Techno' is a job designation."

"Excuse. I am a roughneck steppe dweller. We tend to t'ink of a person in terms of w'at he does." Duna's stumpy bowlegs carried him less gracefully across the floor than Roban had become able to move in this gravity. "You admire de scene?"

"Yes. *When are you going?*"

Duna took stance beside him. "Dat is not common for my folk. We live too close to nature, most of us, even today, for seeing it as a subject for poetry or tourism. I doubt you did, eider, w'en you was a sailor boy. Dese days you live more comfortable, more intellectual, and it gets different. Maybe my grandchildren, dey have a Horace or a Virgil."

"A what?" The question escaped Roban's determination to snub the other.

"Roman poets of de late Republic and early Principate." Duna cocked his glance upward at the bigger man. "You don't follow?"

"No. I, uh, I believe I've heard mention of an empire a

long time ago, but" *He won't lord it over my education too!* "—my business is with more important things."

"Ah, dere you make your mistake, my friend. Not'ing is more important. W'ere does de future come from if not de past? W'at is de present more dan deir intersection point? A wise man said in Old America, dose who will not learn history are condemned to repeat it."

Duna laid a hand on Roban's arm. "Here, let us settle and talk," he urged. The cigar wagged between his lips.

"I have to sleep."

"Maybe you do your Order and your home country some good if you hear w'at I got to tell you."

Maybe. Can't hurt, I suppose. Roban lowered himself into a chair. The ancient upholstery crackled. Duna sat down to confront him. "Well?"

"Oh, relax. W'y can we not treat each odder like gentlemen, w'edder or not we agree?"

Roban felt himself blush, and resented it, but managed to nod and lean back.

"I imagine," Duna said, "you wonder w'y a military man like me, a clansman who lives by de Yasa of his ancestors and worships very honest at deir graves each year w'en he goes home for de Grand Hunt—w'y he should know anyt'ing about w'at happened t'ousands of years gone?"

He blew his customary smoke ring. "I tell you," he said. "I got lots of chances for reading. Military life is mostly waiting around, es-specially in peacetime. I am interested. But besides, de Domination tries hard for its officers to keep on learning after dey have left school." His laugh barked. "Partly, yas, we feel shy over being less cultured dan various of our client peoples." Quickly serious again: "However, we got a practical need. We do not want to blunder blind into horrible mistakes like earlier nations did. For having any chance of saving ourselves from dat, we need leaders who can t'ink as well as act. And how can you t'ink unless you know t'ings to t'ink about?"

Roban frowned. He remembered the cries of "Asian barbarians," and unkempt little men in dusty vehicles, and—well, yes, it had been surprising how many of them played a musical instrument; and the Protector had started night classes for them in Seattle, and later for the provincial garrisons. . . . Not that they were any band of geniuses. Far from it. But the lowliest herdboy-turned-grease-monkey respected any educated person.

He met the oblique eyes and said, "You might give a bit of your thought to what becomes of aggressors."

"We do, we do," Duna answered. "Let's not get into de rights and wrongs of our war wit' Norrestland. We say you was making border trobble for us in Alaska, and egging de Tundra Runners on to raid us, and many odder t'ings your government maybe denied. Fact is, dough, your foreign policy was tied to dat of our Latino rivals. And . . . we are not such bad bosses, are we? Before long, Norrestlanders will start getting offered Baikalan citizenship—w'ich will not mean dey have to quit deir own ways of living."

"Until they're told to march out and help conquer the Latinos for you."

"Dey won't be. Not if it can be avoided. Dat is one lesson we draw from de past. An empire gets spread too t'in, like de British, and it evaporates. On de odder hand, de Romans stopped too soon. Dey could have taken Germany, soudern Russia, and de Near East; and dey should have, because dat was w'ere deir later enemies came from. Rome might den have lasted longer dan Egypt of de Pharaohs, and a better world dan ours might have grown up inside de framework. Could hardly be worse, no?''

Roban shook his head. ''I don't know what you're talking about.''

''And still you put your judgment against mine?'' Duna replied, turning severe. ''Besides, you was supposed to have renounced national ties w'en you joined de Order.''

''Well—you can't expect a man to . . . I've family there—''

Duna watched him narrowly. ''I have got reports,'' he said. ''I have seen for myself. Luizo did not pick de best trained assistant he was personally acquainted wit'; he picked de one wit' de best reason to hate de Domination. And he would not wear de mask he does if he was simply learning details about how anodder planet is put togedder.''

Roban swallowed. ''Your, uh, your government will get the information when we've worked it out ourselves.''

''For certain? Brudder, I have been trying to make you see you should cooperate wit' us. Now I tell you plain, you better do it. De Domination wants to be just, but de justice is strict.''

''I don't know anything!'' the techno almost shouted. ''He hasn't told me!'' He realized the implications. ''That is . . . no point in him telling me at the, the present stage of things. He's the only man here who can—'' *Go on the offensive, for God's sake.* "If your government wanted faster results, it could have brought more than one topranker."

"Wit' dat many more chances for trickery?" The tone was a whipcrack.

After a moment, however, Duna smiled and said quite gently: "Please t'ink on it. Ask Primary Luizo to t'ink. You may not like us Baikalans much, but at de last, we are human beings wit' you." He waved around the dome. The sun was entirely down, nothing except that misty half-lens of zodiacal light to interrupt the awful majesty of the stars. "If dis shell around us breaks, we are dead. Dat is a big and strange cosmos out yonder, and it was not made for us; we were made for a single tiny corner of it. Do not take chances wit' our corner."

He rose. "Goodnight," he said and departed.

The Great Bear walked slowly over heaven. When Roban donned earphones to examine the audio component of a message, he would hear the dry, random rustle and hiss that were the stars' way of talking to each other. Once the radioscope had eavesdropped on it and the computers had translated what was heard into discourse of bursting atoms and ghost-thin nebulae and cosmic rays spiraling down light-years-long magnetic lines. But that was before anger and valor drowned reason on Earth.

In another generation, perhaps again.

Luizo began finding less for his helper to do, as the possible manipulations of available data grew exhausted. Roban was not glad. He didn't want leisure to fret over why his chief worked ever more feverishly and withdrew ever deeper into himself. The Norrestlander arranged a few excursions outside, gliding dreamily along the crater floor or riding a moonbuggy to the ringwall for a climb up those gaunt steeps. The trips refreshed him less than expected, and the company of Dominist soldiers was not the cause. He was longing for home—Earth: manhome—gray walls and grave courtyards, gardens, bells at dusk, where Australia Station kept watch from a high hill over intensely green croplands; or gurgle and glitter on Puget Sound, lulling winds, flying gulls and flying sails, little red-roofed villages on the strand beneath pinewoods, odor of smoke and a friendly hail and the brave striding of girls.

Night wore away toward another furnace sunrise. And Luizo said: "We are through here, I believe. We can best finish on Earth. I want to consult my colleagues."

His spare face moved only in the lips, from which the words issued metallic. Roban's heart stumbled.

A call flew from peak to peak to relay satellite to peak until it reached Duna at the base whither he had returned. The colonel's reply was prompt: "Optimum time for raising ship, twenty-nine hours hence. Let countdown begin. I will come bid farewell in person."

Luizo interpreted this for Roban when the officer in charge told him about it at dinner. "For my part," the Primary said, "I shall mostly sleep." His back was slumped, his eyes and cheeks sunken, as if he were hollowed out . . . but by a flame within that was only burning low, that would not die.

When they had eaten, he and Roban sought the laboratory to collect their transcriptions, calculations, ciphered notes, and conclusions. Luizo always took them with him when he went to rest, and never left them alone for any significant length of time. "You may wipe the memory banks of our computers," he said.

"What? But . . . ." Roban gulped. The Dominators' scientists could be almost as indignant at losing those marks along the trail the Communicators had followed, as they would have been at destruction of the message reels themselves.

"I said for you to clear the memory banks." Luizo's voice rose. "To avoid needless duplication where data storage space is short."

That's a command, Roban knew.

Well . . . presumably no one will realize it's been done till we're safely back in Australia. And even if they do, what of it? We need merely claim we took the procedure for granted. Relations are strained enough between Domination and Order that the Baikalans can't afford to consider it a provocative act.

And it'll do them one in the eye.

He laughed. Leaning close: "Sir, can't you tell me now what—"

"No," Luizo said. "The interpretation remains clouded." His thumb jerked toward the wall. *Wait till we're home. Here we too likely have electronic listeners.*

"I, uh, understand, sir." Roban carried the boxes of material to the room the Communicators shared. Luizo reminded him about his key; he had forgotten it once, and found that the Primary had locked him out. Returning to the lab, the techno spent an hour making the erasures.

That left him likewise weary. He started for the wash-

305

room closest to his doss. Rounding a corner, he almost collided with a blocky form. "Oh! H-h-hello, Colonel."

Duna smiled. "Salutation, Brudder. I just got in. Was hoping to catch you two at work. Dey told me you was."

"I . . . have finished." *Thank the fates!* "My superior has already turned in."

"Would you like a drink? I brought a bottle of good gin. Not vodka, gin."

Roban was tempted. But no—not with the enemy—and they'd have taken it in the lounge, which meant sitting under those icily strange stars. "I'd better hold off. You, well, you might tell them not to call us for breakfast but leave some food on standby. We both need ten or twelve hours' rest."

"And blastoff soon after. Very well, as you wish. I will see you before you leave. Nice dreams." Duna waved and continued down the corridor with his horseman's gait.

Roban stared a moment at his back. *Hoy, I did accept a favor from him after all, didn't I?*

Not important. People weren't machines; relationships between them, or between aspects of themselves, had nothing of machine simplicity and invariance.

Nonetheless, the fact that he couldn't really hate Duna— nor really love the whole of mankind—bothered him. And what was in those sendings from Outside, that both troubled and uplifted Luizo?

Sleepiness fled. *Another wakeful nightwatch,* Roban groaned to himself. *God, I can't wait to live again the way men were meant to live!* No caging underground sameness, exterior deadly barrenness; no days which were nothing but symbols and calculators; wind, rain, green grass and thunderous surf, music and ceremonies and tales of desperate bravery, falling in love and children running to meet you, jokes, games, the billion tiny illogicalities of a human existence. Those brought peace.

He let himself into the bunkroom, remembering to relock the door. Luizo had written to him, early in the project, that this was crucial to keeping the papers safe. Roban saw why they must be guarded. Given a chance to photocopy a full record of the Communicators' work, the Dominists could eventually read it; no cipher is unbreakable. And if the masters of the Order should decide to turn in a false report . . . None of the Baikalans had objected, or made any remark concerning the secretiveness. Roban had speculated that they might plan on arresting him and Luizo, acquiring the material by force. No, he concluded, that would bring the ban down on their realm; and they could ill afford to let their rivals enjoy the Order's exclusive services.

The room was a cubicle, sparsely furnished. The sole decorations on its dull gray walls were the official medallion Luizo had hung, four stars linked by trains of waves, and the time-blurred portrait of an unknown woman and child which Roban had sentimentally left in place. A ventilator gusted air that felt a little chill when he removed his clothes; no matter how far they ranged, men did best to take the cycles of mother Gaea with them. Its murmur was soft in his ears. Luizo looked oddly shrunken and helpless, asleep with one thin arm laid over the blanket.

Roban chinned into the upper bunk, turned off the light, and tried to compose himself. Useless. He did not thresh about, for any position is comfortable in low-weight. But too many questions moved inside his head.

Three or four hours had passed when the door opened.

The entry was most quiet. Roban's first intimation was a faint brightening on his lids. He blinked, and saw a line of wan illumination from the hall. *What the demons?* He half sat up. The crack widened and a silhouette appeared within.

They . . . yes, why didn't we think of it, of course they'd have duplicate keys and combinations. Roban rolled over to face the entrance and watched through slitted eyes. He hoped his breathing stayed regular and his heart did not hammer audibly. It prickled along scalp and backbone.

The intruder stepped through and reclosed the door. There was an instant's blackness. A stopped-down flashbeam glowed. Reflections picked Duna's countenance out as a few bony highlights and a glitter of watchfulness.

He padded across the floor and squatted by the lower bunk. Roban risked leaning over the side for a look. Duna held the flash between his knees. One hand grasped a pressure container. From it snaked a tube ending in a bell mouth, that his other hand was bringing toward Luizo.

Roban had done battle in waterfront brawls, and hunted bear with crossbows while the Domination still forbade guns to Norrestlanders, and ridden out gales off Cape Flattery. Only later did he recognize that what flared in him now was less rage than joy.

He swung himself outward in an arc that landed him behind·Duna. The colonel heard the thud, bounded erect and sought to whirl around. Roban caught him in a full nelson. Duna hissed an oath, writhed with astonishing power, and kicked. Pain coursed through Roban's bare shin. He held firm, stood on his unhurt leg and wrapped the other around both of Duna's. "Gotcha, you bastard!" he grunted.

Duna pressed the trigger on his can. A sickly-sweet whiff reached Roban's nostrils. For a second his mind spun, his muscles loosened, and Duna broke free.

A shadow among shadows, the Baikalan snatched for his pistol. Another shadow arose, Luizo, wakened by Roban's massive body striking the bunkframe. The Primary lunged. "I've caught . . . his gun hand. Help!"

Roban shook his head. The giddiness went away. He found the dropped flash and played its beam over the struggle. Duna had lost his pressure can. He wrenched to break Luizo's grip. The old man hung on.

Roban trod forward. His fist smote. The violence of the blow erupted in his own shoulder. Duna's head snapped back. He fell, with the peculiar, buckling Lunar slowness, and did not move.

For awhile murk was, and harsh breath.

Luizo groped to the light switch. The fluorescence seemed bright as topside day. Roban hunkered over Duna. "Is he dead?" The Primary's question sounded as if from an interstellar distance.

"No. Sock to the chin. He should rouse in a minute or two." Roban heaved the Baikalan into the lower bunk.

Luizo peered out. "Nobody else in sight." He shut the door.

"What's this about?" Roban demanded.

"Obvious." Luizo's crisp calm was restored. He stooped for the can, shot the least jet from the tube, and sniffed.

"Yes, pentacycline. A common anesthetic. We would have been unwakeable for several hours, while he duplicated our material and put it back. If tomorrow we suspected, what proof could we bring? I should have anticipated the possibility. You did well, Brother. We may never dare speak publicly of such an incident, but I will commend you to the right people."

At another time Roban might have glowed. On this night he could ask merely, "What do we do next?"

Luizo's dryness restored a measure of balance: "You might start by removing his knife and gun."

Roban hastened to obey. The pistol felt oddly heavy in his grasp. Luizo peered at the colonel. "Ah," he murmured, "he is reviving. Let us see if we can't utilize the initial confusion."

Duna's lids fluttered. He uttered a snoring sound. Luizo asked him a question in Baikalan. He mumbled and tried to sit. Luizo gave him a jet of gas and, as he sagged, snapped another inquiry. Duna mushed an answer and lay back.

Luizo straightened. "He says he came alone, without notifying his fellows. I will assume that is true. Primitive though our narcosynthesis is, we have nothing better, do we?"

More than ever, he appeared like a hawk stooping on prey. And a tingling went along Roban's own veins. Here finally was a time when men must decide and act . . . not any damned machine!

"Let us get dressed," Luizo said. "We want the maximum psychological advantage. He is a tough one."

"What can we do, sir? I mean, he—"

"At worst," Luizo clipped, "we can kill him, move the corpse elsewhere, and hope the death passes for accident or suicide."

Roban was momentarily appalled. "Sir! Is the . . . the issue . . . that important?"

"More." Luizo paused. "I trust murder won't be necessary. The risks are high, not to speak of the moral dilemma." He tugged his beard. "The Domination itself is surely unwilling to run certain other risks. We can try to use that fact. . . . Dress, Brother, and fetch a glass of water. He will need it."

That walk down the hall was the longest Roban had taken. Yet he encountered no soul. The hour stood at midnight over Lake Baikal, and the corridor on this level reached as empty as if nothing remained on the Moon except the unseen, susurrating machines.

When he came back, Duna was hunched on the bunk edge, elbows on knees, face in hands. Luizo offered him the tumbler and, in addition, a tablet from his personal medikit. "Take this. A stimulant and pain killer. You will feel more like yourself."

The colonel did. Presently the slackness left his mouth, the haziness his eyes. Though a bruise had already begun to show among the tattoos on his jaw, he sat straight. Luizo confronted him from the single chair. Roban loomed behind, gun in belt.

"Well," Duna said across the quietness. "You gave me a hard welcome."

"We may have overreacted," Luizo said. "However—" He pointed to the can where it lay on the floor.

Duna grinned, winced, and doggedly repeated the grin.

"An embarrassing situation, right? On bot' sides, I t'ink. W'en I do not soon notify my men I am safe—"

"I doubt your men will worry before mornwatch, Colonel."

Duna stayed motionless. "Ah. Yas. I remember now, from barely awake. . . . You should have been an intelligence officer, Primary."

"Thank you. I assume you are?"

"Not as a regular, or I might have worked more smoot'. Dey figured me for de best qualified man to deal wit' you because I am in a technical corps, and speak not only Inglis but your home language, Primary, w'ich I suspect is de language of your ciphered notes."

Luizo raised brows in an otherwise impassive visage. "Then you have already spied?"

"Glimpses. You gave no chance for more. I had no specific orders, you understand. I was to act at discretion, depending on how you behaved. W'en you showed bad fait', well, I did w'at looked better dan provoking a crisis. I went ahead by myself, for not making any later scandal."

"Why do you accuse us of bad faith? I have explained that translation will be a long-drawn-out process, and that the Order has always been reluctant to announce conclusions until certain they are not premature."

Duna sighed. "Don't let's make insults. You know my government can keep its mout' shut. It would not have assigned me if I could not. You could have told me of your tentative ideas. You did not even tell your assistant."

"Because you might have planted recording devices on us—which you have, in effect, just admitted doing." Luizo stabbed a lean finger at the Baikalan. "What sort of faith does that show?"

Duna scowled. "Credit me wit' having t'ought about w'at I observed."

"I admit I underestimated you," Luizo said. "Shall we call the game quits?"

"No." Watching Duna, Roban suddenly recalled a cougar he had seen readying to pounce.

The attack, when it came, was in words.

"W'en is de Kappan ship arriving?"

"What?" Roban cried. Luizo sat frozen-faced, but hands clenched tight on the arms of his chair.

Duna leaned forward. Triumph blazed from him. "In about sixty years," he said. "Dat is a pretty good estimate, no?"

Through a noise of exploding suns, Roban heard Luizo say—for the first time, weakly—"You must be insane. What gave you any such idea?"

"I tell you." Duna rose. He might not yet have been able to do that under terrestrial weight. Here, though, he stood over the Primary, with legs planted wide, and Roban wondered how the story had ever started that Orientals are expressionless. His hands darted to and fro while he spoke, machine gun fashion.

"I t'ought from your behavior, you must be reading more easy dan you pretended, and it was terrible w'at you read but glorious too. Maybe a weapon you could use for conquering de Solar System? Not likely. Mcn already got lots; and dc Order is not structured for conquering; and anyway, it looks like de star folk don't make war on demselves like us. It has always been men w'at took ideas

313

from de stars and turned dem to war use, like a photon-drive battleship. Right? Well, maybe you saw a doomsday machine in de latest information—but den you should have showed plain fear.

"W'at was a better guess? Well, suppose I was in charge at Kappa Ceti. I would t'ink, here are dese creatures at Sol. Dey don't play question and answer like anybody else; dey are slow to grasp many ideas, and interested in odd subjects like botany and zoology; yas, dey are very strange. Sometimes dey actually stop transmitting for decades or centuries. Dis last breakoff . . . maybe de final message received spoke of a hurricane coming? I t'ink likely so. De last men here before dey evacuated it and went home to die, would dey not have wanted to send a cry across de light-years, 'Remember us'?"

Luizo's gaze dropped. "Yes," he whispered.

The Baikalan pressed his advantage. "Question is, was de language so well developed by den dat de cry could be even half understood? W'edder it could or not, how else to learn de inwardness of dis peculiar race, after it falls silent for w'at might be forever—how else, except go in person?"

Luizo rallied and looked back up. "On what basis do you say your hypothetical ship will arrive in six decades?"

"T'irty-two light-years between. Records show dey sent a reply to de final message from us, and tried again w'en dey got no answer, because deir own last word came in here about a hundred years ago. Well, I allow maybe ten years after de second one drew blank, for building de ship and accelerating to full speed and so on. Dat fits in wit' de date dat last transmission was received, surely announcing dey was on deir way. At one-sixt' light velocity, dey will get here w'en I told you."

Luizo sat in a silence where Roban counted pulsebeats.

Until the Primary said: "The arrival date they gave is fifty-eight years hence."

Duna leaned on the bunkframe and let out a whistling breath.

Almost of itself, the gun moved from Roban's belt and centered on the Baikalan. "Stay where you are, Colonel," said a voice.

Duna congealed.

"What is this, Brother?" Luizo asked, sadly more than surprisedly, and not leaving his seat.

"Can we let him go, sir?" Roban replied.

Duna showed emotion only in the squaring of his shoulders. "I t'ink you damn better," he said.

"Dare we, sir?" Roban begged. "Whether or not we have to die for his death? If the Domination expects them, it'll arrange to meet them alone—tell them lies—get them on its side—"

Duna spoke softly: "W'ereass, if you reach dem first, you can hope for deir help in making independent Norrestland. Or maybe a Norrestlander Empire?"

Roban's aim never wavered. But his tones did. "No! Simple freedom—for everybody . . ." The terror that had made him draw the gun began to fade. "Though maybe it d-d-doesn't matter what we do, we three tonight," he said. "A civilization that old, without war, in touch with its kind across how many light-years . . . they've got to be wise, benign, unfoolable. They've got to come as teachers and liberators—don't they?"

Now Luizo climbed to his feet. He stayed out of the line of fire, but hardened his stare upon Duna. "What *I* fear," he said, "is a hysterical attempt—by your country, by anyone—to destroy the Kappans as they enter the Solar System. It might succeed. They might not suspect defenses are needed. At best, imagine six decades of wrangling, intriguing, probably fighting, over which band of glorified apes shall have the right to meet the Galactic Ancients with what empty pomposities!"

Tall in his robe, he told them both, "One human institution alone is conceivably fit to be man's representative before them. It is for this that the Order of Communicators has existed."

Silence anew, until Roban wondered wildly at the back of his head if the buzzing he heard there was, somehow, the talk between the stars.

Iwan Duna's eyes sought his. "You have read little history, Brudder," he said, almost caressingly. "But you must know legends, you must have imagination. I could tell you how de barbarians overran China or Rome to help one faction against anodder, de English India in deir turn, after deir ancestors took first Britain and den Ireland, how Cortez had native allies dat hated de Aztecs, how de Jovian moon colonies lost deir freedom—oh, over and over, always strangers getting into internecine wars. You can read de books later, dough. Tonight, Roban, t'ink, only t'ink. How easier can conquest happen and *everybody* come under de yoke—dan by one side asking for alliance? Divide and conquer—and dis time de conquerors will not be your fellow men!"

Luizo flung back: "You make the paranoid assumption that a single spaceship represents a menace."

"She does," Duna said, "wit' de knowledge aboard, if we let her."

"You cannot accept that the Kappans are above such infantile games as conquest?"

" 'Conquest' is maybe de wrong word," Duna replied. "Maybe dey t'ink of it as 'help,' like evangelists bringing a true fait' to de pagans wit' fire and sword, or a technologically advanced society choking a pastoral one by sheer weight of economics."

He folded his arms. "Primary," he said, "you could argue for holding de facts from me. But do you mean to keep from Roban de true nature of de Kappans? He could live to see dem come."

Luizo smote fist in palm and said, "Brother, you are right. We have to take care of this man, at whatever cost."

"You can kill me," Duna said, "but den you cannot hear me. Roban, does it mean not'ing to you dat dis ship is traveling at one-sixt' light speed?"

"Be still," Luizo said.

"He has de gun," Duna reminded them.

"I am your superior—" Luizo began, but Duna's voice overrode.

"Organic life cannot survive de radiation. We learned dat. No reason to believe dere were any lies. W'at can, den? Robots. Dat ship is crewed by robots. Computer brains, machine effectors, I don't know how dey work but I do know dey got to be machines."

"And what of it?" Luizo trod toward Duna. The colonel caught his wrist and stopped him, while keeping attention wholly on Roban and saying, in quick merciless words:

"Maybe organic beings would do it dat way. Not impossible. We would, if we had no choice.

"T'ink furder, dough, my friend. W'y is every planet de Order has contacted or been told about—a tiny sample, but consistent—w'y is all but ours so uniform? W'y do dey not take for granted we are interested in living creatures? W'y do dey use computer and physics symbolisms always? W'y never a sign of dat irrational t'ing we call de spirit?

"Oh, yas, you got a few pictures w'at you suppose are of intelligent animals . . . finally, casually, a sop to your odd curiosity. Maybe dose animals are not extinct yet—everyw'ere. Maybe on some worlds dey survive, tame, in small numbers—but makes no difference. Dey are obsolete, dey are being phased out, not by any dramatic revolt of de robots but by de logic of de machine civilizations dey demselves had founded.

"In de end—seems like in dis part of de galaxy, at least—technological society ends inevitable wit' replacing silly, limited organic life by efficient computers and robots. Dey t'ink, yas; dey have awareness, curiosity, a kind of creativity; but all else we care about is dead and forgotten."

Duna swung upon Luizo. "Primary," he rasped, "obviously de Kappans have realized dat we are not machines. W'en dey come, do you hope dey will give us dat same Nirvana?"

Caught in the manacling grasp, the Communicator wet his lips and got out: "He's crazy, Roban. We must silence him. Man isn't enslaved, is he? What danger have we ever been in . . . except from our own lunacies?"

"Maybe dose lunacies are w'at save us," Duna said. "De odder races dat dwell on odder planets, maybe dey are more logical and meek dan de wild hunter man. We get so far in civilization, and den we feel de walls closing in and we revolt."

"And smash the world and start over," Luizo retorted. "Would you keep us forever bound to that wheel?"

"I did not say so," Duna answered, calmer now. "I do not say, eider, we should attack de ship. No, no. Let us be very careful, but let us also learn w'at we can . . . and den, maybe, fare out among de stars and prove on behalf of our poor gone kinsfolk dat once loved and hated and feared and longed like us . . . fare out and prove w'at life can do."

Luizo disengaged himself and turned to Roban. "I do not necessarily advocate anything else," he said. "In fact, it would be folly to try to predict in advance what the Kappan robots can bring us, for good or ill. I do say that none but the Communicators are fit to deal with them."

"Yas," Duna said, "de little, ingrown, order-worshipping Order. No fishermen, no clansmen, no patriots, nobody w'at cares about his ancestors, no poets, no warriors, no lovers, only intellectuals talking wit' machines. Should not de whole of mankind meet dem and decide w'at destiny dey want for deir children?"

"With the Domination of Baikal—your country's oppressor, Roban—their self-appointed spokesman?" Luizo challenged.

"We have fifty-eight years to change dat," Duna said. Then he waited.

After the tears had started to blind him, Roban stammered,

"Sir, we . . . we can't murder; we can't take sides. It's not in our t-t-tradition." His hand shook so badly that he had trouble giving Duna back knife and pistol.

The colonel holstered them and said, "I feel no need to tell w'at has happened between us, after you give me your full report tomorrow."

"I suppose not." Luizo could barely be heard. "Goodnight to you. Eternally returning night."

"How else can dere be sunrises?" Duna asked, and left the Communicators alone.